MW01377611

NEW MOON RISING

NEW MOON RISING

BY MOONLIGHT SERIES BOOK 4

CHELSEA BURTON DUNN

4 Horsemen
Publications, Inc.

TABLE OF CONTENTS

NEW MOON RISING

CHAPTER 1

I t was loud. Shouts, banging, the unmistakable sound of something being dropped and broken filled the still unfamiliar dwelling where Vee sat. Too much sound, too many people, and far too much commotion for Vee who, instead of directing all these people to where things should be going in the new house she was moving into, was fixated on the ornate front door lock she had just pulled out. It was a good distraction. A needed one too. This move had been far from easy, and they weren't even finished with it yet. She was struggling through this day for many reasons, the first of which was the sheer number of people and all their emotions. Mostly frustration and fatigue.

Being an empath in a crowd was hard enough. Being an empath in a crowd of Werewolves was harder. Their emotions seemed heightened with their intense buzzing presence, and the chaos of moving day was not helping with that intensity. Since she had been folded into this pack by way of the bond with their leader, Shane, and by, quite literally, being made pack with blood magic, she had grown much more accustomed to their presence. However, this day was overwhelming enough as it was, and their spiking emotions certainly didn't make her own easier to handle.

So Vee was doing what she did best, distracting herself with locks. Being a locksmith, she was very good at using her work as a way of blocking out her abilities.

"What are you doing on the floor, Vee?" came a familiar voice from above her. Apparently, she was blocking a bit too much. Normally she would have been able to anticipate this intrusion, but she had been lost in the metal pieces that made up the old deadbolt in her hands.

Vee glanced up, looking into the face of Toby Curtis, her friendly acquaintance who kept her shop supplied with antique locks that needed restoring. His renovation company was working on a few modifications that Shane had requested on the new house. But they hadn't quite finished one of them before the move-in date, hence why he was there on moving day, thrown into such chaos and standing in the open doorway, looking down at her.

"Looking at the lock?" she said back, a question in her voice, since it seemed obvious to her. She was, after all, holding the lock's innards before her.

"Why?" His boyish sideways smile crept onto his face. There it was, that thoughtless flirtation she hadn't noticed until recently. Her almost-son-in-law, Patrick, and her semi-frequent bodyguard and friend, Tommy, had enlightened her to Toby's very obvious feelings for her a month previous, something she had clearly, and willfully, ignored for some years. She fought back a bodily cringe.

"Because I'm trying to figure out if I can adjust the tines and make a new key. Don't need old neighbors or a maid just waltzing into the house," Vee told him, eyes darting back down to the lock itself.

"Why not just replace it?"

Toby was under the false impression Vee was only here to change the locks and other fixtures in the house. She had been, off and on, taking various knobs that she had found particularly wobbly and fixing them to put back in place. A few fixtures that had been replaced over the years, with unfortunate modern pieces, she had swapped for refurbished antique ones that matched, or matched closely enough, from her inventory at her locksmith shop. No one had mentioned to Toby that her presence there was anything other than working purposes, and he had simply assumed she was hired on, just as he was.

Toby knew she did work for Shane and others in his employ. He also knew that Patrick, Shane's son, worked for Vee at her shop. What he didn't know was that Vee and Shane were a couple, engaged to be married, and had bought this house together.

Why did that matter?

Toby was in love with her, and Vee couldn't help but notice it now that it was pointed out to her. She had no idea how to break the news of her relationship to him without losing a friend and a business associate who helped her bring in a decent amount of money. For years, Toby had been bringing her antique locks to refurbish and sell from houses he was remodeling. She had never noticed his feelings before, either because of utter stupidity or because she simply didn't want to know, but Patrick and Tommy had pointed it out to her, and now she couldn't unsee it.

"Shane likes it," she said, her words true but not completely. Yes, Shane did like old things and was happy to let her keep it or swap out any locks that she chose in their house. He wasn't so much concerned about keeping the front door locked, though, and had told her if it was too difficult to adjust, he would rather her replace it. She had seen that as a challenge, but not one she had been originally planning to do in the middle of move-in day.

"Did you convince him to keep it? I feel like his security-obsessed self wouldn't want to waste the labor it will take you," Toby said with a grin.

That laid-back grin and the amusement flickering within him told Vee all of her suspicions of how much he knew were correct. Toby had no idea. No idea at all that Vee and Shane were not just together but engaged. *She* wasn't going to be the one to break it to him, at least not today. Her anxiety about everything increased significantly.

"He likes old things," she murmured, trying very hard not to let on what she was thinking. This sweet man deserved so much, and his feelings for her, which she had willfully ignored, were only growing. Toby had been quite bold, for him, the week before when he was dropping off broken antique locks and brushed her hair off her shoulder. She sucked in a breath at the recollection. She felt nothing but friendship for Toby, but because of that, Vee worried about hurting him. Waiting to tell him about her and Shane was probably not the way to go about it, but she couldn't. She couldn't get the words out when his eyes sparkled as he smiled down at her.

"You seem a little overwhelmed," he noted. She firmly kept her eyes on the lock. The house was chaotic, but his presence there was far more anxiety-inducing than the rest of it had been.

"Noise," she murmured, hoping it was dismissive but not cold. She didn't want him to wrongfully assume she was angry or displeased with him. It wasn't *his* fault, but she doubted Shane would see it that way if he was in the presence of both for more than a minute. Shane would most certainly notice Toby's feelings for Vee, and Werewolves tended to be... well, overprotective would be putting it mildly.

"Hm..." he mumbled, his look showing his doubt at her words as clear as the emotions she felt from him. He wasn't buying that noise was the only thing wrong; it made her feel oddly transparent. But he didn't have time to speculate or question her further, as one of Toby's men hollered his name from somewhere in the house, and he rushed to wherever the voice came from, leaving Vee to her very helpful distraction. Thank goodness.

This day was stressful enough without having male postering to add to the mix. Durran, though usually in female form, and Shane did enough of that already.

Durran, her best friend and Watcher, had decided to make herself scarce for the move, but it had been for the best. High tension and preternatural creatures didn't mix well on the best days, but Shane and Durran had a very tentative balancing act when it came to Vee. They both wanted to protect her, Durran being charged with doing so by the Elder Watchers and Shane having bonded with her initially as a vow of protection. But they were also both in love with her.

Vee got lost in the old lock for a moment, seeing exactly how she would adjust it and envisioning what the new keys she would make would look like to accompany it. The beautiful face plate would be gleaming by the time she brought it back to the house; now if she could figure out how to slip away from all the chaos to retreat to her shop.

Her sanctuary.

She glanced around. No one seemed particularly interested or concerned at her whereabouts at the moment, shuffling boxes to and fro or tramping up with stairs with furniture held in ways no human would be capable of managing alone. Her van was parked on the street just before the cul-de-sac her new home sat in the center of. Vee had parked it there to avoid it getting in the way of the moving vans and work vehicles. She could very easily just wander there and drive to her shop, hopefully not returning until most of the helpers were gone.

She swiftly wrapped the lock in the towel she had set pieces on while she was removing it and tucked it in her messenger bag, before getting to her feet and heading straight out of the house toward her van.

Shane was at the other house, directing the next load to be hauled, so she was certain she would get away without being noticed, until Lori stepped out of the house next door, eyes like a hawk and trained on Vee.

"Vee!" she shouted, now moving rapidly to intercept Vee's path. Her curls bouncing with each step, the locks fading from the once vibrant purple of the month previous to a still rather pretty, pale lavender.

"Hey Lori," Vee said back, waving as she tried for nonchalance.

"Shane said you'd be directing everything being unloaded," Lori said, once she caught up with her. Her curls bounced lightly as her rapid footfalls slowed to match Vee's pace.

"I just need to grab something from my car. Aren't you supposed to be helping your mom?" Vee asked, watching Lori's face blanch at the mention of her mother.

Thomas, Shane's second and Lori's father, had purchased the house next door. While Shane had ordered some renovations done to the house they were currently moving into, Cora, Thomas's human wife, had much more drastic changes in mind. This took much more planning, something Lori, normally, would have loved to take part in, but she was clearly cowed at the way her mother had transformed into a monstrous version of herself once set on her new mission.

"I needed a break," Lori admitted, glancing behind her at the house, as if her mother would burst out the door any minute. Vee smiled sympathetically.

"Me too," Vee whispered, grabbing Lori's hand and tugging her toward the car.

"Grabbing something from your car isn't going to be much of a break," Lori grumbled as she allowed Vee to drag her along.

"We're making a break for it," Vee hissed, quickly rounding the end of the street and seeing her van waiting. Their sweet escape chariot.

"Oh!" Lori said with a grin, happily climbing into the passenger seat while Vee started the van up on her side.

Steadily, to not attract attention, Vee made her way through the neighborhood, turning north shortly into Ward Parkway to head back toward Westport and to her shop. They were a good distance from the house now, both having been holding their breath, expecting to be caught, when they finally let out a giggle.

"So why did you need to escape? This is *your* moving day, after all," Lori said, once the giggle subsided. Vee shot her a glance with her eyebrow raised.

"Too much going on there," she murmured.

"Weres and humans running around. Grumbling and complaining." Lori's eyebrows shot up. "Yeah, that sounds like a Vee nightmare."

"You have no idea," Vee said, a bite in her voice as she turned to park the van in front of her shop. It was a Sunday, so the shop was closed. She had planned this, hoping Toby's crew would be taking a day off for the weekend, but Shane had insisted and paid them extra to get the unfinished project done.

"What project is Toby finishing?" Lori asked, after they exited the van and she watched Vee unlock the front door.

"I honestly don't know. I'm sure Shane told me at some point, but this week my brain has been all over the place."

"Oh, I know. I had three papers to write this week, but I stayed up late to work on them instead of not helping you here just because it's been..." Lori trailed off, looking at the papers scattered over the front counter. Normally Vee was very precise in how she kept her paperwork, quite precise in how she kept everything in her shop, really. This chaos across the normally pristine counter showed exactly how frazzled Vee had become.

"You've put off school?" Vee asked, whipping around to give Lori an accusing glare.

"It got done! Nothing a little coffee couldn't fix the next morning," Lori insisted, eyes turning away from Vee's piercing emerald orbs to see what papers were left out and where she should put them.

Vee's eyes narrowed slightly, but she took a deep breath and moved to the inventory room door to grab the supplies she'd need to adjust the tines on the lock tucked carefully in her bag. She had relied heavily upon Lori this last week, as Patrick had also been quite busy with the packing to be of any extra assistance to her. She cringed thinking of Lori staying up late to finish her schoolwork. The school year had only been in session for a month. As usual, when chaos came to call, it came in droves.

Vee and Shane had purchased the house, which was currently filled with irritable Werewolves carrying large things, because their previous home had been compromised. Vee had been followed—scented home by the master Vampire of the local nest almost a month before. They also had, sort of, solved the mystery of what Vee was preternaturally. Though it had been an intriguing mystery to Vee, one she absolutely had planned to eventually get to the bottom of, they had not been given the choice of her finding out at the slow pace she had in mind.

The Elder Watchers and the Sha had both demanded to know who and what she was, and that had been put at ease, for the time being, by their trip to the Sha realm at the same time. Vee had met her real father, been brought into the pack, and also been attacked and nearly killed by the Vampire who had endangered their home and pack headquarters. All these things culminated in the very harried life Vee had led since. There had been a whirlwind of activity to where she scarcely felt like she could catch her breath, let alone feel any sort of normalcy and cadence to her new life.

Originally, when she had moved in with Shane, she had reasoned that she would find a new sort of normal that she would become accustomed to if she had allowed herself to feel comfortable, but now, especially with the revelations they had most recently had about who and what she was, she wasn't sure a calm and uncomplicated life was in the cards.

It was unlikely someone who was destined to hold their own fate in their hands and who was told her choices would change the course of the world would be capable of hiding away and living simply as she once had.

But Vee still had her distractions. The lock before her was a task she could easily lose herself in and let the troubles of her life fade away, if only for a time.

"You thought anymore about your birthday?" Lori asked, as she separated the once scattered papers into more cohesive piles on the counter so she could file them away appropriately. Vee's eyes snapped up to glance at Lori from over her magnifiers.

Her birthday was only next week; this would be the first birthday she even considered celebrating since her adoptive parents died. No one had been pressuring her, but they all wanted to do something, anything, other than pretend it was just another day like she typically did.

"Too much going on," Vee murmured back, looking back at the lock before Lori's sympathetic eyes met hers. Lori didn't push, which was somewhat unlike her, turning to take the papers into the inventory room and letting Vee zone into the lock.

"Patrick texted a minute ago. Said he and Shane are headed back to the new house," Lori said when she reemerged, causing to Vee to straighten up. She had, only moments before, finished adjusting the tines and only needing to put the plates back over the lock.

"They'll wonder if I'm not there," Vee grumbled, realizing there was still the matter of making the keys. No way for them to get back before Shane got there; that could either be good or bad. Maybe Shane would be able to send Toby away before she returned, or perhaps Toby would be finished. She could only hope.

"And Shane and Toby will both be in the house soon," Lori said, seeming to have read Vee's thoughts.

Vee glanced at her guiltily. Ever since it had been brought to her attention the truth of Toby's affections for her, Vee had been uneasy. Shane had a hard enough time grappling with the fact that Durran was in love with her. She wasn't sure how well he would handle the same being said for her work acquaintance. Vee didn't want to hurt Toby's feelings nor did she want to push away the delight and additional income of restoring the old locks he brought her, but she knew Shane.

"I don't want to hurt his feelings," Vee said, looking up at Lori's sympathetic face.

"He has to know eventually," Lori said, with far more wisdom to her words than a girl of nearly seventeen should be able to muster. Vee nodded, giving Lori a weak smile before she snatched the uncut keys she had decided for the lock from their spots along her key wall and went to the back to cut them. Vee had just finished the first key and came back to try it in the lock when her phone rang.

"Hello, Shane," Vee answered, wedging her phone between her ear and her shoulder as she resumed the fitting. It was a little stiff, so just a slight adjustment needed to be made.

"Why, if I may ask, are you not here?" Shane asked, not bothering to greet her, simply straight to business, as usual. She let a small smile grace her lips at the sound of his deep voice, velvet, even through the phone. If there was one thing she didn't feel any trepidation about, it was her feelings for him.

"Adjusting the lock," she told him. Truth. Not an ounce of a lie in that, since that was, in fact, what she was doing. She just didn't mention she was doing it to avoid everything else.

"There's about twenty boxes that are stacked in the entryway because someone wasn't here to tell them where to put them."

"I'll move them when I get back," Vee promised, trying for nonchalance but clearly failing. Shane knew her too well.

"Got a little overwhelmed?"

"Needed a more … quiet project," Vee told him with a bit of hesitation, as she moved back to the inventory room to shave down a few rough spots on the new key. The bond between Shane and Vee opened up a bit, as she felt Shane's reassurance, comfort, and love warming her. She didn't realize she had needed it until then, both having shut their end of the bond down over the course of the last week with all the chaos. Each of them had been tense on their own and hadn't wanted to increase the anxiety of the other by combining it.

The couple had become like two separate islands joined by a watery land bridge. They could feel each other, could tell the other one was still connected and within them, but they were cut off beyond that. Vee didn't realize how much she had missed the full bond with Shane until she felt it open on his end, blossoming within her. She could almost smell him surrounding her while they talked.

"How much more time do you need?" Shane's voice had grown much softer now, and she suddenly didn't care what awaited her at the house; she wished she could fold herself into him. The comfort of his voice and the open bond felt so good that she didn't want to think about anything else, but she knew realistically they needed keys and a functioning lock.

"I need to make at least two more keys, and then Lori and I will head back," she told him, taking the now much smoother key back to the lock for another test.

"I'll get these things unloaded and try to send everyone home before you get here."

"I think that's the most romantic thing I've ever heard you say," Vee murmured with a smirk.

"Romantic, was it?" he asked with a chuckle. His laugh was rare, and the deep vibration over the phone made her face feel hot.

"Mhm. Almost seductive," she said, trying not-so-subtly to do to him what he had unintentionally done to her. She was rewarded with a deep growl from the other end.

"I will *make* them all go home before you get here," he amended, his voice still nice and gravelly against her ear.

Lori made giggling faces from the other end of the shop, but Vee only grinned. There hadn't been much opportunity for alone time between her and Shane the past week, and she was now eagerly awaiting going home.

Home.

Shane's house hadn't felt like hers, but this new house, though it was much grander than her old, tiny apartment by a mile, something about being able to choose it, knowing she, Shane, and Patrick would be putting it together, made it hers, made it home.

"Good," she said, but just as the word left her mouth, she felt something at a slight distance from her shop. A Were.

All the pack wolves were busy helping the move, helping Cora with demolition, or at their human jobs. Not one pack member was free on this chaotic day to roam about Westport. Vee shot Lori a glance and moved her eyes to the front windows, indicating which direction she felt the presence coming from. Lori sensed the unease from Vee. The way the little locksmith's muscles tensed, a specific look of anxiousness that Lori only associated with when Vee felt threatened crossing over Vee's features. Lori immediately straightened, her body going on alert as she moved silently toward the windows, peering out briefly before stepping through the door.

"What is it?" Shane asked quietly, having been clued into her sudden change in emotion.

"There's a Were here. Lori's taking a look," Vee said, quiet enough that only Shane would be able to hear, as her eyes focused unblinkingly toward the teenager who had just stepped out, without hesitation, to protect her. Shane's breathing changed on the other end of the phone; there was nothing he could do from where he was.

Lori and Vee were, unfortunately, alone.

CHAPTER 2

V ee pushed Shane's emotions she had just been basking in aside in favor of focusing on Lori and the unknown Were presence, though it was now feeling more familiar. The tone of the vibrations was one of low-lying but chronic frustration, much like a sound that is constant and steadily in the background, which you find to be annoying at first but as time goes on, you start to be able to ignore its presence. Vee knew only one person who made her feel that way. An odd relieved, and then confused, expression on Lori's face confirmed the suspicion immediately.

"It's John Meyers," Vee said into the phone to Shane.

Shane let out a breath, then a very low, almost inaudible noise came from his throat, indicating his displeasure.

"Set the phone on the counter. He was supposed to be going home after he helped load the last truck. There is no reason for him to be there," Shane said after a moment. It seemed he too had been relieved, and then suspicious.

Vee set the phone face down on the counter before watching Lori gesture for John to join her inside the shop. Vee busied herself with pulling blank keys from the wall to make duplicates of her new house key instead of staring at them as they entered.

"Apparently Shane told John to swing through and check on you here at the shop before heading home," Lori said, doing a fantastic job of keeping her face neutral despite the waves of distrust Vee could feel coming from her. John smiled broadly, overly friendly, but nonetheless handsomely. He was conventionally attractive, attractive enough to have been a model or an actor if his longevity didn't have to be kept a secret. His dark blond hair, blue eyes, and face that matched the Golden Ratio were not enough, however, to sway Vee into thinking he had anything other than something sinister on his mind.

While Vee and Shane had been tracking down her parentage and past, John had been quietly seething that she had been capable of bonding with Shane. John, having married a human wife without even a touch of magic within her, was incapable of bonding. It was a miracle that given her lack of magic, the couple had produced children who were born with the Werewolf trait, two of the three. Vee had not been aware of his animosity toward her until their pack protection on the homes surrounding Shane's had been broken. He

was immediately enraged, blaming her for all the mis-
fortune that had befallen the pack.

She couldn't deny that John was somewhat right. If
she hadn't been part of their lives, they wouldn't have
had to go to battle with Gwen Tallon's coven. Nor
would they now be threatened by the Vampire master
of the local nest. But without her, they would have
had a very large problem on their hands when Lori
had unexpectedly changed a little over a year before.
Lori's change could have exposed the preternatural
community to humans. Vee helping Werewolves was
the reason she was even in their lives at all, not the
other way around.

John's hatred of her, or his frustration at Shane, did
seem to ebb a bit once they returned from the Sha and
told the pack that Vee's father was a Sha. Shane also
happened to give an ultimatum, plainly stating that
anyone who didn't accept Vee could leave the pack. It
wasn't perfect; John still resented her for being able to
bond with Shane, but it had seemed better, more subdued, this past month. Now with his unexpected arrival
at the shop, she wasn't so sure.

"We're fine. I'm almost done, and we're going back
to the house. I'm sure Shane would be fine with you
returning to Susan. Not that I think I need it, but I
have Lori here if someone tries to threaten me in the
middle of the day," Vee told him. Shane's guard wolves
were a source of contention between Vee and Shane,
and everyone in the pack knew it. She despised having
babysitters, and they were often unnecessary. Only a
very few times in the total number of days Shane had

someone stay with her had there actually been any sort of a threat.

"Is that why Lori's here?" John asked, a hint of condescension in his tone. He, like many men of a certain era, seemed to think female Weres were somehow weaker than their male counterparts, when, in reality, they were equally as strong and fast. The only thing they lacked was size in comparison to the males. Lori was quite formidable, according to Patrick and Shane. She was even faster than most of the pack, save for Frida, their best scout.

"Vee offered me an opportunity to take a break from my mother, but I don't mind keeping her safe if it's needed. Pack and friendship mean having each other's back no matter what. Right, John?" Lori asked, crossing her arms to hide her tightening fists but managing to keep her face pleasant and happy. Her face may not have been letting off her distrust, but Vee could feel every ounce of it as it flowed off her. She imagined there might have been a smell associated with it too, since John seemed to prickle a little.

John's mouth twitched at the little dig Lori's words made at him. He had been behaving selfishly, that much had been clear to everyone.

"I suppose I'm not needed then." John shot Lori an odd look, with a mixture of annoyance and mild humor. Lori's presence had certainly thwarted whatever plans John had, but apparently it wasn't enough to cause him to become overtly frustrated.

"I'm sure Susan will be happy to have you come home so early. Cora told me this morning she was planning on spending the whole day packing by herself,"

Vee said, trying to not-so-subtly let on that she knew what was going on within the pack. She may not have been privy to every piece of information, but she knew most things, including what was going on in his house. John didn't seem to gather what she was saying though, since his smile broadened, and he opened the door to take his leave.

"I'm sure she will." And with that, he was out the door and walking the opposite way from where he came.

This interaction told Vee two things. One, that John was very unfamiliar with subtleties, either in his actions or others. His not seeming to understand that Vee and Lori knew something wasn't quite right with this entire interaction was seemingly lost on him, as well as not being able to pick up on Vee's hint that she knew he had been lying. Two, that John was indeed up to something nefarious, whether it was just toward her or the pack in general, Vee wasn't certain, but she was still considered the weakest member since she didn't have full control over her abilities.

Vee finally picked up the phone from the counter once she could barely feel John's presence to see Shane was still on the line.

"He's gone," Vee told him.

"That was, by far, the oddest conversation I've ever had with John," Lori said, eyes still on the window where they had both watched him walk away.

"Don't leave until Tommy gets there. I'm not risking it. I thought when he decided to stay in the pack after the altercation last month that he had accepted the situation … apparently, I was wrong," Shane murmured into the phone, the sound of skin rubbing on skin quite clear.

"You'll rub a hole in your forehead if you keep that up. We can speculate on his reasons later. Right now, I need to finish making the other keys before Tommy gets here so we can all get into the house when we need to," Vee told him, smiling a little at the quiet chuckle he gave her for her initial admonishing tone.

"We certainly won't be leaving the door unlocked."

Tommy and Durran seemed to show up at nearly the same time. Vee had just finished making a few additional keys, one each for Shane and Patrick, and a handful of spares for pack members, like Thomas and Margaret, who were second and third in the pack hierarchy respectively.

"Did Shane call in *all* the reinforcements?" Lori asked, eyeing Durran as she came through the shop behind Tommy. Durran narrowed her eyes at the teenager for a moment before leaning against the opposite counter.

"Why is Shane calling in reinforcements?" Durran asked, her glance now darting to Tommy, who plunked himself down on his favorite stool by the door while they all waited for Vee to come out of the inventory room, with four precise keys in hand.

"John Meyers came by when he should have been home helping his wife pack. Shane happened to be on the phone with me when it happened and decided that he's up to something. I have to agree. But unfortunately, that means that I have to have bodyguards until I get home," Vee told her, as she stuffed the keys in her pockets before carefully covering the lock and its bits with the towel she had brought them in.

"Ah. So a normal day for Vee, then," Durran said, turning back to Lori, who rolled her eyes. Durran let a rare smirk grace her lips briefly.

"Pretty much, yeah," Vee confirmed, slipping her messenger bag over her shoulder and heading to the alarm panel. "Everyone ready?"

With no answers in the negative, she set the alarm, and they all filed out.

"I'll ride back with Vee, if you two want to follow us," Durran said, gesturing to Tommy's truck. At one time, someone would have questioned how Durran would be returning if she didn't take her own car, but she would either not answer or simply tell them she would fly back. Now they didn't bother. Even if it was still clearly daylight, she had her ways that even Vee wasn't privy to.

Vee started up the van and began driving to the new house. At first, she thought to question Durran for coming to the shop, as if everyone could predict her behavior before she had formulated her thoughts, but she recalled she had promised Durran to meet her at the shop at some point in the day. Now that Vee was officially pack, once the pack protection had been placed around their home, even as her Watcher, Durran could not go there without Vee. That could prove to be extremely dangerous if they let it go on too long. Having Vee escort Durran and "inviting" her within the protection meant she would no longer be barred by the magic, or that's what Shane had told them.

The certainty of the old rules of Were magic was a bit hazy. Vee had changed something within the pack. With her being brought into it, some of her had seeped out through those new bonds, and the magic of the pack was different. No one was sure what that meant, and thus far everything had seemed to remain as it had been, but Vee, Shane, and Durran were waiting for those changes to reveal themselves. To Vee, it seemed that she was now always waiting for the next shoe to drop, sending her life into more violence and chaos.

"We never set a time to meet today," Vee started to say to Durran, half apologetically since she realized she had been so preoccupied with the move she had barely looked at her phone.

"Well, I knew eventually you'd need to get away," Durran started, grinning at the grimace that flashed across Vee's face. "But more truthfully, I felt it when you left the barrier. I could find you again."

Durran had been much more forthcoming about her abilities and connection to Vee since they'd returned from Colorado. Durran had told her that Vee had changed her as well as the pack. It was unsettling to know Vee had the power to change the magic within another being, but because of that, Durran's tendency to be secretive about the Watchers was waning. If Vee, Durran, and the pack were to be a team, everyone needed to be on the same page.

"You'll always be able to find me soon enough," Vee said somewhat begrudgingly, as they paused at a red light.

The remainder of the short trip was driven in silence, both listening to the local radio station that Durran had switched on as soon as they got in. For the last month, Vampire attacks had been on the rise. They had started as assaults, humans waking up bruised and bloody with very little idea of how that had come to pass. The news speculated it was a small gang of youthful miscreants, until the word "injured" in the headlines changed to "dead." Kansas City's murder victim totals had nearly doubled in the last month alone.

Vee, Shane, and Durran all knew what was happening. It was exactly what Anton, Vee's unlikely Vampire ally, had warned them would happen. Lazare Duflanc, the master of the local Vampire nest, had disappeared following his attack on Vee. Her blood, like the blood of her mother before her, seemed to have driven him to a sort of insanity, one that Anton had helped him through years before. Anton had chosen to remain rather tight-lipped about the status of the nest, only having warned them what *might* happen if Duflanc was away too long.

Vee suspected Anton had gone off searching for him, leaving the nest of relatively young Vampires to fend for themselves, which accounted for the steady increase in brutality they were seeing from these attacks. Werewolves were not permitted to step in unless there was a threat of exposure, something which was becoming a very real possibility as more bodies turned up.

"Shane is going to need to appeal to the Sha, to ensure he has their protection and support before he takes out those younglings," Durran murmured, after the radio host described in horrifying detail how the most recent victim had been found. Her feet and hands had been removed, no blood on the scene, and what seemed like odd puncture marks at various places littered her body: neck, inner elbow, inner thighs.

"I mean, what does that sound like to you, Doug? If not vampires!" the radio host said, followed by a roar of laughter from his cohost and some others in the background.

"Vampires! Can you imagine? What's next, Werewolves roaming the streets? Witches cursing our city?"

The laughter continued until Vee shut the radio off and turned to Durran. They exchanged dark looks.

"Yes, Shane does need to appeal to the Sha. We haven't really talked to any of them since we returned home," Vee said, deciding to pull into the cul-de-sac, now that the moving vans and trucks wouldn't need to be coming and going for the rest of the evening.

"Not even your father ... or Min?" Durran asked, a bit of tenseness in her tone as she ground out Min's name. They hadn't gotten off on the best foot, Durran and Min, so it was understandable for Durran to have that reaction at his mention. If Min had gotten his way, Durran would have been taken out for knowing the location of the gate to the Sha realm. It had only been Vee and Shane's assurances that Durran would not take advantage of that knowledge, and them subsequently fighting off Duflanc as a team, that held Min back.

"I suppose Aho has text me a few times, mostly just promises to come visit us at some point, but otherwise, no ... no contact." Vee hadn't expected any sort of normal father-daughter relationship with Aho, but she had been thinking there would be a bit more than a random text here and there. She still had plenty of questions for him, but somehow, she felt it made more sense to ask them in person.

Vee turned to Durran once she shut the van off, having parked in front of her new home.

"We have arrived," Vee said with a little smile. Durran glanced at her, then followed her gaze, turning to take in the building.

It was quite a far cry from the place Vee had called home for the majority of their friendship. The dark stone rose up the first floor and bordered the second on the front, with stucco at the top. It was tall, imposing, looking old for the homes in the city and regal, though not overtly ornate and much larger, even than Shane's previous home in Brookside.

"I'm surprised you agreed to this," Durran said, eyes impartial as they looked over the façade.

"Many reasons," Vee mumbled, opening the door and climbing out of the van. Durran met her on the sidewalk, and the two of them stood side by side as she continued to look it over.

"More space for the pack, I imagine," Durran said, watching as a group of five pack members wandered out the front door to the last remaining moving truck, presumably to get the next load. Tommy was among them, seeming to have parked and jumped right back into unloading the last truckload as soon as he and Lori arrived. He spotted them and waved cheerfully, as usual.

"That's most of the reasons," Vee admitted with a sigh, walking through the still open front door. Though what Vee didn't say was the moment she saw the pictures of this house, she had known it was supposed to be theirs. She had been completely taken by the mental image of living there with Shane that there was no denying this was where they needed to move.

Just as they passed through the threshold, Shane seemed to materialize from nowhere, but she imagined he sensed her presence as she got closer.

"John is definitely up to something," Shane said, nodding to Durran as greeting as she stepped in behind Vee.

Oddly, Vee could feel the pack magic accepting Durran as soon as they pulled up. It was like an extension of herself and the oneness that she felt with the pack now that the bond had settled there. It vibrated within Vee, as if it was trying to rattle her bones, but it was intimately part of her too. Occasionally, she would feel the individual pack members, even at a distance. Vee felt their presence within her, much like she did when she was in the same room with them. Shane told her they felt differently to him, but they had both assumed the difference was due to her own abilities. How she perceived magic was different in general.

The pack magic had seemed to swell in intensity once Durran passed through the border. It resisted, not angrily since Vee's presence with Durran was indicating this was a welcomed presence, but it seemed to snap back once they were in front of the house.

Resistance gone.

Durran was accepted.

She wondered if Durran had felt repelled at all as they drove up. If she had, Vee had not been felt that impression. Many aspects of magic still confused her, and now that she was much more aware that she had her own magic within her, she found it far more confounding than her vague notions of it had been.

"Other than trying to get rid of you, Shane, what could he be up to?" Durran asked, as she looked around the house with mild interest. The house was still in quite a state of chaos, what with the boxes stacked and furniture haphazardly placed in rooms where they belonged. It would take quite a while before it was fully livable. Vee did not anticipate enjoying the time-consuming process that would be.

"It's still in that line of thinking. Using Vee as a way to get to me," Shane growled, pulling Vee against him and taking in a long inhale of breath to catch her scent. They both felt the added torture of each other's touch and scent. Not long now ... and they'd be alone. They still had a million things to do, but now that their things were moved, all that could wait.

"Whatever his plan was, it was foiled. I'm still just wondering how he knew I'd be at my shop," Vee said, taking only a moment to relish in the feel of Shane's arms around her before stepping away reluctantly and pulling off her messenger bag.

"There was a bet," Tommy said, as an answer, having barged back through the front door holding two large boxes stacked on top of one another. Shane cringed and Durran's lips twisted, clearly trying to subdue a smile.

"Excuse me?" Vee asked, freezing halfway through unwrapping the lock from the towel to glare at him.

"Oh yeah, everyone bet on how long it would take you to ditch and go hide in your shop today," Tommy said with a wide grin, setting the boxes next to the ever-growing stack in the entryway. "I think I was the closest. Pretty sure I won," he said proudly.

"I gave you six hours, but you surprised us all with eight," George said, having come behind Tommy with a box of his own. His usually perfectly neat hair was tussled from exertion, but he somehow still looked far more put together than Vee did in her torn jeans and rust smudged T-shirt.

Vee's emerald eyes darted sharply to Shane's guilty face, a thin rim of amber flashing momentarily.

"Did *you* bet, Shane?" Vee hissed, the question coming from between her teeth.

Without an answer, Shane turned to Tommy, instructing him that once the truck was unloaded, everyone needed to pack up to leave. Vee narrowed her eyes but set herself on the task of reinstalling the lock and, once again, making sure the new keys worked. Durran leaned down, careful not to jar Vee while she was working on the lock and keys. "I bet too," she murmured in Vee's ear, making Vee's face flush with restrained rage. Vee ignored the comment, keeping her eyes firmly glued to her task.

Of course, they'd all placed bets. Werewolves were notoriously competitive; they would, quite literally, make a competition out of everything, but for Durran to have gotten in on the bet—well, she hadn't expected that in the least. On the one hand, she was surprised. Durran involving herself with the pack members without Vee was not something she would have done just a month ago. On the other hand, Vee was quite happy. While it didn't seem like much, Durran getting in on the bet meant not only was the pack accepting her more, but that she was accepting the pack.

Vee smiled to herself as she continued adjusting the lock and making sure the fit was snug. Once she was satisfied, she turned back to Durran and Shane, who were discussing the Vampire situation, as well as John.

"As long as we keep John at bay until we can square away the Vampires, I don't think we'll have a problem. Min and Aho were planning to come see the new house and visit next week anyway, I'll see about appealing to them then," Shane told Durran, who nodded, seeming pleased by Shane's decisions. They had grown far more comfortable with one another more recently. Not that there wasn't still clear tension and jealousy on both their parts, but they managed to keep it civil, even occasionally friendly, which was always a pleasant surprise to Vee, even if it was often at her expense.

"I suppose I should give you a house tour," Vee said, sighing at Durran as she handed Shane his new key. It wasn't the wolf head that she had made for his previous house, but she hadn't had as much free time to make or restore things as she usually liked to, so it would have to wait. Durran raised an eyebrow at the strained look on Vee's face.

"Another time, perhaps. You look like you might short-circuit if you have to do one more thing." Shane grinned at Durran, clearly in agreement.

"I did want to show you something before you go, Durran," Shane said, gesturing out the front door. Vee followed with reluctance and curiosity, having no idea what Shane was planning to show her Watcher, but that seemed to be a theme lately, especially since their bond had been closed down. Shane had plans that he just didn't seem to let her in on, either as a surprise to her, or perhaps partially because he hadn't had someone to share all these things with in quite some time. It was hard to adjust to being in a relationship and having to communicate and confide when you've been alone for so long. Vee knew that better than most, and yet, she felt like she was better at adjusting to the communication part of a relationship than Shane.

The three walked along the stone path that cut to the side by the garage. Vee had seen the garage, of course, but she had no real use to go there since her van was a bit too tall to park inside. So, when Shane brought them around to the side, she was a bit shocked to see a nice set of stairs winding up to a second floor. The garage had an apartment. Somewhere in the back of her mind, Vee recalled that feature being listed on the description when they were deciding on a new home, but it hadn't seemed important to her at the time. Now she realized what Shane was offering Durran, and her heart nearly stopped in her chest.

"It's yours if you want it. You may not be officially a member of the pack, but you are part of Vee's. I understand you would want to stay close," Shane said, holding out a key for the apartment door to the brooding, dark Watcher. Durran looked at the key and then at Shane. Her red-tinged brown eyes widened ever so slightly at the gesture. With mild hesitation, Durran reached out her hand, glancing at Vee's shocked face before letting Shane drop the key into her palm.

"I ... I'm not sure what to say," Durran murmured, her face struggling to resume its normal neutral expression.

This was quite a gesture; this was acceptance. A white flag of peace when they had been teetering on the edge between hatred and allies. Despite Durran's feelings for Vee and the jealousy she still inherently harbored, she also knew Vee loved Shane. Vee had chosen Shane. Taking this key would be a symbol accepting that.

"You don't need to say anything or use it. But the space is there if you need or want it," Shane said.

Vee hit Shane on the arm, making both of them turn to her, Shane with surprise and Durran's expression unchanging, as she moved the key between her fingers.

"Why didn't you tell me about this?" Vee hissed, glowering at Shane.

"You don't want Durran here?" he asked, his tone having become rather provoking now. Irritation flashed within him at her anger. What about offering Durran a place close to them was worth her being upset about?

"Of course I do! I just..." She trailed off, not wanting to start an argument about proper communication in a relationship right in front of Durran. Durran, of all people, would relish an argument between them.

"We don't know what's coming, and I'd rather keep our pack, our family close," Shane told them both. It wasn't that Vee was unhappy with the gesture, but the swell of anger that flared in her made her close down her side of the bond. They had been busy. They had been overwhelmed. But he was omitting a great

number of things recently from their conversations, and she needed to find a way to remedy that, but until she did, her immediate response was fury.

"I think I'll head back in," Vee muttered through clenched teeth, turning briskly and going down the stairs, leaving Durran and Shane in startled silence on the landing.

CHAPTER 3

Patrick was in the kitchen, looking over the piles of boxes and crates that were piled there, when Vee stormed through. The kitchen was huge. It had two wall ovens, a six-burner range, and counter-space galore. Though Vee did small, what she considered mediocre, cooking, she had never cooked in a room like this. She was quite certain that Markus was going to be pleased; he tended to be the go-to pack cook for gatherings.

"Just thought I'd at least get the coffee pot set up so we can all function tomorrow morning," Patrick said without turning around, having sensed her come through the door.

"I might need a cup now," Vee admitted, moving to the box labeled "mugs" and starting to pull the tape off.

"How did Durran's surprise go?" Patrick asked, moving to try and find the boxes that contained the actual food products. They wouldn't be able to make more coffee if they couldn't locate it first.

"If I hadn't gotten irrationally angry, it probably would have gone well," Vee told him, having pulled three mismatched mugs from the box and setting them on the counter, perhaps a little harder than she intended, since the bottom of the third one chipped, the broken shard scattering across the counter and onto the floor. Vee looked mournfully at the mug that had chipped. It was one of her favorites, a teal cup that once sported the words, *I don't speak to anyone until I've had my coffee.* Over the years, some of the words had worn off, leaving, *I don't speak to anyone   my coffee.* Vee liked it better that way.

"Irrationally angry?" Patrick asked, glancing to where the ceramic piece landed.

"You seem to know a great deal more about what your father has planned than I do," Vee grumbled, choosing to dig through another box to find the coffee grounds a bit more carefully than she had with the mugs.

"I thought he had told you," he said quietly, eyeing her for a moment before he started filling the carafe with water.

"He did not," she said through gritted teeth.

"Not a good surprise then?"

"It's not that I don't want Durran here. He just … he's keeping things from me."

"It's not on purpose, I don't think," Patrick murmured, taking the coffee grounds from Vee's hand as she slumped into a barstool.

"Probably not," Vee said, resigned. She had wanted to have a thought-free evening, but with her slight outburst, she knew that would not be the case. Inevitably, she and Shane would have to have a conversation about what she expected as far as communication between them. Confrontation wasn't her strongest attribute, and the thought of an argument when she was already so exhausted and overwhelmed didn't sound appealing.

Vee's phone rang in her pocket as she heard Shane closing the front door behind him. He was alone, so Durran must have left or remained in her new apartment above the garage. Vee wasn't quite calm enough to have a thoughtful conversation with her fiancé just yet, so she welcomed the phone call, expecting it to be a house call or something. She was far too tired to take the business, but she could at least use answering it as a momentary distraction from Shane's questioning.

"Vee," she said, as she answered the phone without looking at the caller ID.

"Hey, Vee!" came the familiar voice of her old neighbor Una. While Una hadn't necessarily been Vee's friend, she was about as close as Vee had let anyone get to her in the time before Shane. As far as Vee had been concerned, Durran had been her only true friend. A fact that still filled her with a twinge of bitterness, now knowing Durran had been ordered to get close to Vee by the Elder Watchers. Una had been a neighbor, a quiet and thoughtful one at that. She never pushed a relationship on Vee, but she also didn't actively avoid her as most of their neighbors had. Una's cat Midi had been a wanderer, getting out of her second-floor apartment more times than Vee could count to greet her.

Vee had missed the little black cat and her eccentric owner over these past months.

"Una! How are you and Midi?" Vee asked, more excited to hear from Una than she would have thought.

"Mostly we're fine. She sits at the window a lot. I can tell she misses you." Vee's heart stung a little. She had wondered off and on if Midi was being left out too long now that Vee wasn't there to bring her back in. "It has been kind of crazy around here. I feel like the whole city is falling apart with all those attacks."

"I know. I want you to be extra careful right now, especially since you live alone," Vee said, a pit forming at the bottom of her stomach just thinking about Una being by herself. No one would realize she was gone for quite a while if something happened to her.

"That's actually partially why I called. I should have texted you more often, I feel so bad to call just to ask you for something," Una said, her voice pained.

"Don't feel bad! I haven't texted or called either."

"That's more to your character, though," Una said, chuckling lightly. Vee glanced up at Patrick, who was clearly listening in on the conversation while he quietly rummaged through the boxes labeled *kitchen*. He had finished setting the coffee to brew and was making himself somewhat useful until it was ready. Shane had yet to make an appearance, but she assumed he wasn't far, listening in as well.

"So, what's the other part?" Vee asked, smiling at the sound of Una's chuckle, but hearing the uneasiness simmering under the surface of her lightheartedness. A shaky sigh came through, and Una was silent for a moment.

"I think someone is stalking me. I keep seeing the same guy at my work and sometimes out front of the apartment. Last night, my keys weren't in my purse under the counter when I was getting ready to leave, and they miraculously were returned by a customer to my coworker after I had been looking for a half hour. I think it was him. The stalker. I'm scared he made a copy of my apartment key, Vee," Una said, her voice growing shaky the more she spoke.

This, unfortunately, wasn't unheard of. Una still lived in Midtown and had started working a few nights a week at a bar to supplement her income not long before Vee moved. Predators of the human male variety were known to take a shine to the bartenders and servers of the establishments that they frequented. Vee had changed many locks for the women in the neighborhood for the very same reason.

"I'll come over first thing and switch it out for you. We'll put in some additional locks too," Vee told her without hesitation.

"I didn't want to have to ask you," Una said apologetically.

"I would have been more offended if something happened and you hadn't asked me. What's the earliest you are okay with me coming over?"

Vee got off the phone, having darted from the room to snatch her bag from the entry so she could write the time Una had requested as well as everything she'd need from her shop before she went over. She wandered back into the kitchen blindly, still looking down at her notebook and writing when she felt Shane's overwhelming heat come behind her. For a moment, lost in her own little bubble of distraction from Una, Vee merely basked in the heat and his presence being so near. But it didn't take long with her feeling the small hint of his emotions, since their bond was still closed, to snap her back.

"It's a little late for coffee for you, Patrick," Shane said, as he entered the kitchen behind her, stepping around without even brushing against her. Vee stopped writing to glance at him. No hint of the irritation that had been on his face when they were outside with Durran, but she could still feel it there slightly, despite having closed off their bond.

"I have homework to finish for tomorrow," Patrick said sheepishly.

"I thought you'd finished it up on Friday so the weekend was free," Vee said, eyes narrowing as they focused their attention on Patrick's guilty face.

"I'm going to get it done!" Patrick insisted, raising his hands up in surrender. "I was hoping we'd have food, though."

Shane grimaced as he opened the very sparse refrigerator; the contents amounted to condiments. They had purposefully cleared the house of leftovers and perishables, not wanting to have anything spoil if it sat in a truck too long, but two Werewolves in a house meant they would need to restock quickly. Not something that could happen right at the moment, though.

"I'll go to the grocery store after I change Una's locks tomorrow," Vee told them both. She knew she didn't need to give further explanation; both had heard the entire exchange.

"We'll order something to be delivered tonight," Shane said, gaining sounds of both hunger and relief from the other two. Patrick handed Vee a full mug of coffee as she finally stashed her notebook back in her bag. She glanced at the mug with suspicion, as she realized it was the one she chipped.

"It won't leak; I checked before I filled it with the coffee," Patrick assured her, before snagging his backpack that was set precariously atop a stack of boxes in the corner of the room and leaving the kitchen, most likely to his new bedroom.

Shane waited a beat to make sure Patrick was well out of earshot before he looked at Vee and raised an eyebrow.

"Order the food first," she said, returning the raised eyebrow that he gave her as she took another sip of coffee. His grunt in response was both affirmative as well as grumpy. This was going to be a fun conversation.

Instead of waiting in the kitchen while he placed the order, Vee snatched her mug and made her way up to the room that was to be theirs. She hadn't been in the room since earlier in the day when she and Margaret had decided what spot would be best for the bed to go. Otherwise, she had spent most of her time giving instructions from the hallway until she had decided to lose herself in the front door lock.

She opened the double doors that lead to the primary suite and glanced around at the stacks of boxes, bags, and luggage that were piled around the parameter. The bed frame was put together with the bare mattress on top of it in the spot that Margaret had suggested. Vee had been mostly indifferent, but she did like that the bed was an against exterior wall, much like the bed at the Pleasant Hill property. Light would stream in from the windows, both sun and moon.

Vee looked out the windows at the darkening sky and let the weight of the last few weeks fall away. The conversation with Shane would probably be unpleasant, but it was necessary. The hardest part of this move was over.

She thought back to what had been causing her anxiety to spike so much, other than the overwhelming revelations that she had when she met her *zi*. Something about her powers had caused the ritual to place the new pack protection around their and Thomas's new homes to amp up from what it had been at Shane's old house. It was the first time since she had been brought into the pack that Vee was involved in a pack activity, having decided against going on the run when they returned from Colorado.

It hadn't been a full moon, but the sky was clear. It seemed like it was reaching out and touching them all, caressing them with her light, even with the light pollution of the city surrounding them. The pack stood in a circle in the extensive back yard. No one was touching, but their bonds seemed to vibrate more intensely, as Shane spoke.

"We place protection here. Eyes don't see. No path to turn. No scent to track. No magic to cast unless it is ours and we will it."

Vee felt her heartbeat changing within her chest. It was pulsing with a beat that was resonating within the bonds. The pack magic, their unity, was coming through. She could feel them all on the precipice of change. The beasts were at the surface. The circle was glowing as their eyes revealed their wolves within. Her fists clenched as she felt her body urging her to … to do something. She wasn't sure what. All she knew was she needed to give, to take, to change.

She looked down at her fingers as her breath came out in short, raspy grunts. She could hear similar sounds from everyone else around her. Her hand was shaking, and she could almost see her skin shimmering under the moonlight.

Change.

She heard the call in her head. She watched, as one by one, the pack members dropped to their knees and began changing into their wolves. It wasn't the call of the moon; it was the call of their Leader.

She turned her gaze to Shane, who seemed to be radiating in his power. He was taking in the magic, magic gifted by the others with their bodily transformations, and using it to create a barrier. She had never noticed the protection surrounding Shane's home before, but now she saw it. It was like a translucent shimmering curtain that was swelling from the circle of Weres and moving outward. She had no change to give; in fact, she could feel the power filling her up as well as Shane, and like a small stream, it flowed out and into him from her as well.

This protection can be stronger.

She knew it instinctually. Without another thought, she turned to Shane, whose eyes were unfocused, glowing vibrant gold. They, alone, were the only two not in wolf form, but he looked as if he was barely holding onto his human shape.

She reached out, moving by instinct alone, and clutched his forearm roughly. His head jerked, just slightly, but he didn't turn to her. With the contact, the power filling them seemed to explode forth. Vee could feel it pulling from her and joining the shimmering veil that was now encompassing their new home. Bigger and stronger than it had ever been. How she knew this, she wasn't sure, but it would be impenetrable.

Shane's skin shifted under her touch, his flesh turning to fur beneath her fingers. She could not look down or change her focus to see, but she knew that he had finally succumbed to his change. She, alone, was standing in the circle of wolves.

The air was different. Shane was still their Leader ... but something had shifted.

Without hesitation, she let her head lift to the moon and as one, they howled, sealing the protective magic around them.

"You could have changed. I could sense it through the bond, even though you resisted," Shane said, breaking her out of her memory of the week before.

"I don't think I could have," Vee said, turning from the window she had been staring out.

"You don't remember it, but you have before." His smirk both irritated and heated her in opposing ways.

"That whole experiences was mind-bending. I don't know if any of us remember it as it truly was," Vee grumbled.

It was hard for her to believe she had changed into not only a wolf, but a crow and a cat as well, but it wasn't just Shane who told her she did. Aho and Min had also confirmed that fact to her. She had no idea how she had done it, but when she went through the full moon without any urge to change shortly after they returned, she had convinced herself she wouldn't again.

"Deny all you want, but I know you believe me," Shane murmured, turning to the box labeled *sheets* to begin making the bed.

Vee set her coffee on the bedside table to help him, the two of them working silently, performing the motions as they had many times since moving in together. It was an odd familiarity in an everyday task. One of the parts of a relationship you don't necessarily think about but turns out to be strangely intimate. Who else sees you changing the sheets but the person you live with?

Vee was halfway through pulling the pillowcase over his pillow when he stopped her.

"Are you going to explain your reaction, or am I supposed to figure that out?" Shane asked, his tone mildly patronizing.

CHAPTER 4

V ee's anger flared with the question. Everything about how he said it to her was laced with condescension, from the way his mouth tightened to his arms crossed across his chest. Though she knew he was physically tired and mentally exhausted, like she was, it wasn't an excuse for him to have that reaction to her.

"Not if you ask me that way," she hissed, throwing his pillow at him. A small growl escaped his throat as he caught it just shy of his face.

"You don't want Durran living here?" Shane asked, his voice gravely with anger.

"That's not even remotely the problem."

"Then what is? What is the problem, Vee?" he roared, causing her to tense, clenching her fists into the comforter she was about to spread over the bed. Her eyes glowed amber as she glowered at him. She took a shaky breath, willing herself to let the words she was about to say come out spoken, instead of screaming. His anger was piling onto her own, and she swallowed it down just enough.

"Why didn't I know about it before today?" She spoke slowly and quietly, words overly enunciated, making her voice low and dangerous.

Shane's face narrowed slightly as he took in her question. In his mind, he had already discussed it with her. It had made perfect sense to have Durran live there, separate but close by. They had no idea what was coming in the future, and though Shane didn't particularly like how *attached* Durran was to Vee, she would do everything in her power to keep Vee safe. That much Shane was certain of. But though he had thought this over a multitude of times, and even mentioned it repeatedly to Thomas and Patrick, Shane realized after a few long moments that he had, in fact, never talked to Vee about it.

The past few weeks had been chaotic. Messy even. Most days, one of them was asleep in bed before the other even came up. Vee had been working and coming home to pack, while Shane was simultaneously working with clients and overseeing the renovations. The security company had also seen an end-of-summer boost in business with concerts and festivals that took most of the pack, off and on, to coordinate. Not to mention the additional patrols until the new pack protection was put up and the increased Vampire attacks.

No, they'd had so little time together in the past few weeks, Shane had found himself slipping into his comfortable pattern of confiding in Patrick and Thomas, even through text messages, and not Vee.

"I..."

"I feel like an outsider. Not that I didn't before, but at least you usually let me in on what was going on. Now, I have no idea what the plans are. I only knew about the pack protection ritual because of Tommy and Lori. Were you planning on just springing that one on me too? And what about all these renovations? I thought Toby was only putting in more outlets and upping the AMP service. What project has his crew been working on that couldn't be finished before we moved today? What else are you not telling me, Shane?" The words burst from Vee's lips and just continued tumbling forth without her control. Her voice had started shaky, but remained calm, but as she spoke, the anger started seeping through, and her eyes began burning an even more brilliant amber than they had been. Shane's had dimmed down so there was only a small ring of gold circling his irises, his anger dissipating as he realized the error in his ways.

"Vee..."

"And I know it's probably because you haven't had a partner in your life since Patricia. You haven't had to confide and share with someone like me for years. You are comfortable doing that with Thomas. I understand that, which is why I'm so angry at myself for this reaction. But today..." She took in a deep breath and let it out quickly, her dark bangs fluttering away from her forehead with the force. "Today with Durran, I just couldn't help myself. It's not an excuse to be overwhelmed with all the changes, but damn it, Shane! You blindsided me! Durran isn't yours. She isn't your pack. She isn't even your friend. She's mine. And you didn't even tell me before you did it!"

Vee was pacing now; her fingers having released the comforter but only so she could once again fist her hands as she walked stiffly on her side of the bed. Shane watched her thoughtfully for a moment, making sure she wasn't going to start yelling again. Not that he hadn't seen her yell before, and not that he hadn't been on the receiving end of it many, many times, but something about this was a bit more breathtaking than it had been in the past.

She wasn't angry at him for overstepping, necessarily. It was that she wasn't involved in the process, that he hadn't talked to her about it. She was thoroughly invested in this relationship, to the point that the idea she wouldn't be informed about things, even non-life-threatening things, like what projects were being done around the house, infuriated her. And she'd even waited until they were alone before addressing it. In the past, she would blow up at him, damn who was present to witness it. This time, she made sure they were alone.

Something about that and the absolute heat that radiated off her when she was angry ignited Shane, but not in anger.

"I'm sorry," he said quietly, watching her as she paused in her pacing.

"What?" She whipped her head over to look at him.

"You're right that I fell into comfortable habits. And I didn't think before springing that on you. I know how much you hate that. So, I'm sorry," Shane said, moving around the bed so he was standing close, looking down at her with a simmering gaze. Vee let her shoulders soften a little as she looked up at him in disbelief. She was expecting him to fight her. To tell her to get over it. That *she* was in the wrong.

"Wh—?"

"Let me in there," he whispered, cutting off her stammering as he lightly touched her temple. If he could have wrapped himself in the comfort of their bond flowing freely, he would have. To have it reopened that day after weeks of shutting it down, and then quickly slamming it closed again, was rough. He had missed the feel of Vee fully there, fully present within him. He missed their wordless, subliminal communication throughout the day that they had started to grow accustomed to. And it wasn't just the bond that he missed. Busy as they had been, they had barely touched, let alone kissed.

Vee didn't fully have time to process her thoughts before her instincts took over. Her hands snaked up his chest, his shirt still mildly damp from exertion throughout the day. She had been getting better at using her other senses, especially her nose. She could feel his desire, through the bond and her ability, but she could also smell the tangy scent of it as well.

She let the bond reopen from her side, letting him feel her in her entirety. He took in a sharp breath at the suddenness and the feel of her own desire, but she moved first, hands sliding up his neck to thread her fingers through his hair. She yanked his head down to hers, drawing their lips together.

A growl rumbled in Shane's chest as he lifted her up, loving the way her legs immediately wrapped around his waist as they deepened the kiss. The electricity seemed to spark between them, breaths coming out as shallow pants, before going right back to devouring each other.

Shane just held her, squeezing at her back, hips, and cheeks, unsure if he wanted to take her on the bed, the floor, against the wall? But nothing was soon enough.

"Take your shirt off," Vee growled, pulling her legs down to stand once again. Shane chuckled as she yanked at the offensive material for a moment before he whipped it over his head.

"Yours too," he said, eyes glowing bright as he watched her pull hers over her head without a second thought.

He bent down, grasping behind her thighs and taking her feet out from under her so she fell back on the bed. The laugh that came from her made his entire heart glow. He tugged roughly at her pants. He'd been making attempts to keep from ripping them off her recently, but they'd gone so long now...

"Just rip them!" Vee growled. He didn't have to be told twice. They were off her the next second. She practically purred, smiling as she looked up to him, now bare. He grinned back at her, climbing on the bed over her and running his nose over her neck.

"How long until the food comes?" Vee panted, as his hand slid around her, undoing her bra, and his lips trailed fire over her neck and chest.

"Patrick will get it," he grumbled, as the bra came free.

Shane brought his lips back up to hers, grasping her hair roughly to angle her head better for him to devour. The kiss became frenzied. Nothing mattered more than feeling one another. Vee's hands raked over Shane's back as he pulled her head back to have better access to her neck. They were basking in each other after having so little touch, but it still wasn't enough.

Shane pulled away from her for just a moment to look into her amber eyes before he pushed forward. They joined together for the first time in weeks, and it pulled a gasp from them both. Their bond seemed to reinforce itself, overloading them with pleasure and completeness. They continued to clutch at each other, like they couldn't stand to have even an ounce of their skin not touching. But as they reached that peak that was always baffling, Vee's back arched up off the bed as Shane bit into her shoulder, and they both found oblivion.

They lay there for several minutes, just breathing each other in as they returned to reality.

"I don't think we can ever go that long again," Shane said, his voice muffled in the crook of her neck.

"We better never need to move again," Vee said, running her hands through his hair. His stomach growled, and then hers did immediately after, making them both chuckle. Moving day meant eating at odd times, and Shane didn't know Vee had skipped breakfast and lunch, partially because she was busy, and partially out of nervousness. Anxiety could sure be an appetite killer.

"I should check and see if the food's here," Shane said, reluctantly pulling away from her, but not without giving her a quick kiss.

Vee decided she needed a shower. She was covered with sweat, dust, metal shavings, and now Shane. Even though she knew she'd just shower again in the morning, she felt she needed to be clean to sleep at all tonight. She rummaged through the duffle bag for some of the clothes she had dropped in there when she and Margaret had been in earlier and grabbed a pair of shorts to slip on under the band T-shirt of Shane's she'd made hers over the last few months. He didn't seem to mind, not even bothering to put it away in his dresser anymore. Though she had been the only one to wear it for some time, it still smelled like him whenever she slipped it on.

Vee heard the knock on the front door as she put her now clean wet hair in a braid, realizing that had to mean their food was finally there.

"I'll get it!" Patrick yelled to the whole house, shortly before she heard him sprinting down the stairs.

She looked around the still not-put-together bedroom but sighed happily. The hard part was over, the move. They were in their house. Her and Shane's house. She couldn't help the smile that spread over her face as she wandered down the hallway to get back to the kitchen. The smell of the food hitting the air as she got closer made her stomach clench, like it was trying to digest the scent. But she was stopped dead in her tracks as she got halfway down the stairs, and Toby was standing in the entryway.

"One second, Toby," Shane called from the other room. Toby's face seemed to take her in and contract. Like seeing her there was so confusing, he didn't know how to process it.

"Hey Toby," she said quietly, trying to smile, though his gaze was uncomfortable. Eyes moving from her face to her wet hair and down to Shane's T-shirt that hid her shorts, settling on her thighs, then finally her bare feet, before snapping back to her face. She was *very* uncomfortable, and Shane seemed to reappear in the room, his eyes finding hers with concern and a questioning feeling tugging at her through the bond.

"What's Vee..." Toby started but let his words trail off as he seemed to let the pieces click in his head.

"Here's that list of equipment," Shane said sharply, turning his eyes back to Toby, though a ring of gold had formed around his irises.

"Oh ... yeah. I'll get right on this," Toby said, clearly taking effort to rip his eyes from Vee and to the paper Shane held out to him. "I'll call you when I get these to set up when we can bring them by," Toby said, keeping his eyes down as he turned toward the door.

"That would be great," Shane said. He was clearly trying to keep his voice normal, but to Vee's ears, it was wildly unsuccessful. The rumble that came from him made Toby cower; it was an instinctual thing. He knew, somewhere within him, that Shane was a predator, and he, the weaker animal.

But that didn't stop Toby from turning back after he had opened the door, eyes glancing up at Vee and then Shane.

"If I had known..." he started.

"You know now," Shane rumbled deeper.

The door closed with a snap, and they waited a beat for Toby to get into his truck and drive off.

"He's in love with you," Shane growled, fists clenching at his sides.

"Oh yeah, everyone knew that ... except you and Vee," Patrick said with a mouth full of noodles, as he walked back into the hall from the kitchen. Shane turned sharply toward Patrick and glared.

"You should have told me before I had him work on—" Shane stopped himself mid-sentence.

"Had him work on what, Shane?" Vee asked, narrowing her eyes. She had brought up the secret renovation project more than once and still hadn't been told what was going on. Patrick grinned broadly with full cheeks, turning and walking back into the kitchen.

"I'm hungry," Shane grunted instead of answering, heading toward the kitchen with Vee hot on his heels.

"Why won't you just tell me?" she snapped, as Patrick slid the box of fried rice toward her.

"Does the word 'surprise' mean anything to you?" Shane asked, shooting her a glare.

"She doesn't like surprises, Dad," Patrick said, barely containing his laughter.

"You are just as much in on this as me," Shane growled.

Vee glared, Patrick cowered, and Shane silently ate a crab rangoon, crunching it loudly.

"You're really not going to tell me?" she asked the two men, who simply said nothing to her.

They finished eating, Shane and Patrick discussing how they would unpack the house into sections, while Vee sat silently fuming at them. But she was too tired to argue, tossing her leftovers in their barren refrigerator and heading up to bed without a word.

They still hadn't finished putting it together; the fitted sheet was on, and Shane's pillow had a case, but the rest had been happily abandoned earlier. Vee stared at the comforter she had dropped on the floor and frowned before she picked it up. Now Vee was back to disgruntled. Shane came up as she was pulling it on and closed the door slowly.

He knew she was mad. He could feel it through the bond that she was, surprisingly, still keeping open, but more than that, in the tense way she was holding her shoulders.

"Don't be mad," he murmured, walking closer to her as he moved to his side of the bed to look across it at her.

"I'm trying," she said, pushing the comforter aside to climb in.

"I should be allowed to surprise you on occasion."

"You like to do that," she murmured, turning to face him as he climbed in on his side.

"I do," he said with a smile, brushing her hair over her shoulder as he propped himself up on his elbow.

"I don't like surprises," she said, narrowing her eyes.

"I know," he said chuckling, as he leaned forward and kissed her lips softly. "But you'll like this surprise. It's just not ready yet."

"I'm too tired to complain at you, anyway," she said, some of her irritation letting go as she looked at his face. The only thing she saw there was love and amusement. How could she be angry that *this* man wanted to surprise her?

"Me too," he said, grabbing her at the waist and pulling her close.

"You're lucky I love you," she whispered as her eyes began closing, the steady vibration of Shane lulling her to sleep.

"I love you too," he chuckled lightly, closing his own eyes. She fell asleep with her head against his chest, breathing in his scent and feeling so much more at peace than she had for quite a few weeks.

CHAPTER 5

V ee woke up to Shane's lips on her forehead. She cracked open her eyes and looked at him as he stood at her side of the bed, buttoning his shirt. He smelled like he had just showered, and she noticed a steaming mug of coffee sitting on the bedside table.

"Where are you going so early?" Vee asked as she sat up and snatched the mug, bringing it to her lips as Shane turned to grab his jacket from a box it was draped over.

"I have an early meeting with a client. Then I thought I'd try to track down John and have a chat with him," Shane said, his eyes hardening a little as he brought him up.

"Is Patrick off to school?" she asked, glancing around and noticing there were no clocks set up.

"Not quite awake yet. I thought I'd wake you. I know you need to get some things before you head to help Una," he said.

"What time is it?"

"Seven."

Quite late for Vee, but she wasn't planning on opening the shop that day. Too much to do. She would take house calls if anyone rang, but with her helpers in school and whole house to unpack, she figured she could keep it closed one more day.

The horrible sound of Patrick's alarm going off down the hall made them both cringe. It died after an inhuman roar from Patrick and loud crashing sound.

"He didn't fix the volume," Shane rumbled, glaring at the door. Sensitive hearing meant alarm clocks for Weres were turned all the way down. Apparently, that had slipped poor Patrick's mind when he'd set it up the night before.

"I suppose I'll get him a new alarm clock when I go to the store today," Vee murmured, envisioning the wreckage of plastic and metal across his room and the potential hole in the wall Patrick had just made. Shane grinned, moving close to the bed once again to kiss her lightly on the lips.

"You planning on being in the shop much today?" he asked, his desire blossoming as he looked at her, still slightly disheveled from sleep.

"After Una and the store, I'll just be home unpacking," she said, letting a wry smile twitch into place.

"Home," he hummed, liking the way she said that. She had never called his other house home. "I'll try to make this business with John quick."

"So you can set up your office?" Vee asked, playing dumb. He growled.

"So we can be alone in this house for a few hours," he murmured, pressing their foreheads together and taking a deep inhale of her scent. Vee grinned, taking the additional kiss he pressed to her lips happily before he tore away from her.

Vee had just pulled up to her old apartment when a text message buzzed on the phone.

[Durran: Why are you at your old apartment?]

[Vee: That would have been creepy if I didn't know you were my Watcher.]

[Durran: I don't think it's safe to go back there. Too exposed.]

[Vee: Daylight. Plus, Una needed my help with something. Shouldn't be too long.]

Vee snagged her bags with supplies and wandered up to the familiar building. The landlord had insisted she keep the main door key, deciding that having a locksmith in his back pocket might not be the worst idea. She hadn't been called over to change any locks yet, but she hadn't minded. She knew the landlord and this building; it wasn't her little fortress of solitude anymore, but it still held years of good memories.

As she went to unlock the door, Midi appeared, rubbing against her leg and purring loudly.

"Oh, Midi," Vee said happily, crouching to scoop her up. "I've missed you."

"She definitely missed you too," came Una's voice from the window above.

"I'll be right up," Vee said with a grin, looking up at the only neighbor she had ever gotten to know.

She went up to the second floor, and Una was there with the door open. Her hair was bright red this time and longer than it was when Vee had last seen her, but she supposed it had been six months. She felt a pang of guilt that she knew wasn't necessary. Una understood Vee and her rather reclusive ways. It hadn't been a shock to her that Vee hadn't reached out since she moved away from the building.

"Like old times," Una said, reaching out her arms for Midi to jump into.

Vee stepped inside the apartment that she had only seen from the vantage point of the front door. It was the same layout at Vee's old apartment, but there was so much more going on in the space. Colorful tapestries and posters lined the walls, floor to ceiling bookshelves with books, DVD cases, and knickknacks lined one wall. She had an old velvet couch that looked like it had been burnt orange at some point, but there were quite a few pillows and blankets covering it, and a low coffee table where a very intricate-looking incense burner sat, smoke curling into the air.

"I'm sorry I didn't really get a chance to pick up in here," Una said sheepishly, as she let Midi down and moved to grab a few cups and a bowl that were on the coffee table.

"No need to apologize," Vee said, setting her bags on the ground beside the door and going to look at the lock.

"So ... I know we didn't exactly share much when you lived here, but you never did tell me why you moved," Una said when she returned from the kitchen. Vee couldn't help the way Shane flashed in her mind, warming her before the rest of the chaos that had ensued over the past year and a half seemed to crush the nice thought.

"I know it's surprising, but I met someone," Vee said, starting to unscrew the lock from where it was nestled in the door. Someone had definitely tampered with it. There was some residual marks left on the outside that were telltale signs, but there was no way to know if it was from recently or not.

"Vee? Met someone? I wondered when I started seeing all these people hanging around the building. Who is he? Some mob boss?" Una said sarcastically, chuckling.

"He owns a security company," Vee said, glancing over at Una's cheeky grin.

"Pretty serious if you moved in together."

"Getting married even," Vee said, pulling the new lock from her bag. It wasn't strange to say that she and Shane were getting married when it was in her head or to pack members, but to someone who had only known her from her solitary life before, it felt foreign coming from her mouth. Shane and the pack were a different facet of her. He brought out a different version of her, the real her, that no one else had really gotten to see, except for maybe Durran.

"I would have never thought," Una said, not keeping the grin from her face as she watched a light blush come to Vee's cheeks. Una was truly happy for Vee; the feeling flowed out from Vee's former neighbor like warm rays of sunshine.

"What about you, Una?" Vee asked, giving her a side eye. Una seemed to get slightly embarrassed, her cheeks filling with color. She had also been quite solitary for the years when they shared the building.

"There is this guy. Not the stalker, thank goodness, but another customer that I've been considering letting him take me on a date," Una said, grabbing her coffee mug from the table and fiddling with it.

"Tall, dark, and handsome?"

"Tall, blond, handsome, and foreign. He said he came over to the States for business a long time ago. I can't believe he seems interested in me. We are polar opposites," Una confessed, twisting a piece of her brightly dyed hair in her fingers.

Something about the way Una described the man made the hair on the back of Vee's neck rise. She wasn't sure why. Kansas City, though completely at the center of the country, got quite a lot of foreign expats moving here for business. It shouldn't have made her suspicious, but her mind was swirling with possibilities.

"I'm going to add some extra locking mechanisms, just in case," Vee said, when she finished checking that the lock lined up and the new key worked.

"I know you don't really go out, Vee, but you could come by while I'm working. Maybe I could meet this guy who managed to snag your attention," Una said, as Vee pulled out a U-lock and was setting it against the door and frame.

Vee thought about Shane meeting Una and thought it wasn't the worst idea. She and Shane hadn't really gone on many "dates," and now that Una was back in her life, despite her being completely human and not at all capable of being part of Vee's whole life, she liked the idea of being able to call her a friend. She should have years ago.

"When do you work next?" Vee asked.

Una told Vee about her irregular schedule, but she usually worked every Friday night. The idea of being in Westport on a Friday made Vee's stomach roll, but she could do it once, at least, for Una and Shane. Shane didn't deserve to have to cower away from anything fun and exciting because Vee couldn't handle a crowd.

"Friday," Vee said with a smile over her shoulder, making Una positively radiate with joy.

Vee finished up, taking a minute to pet Midi, who purred happily, before refusing any payment from Una and making her way back to her van. Durran was leaning against it, her usual black duster against the black van should have been too hot on this eighty-degree September day, but Durran looked unfazed as usual.

"You couldn't keep from coming, huh?" Vee asked, as she set her things in the van's back.

"It smells like Vampire out here. Fresh," Durran said with a grumble.

"Well, they've been all over the place these days. I'm not surprised," Vee said, but that eerie feeling immediately came back. She glanced at Una's window before moving to get in the van. Durran climbed in the passenger seat as Vee started it up.

"Shane needs to appeal soon. This is getting out of hand," Durran grumbled as Vee headed back toward Ward Parkway. Groceries and an alarm clock meant either two stores, or she could go to Target, which was much closer to her house. She was choosing Target and a one-stop.

"Shane said Aho and Min are coming. I guess I could see when," Vee murmured, grabbing her phone while they were at a red light.

[Vee: Shane said you were coming to visit soon. Can I ask when? I made some plans and don't want to be a bad host.]

That text served several purposes, one saying she didn't exactly appreciate Shane knowing more about when her father and brother were coming to see them, while also trying to determine when.

[Aho: Some things are being settled. I'll tell you when we are close.]

Vee rolled her eyes, shoving her phone at Durran to read as the light turned green, and she continued South to the Ward Parkway shopping center. All these cryptic preternaturals Vee had to deal with would be enough to set anyone on edge. Unfortunately, she was rather used to it at this point.

"I can see why you get frustrated with me," Durran said, after reading the message.

"Interesting how you only catch that when the tables are turned," Vee said, glancing at Durran with a smirk.

Vee pulled into the Target parking lot, which was surprisingly sparse.

"Vee, I wanted to make sure you're okay with me staying at the house," Durran said suddenly, as Vee turned the van off and put her messenger bag over her head. She stopped and looked over at Durran, whose eyes held just the smallest amount of pain as she held out the key to Vee.

"I want you there, Durran. My outburst was more about Shane's lack of communication," Vee said, pushing Durran's hand back toward her. "If I had known that's what he planned, it would have gone much differently."

"You're sure? I know you like your solitude." Vee laughed, opening the door and climbing out.

"There's no solitude in a pack house, Durran. If you plan on staying, you'll find that out soon enough."

Vee, and oddly Durran, who had decided to join Vee in her shopping adventure, were staring at the alarm clocks when Vee's phone rang.

"I just thought I'd tell you I'm headed to John," Shane said as soon as Vee answered.

"I'm at the store now. Durran is with me," she said, wedging the phone between her shoulder and ear as she picked up one of the alarm clock boxes, looking at the features.

"I'll try to make this quick," Shane said, sending her a little twinge of desire. She glanced at Durran, who seemed unperturbed but she felt the jealousy bubble up under the surface.

"See you at home," Vee said, hanging up before Shane could say anything more. "I'm sorry," Vee murmured, picking up a different alarm to see if its features were less flashy. The price certainly indicated it was.

"You don't have to apologize," Durran said, but her hand tensed around the box she was holding. "You are allowed to love him, Vee. I may have been a fool, but that's not your fault," Durran murmured before moving down the aisle.

Vee's heart ached a little for Durran. In a different life, Vee may have chosen her. Her life before Shane, she would have never entertained the idea of being with someone, and Durran had kept herself at the arm's-length distance Vee had demanded. When Shane came along, Vee had fought her feelings as long as she could, but there was no escaping it. True Mates were inevitable.

The subject was dropped, and Vee and Durran loaded the back of the van full of groceries, and the only alarm clock that wasn't loaded with additional unnecessary functions, when Vee felt the pack protection protest violently and ripple, like something hit it and the aftershocks could be felt in waves. She gasped, dropping the milk, which Durran caught before it hit the pavement, and braced herself against the bumper.

"What is it?" Durran hissed, watching Vee's face contort with discomfort.

"Pack protection," was all Vee could say, as she slammed the doors to the back of the van and raced around to the front.

It was probably the fastest Vee had ever driven on Ward Parkway. She came around, entering the cul-de-sac with a squeal of her tires, just as she saw Shane getting out of his car parked haphazardly in the driveway.

"Where?" Vee asked as she jumped out, Durran hot on her tail.

"The back yard," Shane growled as he raced around the house. The pack protection wasn't broken, but it had been breached. Vee wasn't sure how she knew that, but she followed Shane and Durran.

The back yard was huge, a massive amount of land for a house in the middle of the city. They had torn the fence that separated their yard from Thomas's down so the pack would have a large swath of terrain to run on in a pinch, but because of the size, there was no telling where amongst the tree clusters dotted around the breach had occurred.

Vee stopped about halfway, watching as Shane and Durran split to check the perimeter. Her heart pounding in her chest; she felt it when the protection stopped fighting and seemed to accept whatever was pushing their way in. The unmistakable feeling of Sha magic came like a short wave through the protection, just before her phone buzzed in her pocket.

She snatched it, her breathing still erratic from adrenaline and running faster than she ever had before.

[Aho: We'll be there shortly.]

As she looked up into a cluster of trees, she saw the familiar shimmer of magic between two old oaks to her left. Her eyes narrowed as she watched Aho and Min step out through the gate that had just formed.

CHAPTER 6

Durran came out of nowhere, slamming Min into the nearest tree by his neck.

"Durran!" Vee yelled, immediately sprinting over to them.

"Get your hands off me, Watcher, if you don't want to lose them," Min growled, his eyes glowing amber.

"Perhaps we should have told them our plan in advance," Aho said with humor, as he watched Durran rip her hand off Min's throat.

"That might have been helpful," Vee snapped as she got closer. Shane burst through a moment later, eyes still glowing golden.

"What's the meaning of this, Aho?" Shane growled, not able to reign back his wolf form that had been so close to the surface.

"The others thought we needed to change the gate location due to recent events. It made the most sense to have it closer to your pack, now that so many changes have been taking place," Aho said, eyes falling on Vee who moved closer to Shane, threading her fingers through his as his breathing started to slow.

"You couldn't have warned us first?" Shane asked, his voice a little calmer as he tightened his hold on Vee's hand.

"We weren't sure it would work. The gates haven't changed locations in quite some time," Min admitted, still glaring at Durran.

They all just stood there for a moment awkwardly, as everyone tried to reign in the adrenaline that had just spiked. Shane's phone rang, and a series of text messages started coming through on Vee's phone.

"It's fine," Shane snapped, after answering his phone.

"You don't need backup?" Thomas asked, his voice low and dangerous. Vee could hear the sound of his engine pushing its limits as he drove from the West Bottoms.

"It's Aho and Min," Shane grumbled, glaring at Aho, who simply stared back at him. "They moved the gate here."

"Moved the gate?"

"Apparently. Don't worry about us. I've got it," Shane said before hanging up.

"Are you going to invite us in?" Aho asked, glancing up toward the house.

"I have groceries to put away," Vee said, realizing they were rotting in her black van as they stood there.

"I'll help you," Durran said in a low voice, moving away from Min but keeping him in her peripheral.

"We can all help," Aho said, almost cheerfully.

It felt strange to have everyone waiting as she handed out bags of groceries. Stranger still when they all wandered through their chaotic, unpacked house to the kitchen. Thankfully, it was big enough to hold quite a number of people, but it still seemed crowded when Vee started to pull things from the bags they all left on the counter.

"Your protection felt different," Min said, sitting at a stool as Shane pulled the packages of steak from a bag and handed them to Vee at the refrigerator.

"It resisted a lot more than we anticipated," Aho said, picking up a jar of peanut butter and turning it to read the ingredients.

"Vee's magic," Shane grunted out.

"You keep your Watcher around all the time, Vee?" Min asked, his voice laced with venom as he glanced at Durran, who was leaning against the counter across from him.

"She's living here now," Vee said, not seeing the way Min's eyes widened and then narrowed.

"You let an outsider amongst your pack, Shane?" Min asked, his voice as antagonizing as his gaze.

Shane stopped handing Vee things, bracing his hands on the counter and taking a deep breath.

"Durran is important to Vee. Vee, who is your sister, also happens to have been an outsider, and yet she's now my mate," Shane said coldly. Durran seemed to bristle a little at Shane's defense of her, and Vee let a small smile settle on her lips as she continued arranging the refrigerator.

"Your pack is growing, and not in expected ways," Aho said, his eyes twinkling with that same amusement and joy that it often did.

"Unnatural ways," Min grumbled, turning his glare at his father. "The other Sha will—"

"The other Sha will learn to deal with it. It's how things are supposed to be," Aho interrupted.

"Sandwiches?" Vee asked, after the silence stretched uncomfortably.

"I'll go," Durran said, pushing off the counter and heading out the door with Min's eyes laser-focused on her as she left. Vee knew better than to inquire, and if anything, Durran was helping make the tension in this room decrease by stepping aside.

They heard the front door close, and Shane started clearing the empty grocery bags.

"A Sha gate in our back yard," Shane grumbled under his breath, as he stuffed the plastic bags into the trash bag.

"We felt it would be better if your pack had direct access to us with what seems to be a never-ending stream of difficulties you're facing," Aho said, taking the plate that Vee offered him.

"Feels a little intrusive," Shane said, not turning around but instead staring out the back window at the group of trees they had come out of.

"We won't interfere," Aho said, watching Vee silently gather bread and meat.

"You wanted us to come, didn't you?" Min asked as Shane turned around.

"We have a Vampire problem that needs addressing," Shane said, nodding.

"Duflanc?"

"He's disappeared; it's what's left of his nest that seems to be the issue," Vee said, as she passed out knives to Min and Aho.

"Their attacks on humans have become increasingly less controlled. We're looking at an exposure if we don't get a handle on it," Shane told them seriously.

"You want our help or our approval?" Min asked, starting to build a sandwich on his plate as Aho took a bite of the one he had just finished putting together.

"I don't think we need your help. We outnumber them; we just don't want any trouble when we have to wipe out a whole nest," Shane said with a smirk.

"We'll let the High Vampire Court know what's happening, although I'm sure they already know and are just choosing not to sully their hands," Aho said, unable to hide the curl of his lip as he talked about them.

"High Vampire Court?" Vee asked, turning around slowly from the box labeled *glasses* she was digging through.

"You still haven't explained all these things to her?" Min asked Shane in a condescending tone, raising his eyebrow. A line showed in Shane's jaw as he clenched his teeth.

"We've been a bit busy this last month." Min smirked, taking a bite of his sandwich and glancing at Vee's expression, which had changed from surprised to aggravated. She shouldn't have been surprised that there was more to the preternatural world she didn't know. It wasn't long ago that she thought the Morrigan was simply a fairy tale. It did irk Vee that it seemed like she was always missing a vital piece of information about the structure of everything when she needed it. She wished there was some sort of manual to read so she'd be prepared the next time some issue came up.

"Always in the dark," she mumbled, pulling out the glasses and setting them on the island a little more carefully than was needed. She didn't want a repeat of the night before.

"How long are you staying?" Shane asked, trying to ignore the string of emotions coursing through the bond from Vee.

"We only wanted to see if this worked. We should go let the others know about the Vampires here," Aho said, as Vee pushed a glass of water his way.

"Finish your sandwiches," Vee said, feeling a little pleased that she could feed Aho a sandwich upon his arrival in her home, much like he did when she first came to the Sha domain.

"I like this house," Min said, now looking around the kitchen a bit more.

"You didn't like my other one?" Shane asked, as he started making his own sandwich. Min rolled his eyes, taking another bite instead of saying any more.

"So, have there been any more developments with your magic, Vee?" Aho asked. She felt genuine curiosity there in this question and supposed it only made sense. There was no one else who was like her. Even her mother didn't have the same powers, given Vee was also part Sha. She tried to think of anything other than the pack protection but came up empty otherwise.

"She hasn't been testing it. Like I said, we've been busy," Shane offered, having felt the inner turmoil as Vee thought how to answer the question.

"You haven't changed into anything since meeting your *zi*?" Aho asked, looking her directly in the eyes.

"I've been ... hesitant to try," she said quietly, taking Min's empty dish and turning to the sink.

"It's not the same for you as it is for us. You have no draw, no need to change," Min said, looking at her quizzically.

"I don't have another side to me. There isn't a beast inside clawing its way out, like it is for you."

Aho laughed abruptly, causing everyone but Vee to be startled.

"I think that's the most accurate description of what goes on inside us I've ever heard," he said through chuckles.

"She's bonded with a Werewolf and has empathetic powers. I'm not surprised she has some idea of what's happening there," Min offered, eyes softening more than she had even seen them.

That comment alone made Vee feel that she and Min may someday find a settled place. He didn't see her as a sister, or at least that wasn't the impression she got, just like he and Aho were still a bit disconnected in her mind from being family. Patrick may not have been her blood, but that young man was her family, her son. She hadn't placed Min and Aho anywhere within her little web of family yet, let alone spent enough time with them to develop anything more than acquaintance level comfort.

"We will leave you to your unpacking and go spread the word," Aho said, standing from his seat and hitting Min on the arm to follow.

"I'll walk you out," Vee said, leaving Shane to his sandwich. The reassuring squeeze she felt from the bond made her send him the briefest of smiles before she headed out the back door behind the two Sha men.

Min walked ahead, while Aho strolled leisurely beside Vee.

"At some point I want to teach you more about us, but I know now isn't the time," Aho said quietly.

"I'm not sure what good it would do," Vee murmured. She wanted to know more about the people she came from, but having lived nearly thirty years with nothing, she felt like it was too late.

"You deserve to know where you came from and what parts of it help make you. If I had known where you were..."

"It's not your fault," Vee said, glancing over at him. He didn't show much emotion, his face rather stoic most of the time, but she saw the pain there as she felt it coming off him. The regret that he had missed so much of her life. They were silent briefly while he reeled it in, Min stopping in front of the gate between trees with his arms crossed. Vee glanced at him for a minute before turning back to Aho.

"He'll come around eventually. He didn't hesitate to protect you when Duflanc attacked," Aho said, seeing the skeptical way Vee looked over at Min's posture.

"I don't think he knows what to make of me yet."

"No one does, Vee," Aho said with a chuckle before he moved in front of her, taking her face in his hands and lightly touching his nose to hers. "Goodbye for now," he said, before he turned, and he and Min disappeared behind the shimmering wall of magic.

Vee stood there for a second, just staring at the gate. She didn't know whether to be pleased or irritated about it being in her back yard. One part of her was pleased she had direct access to her long-lost father and brother, while the other part found it to be overbearing. That seemed to be a regular trait amongst preternaturals.

Shane was sitting at the counter, finishing the sandwich he made when Vee reentered the kitchen.

"I don't like that," he said pointedly, staring out the window.

"I know," she said, unable to hide the little smirk on her face.

"You don't like it either," he accused, smirking back at her.

"Not particularly," she admitted, leaning across from him.

"But you kind of like it," he said, raising an eyebrow.

"Only because I *might* get more questions answered if I have easy access to Aho." Shane let one side of his face turn up, as he set his and Min's dishes in the sink. "You didn't get a chance to talk to John, did you?"

"No, I was on my way there when I felt it and immediately headed home instead," Shane said, watching as Vee started putting away the remainder of the groceries she got. There on the counter sat a box with an alarm clock in it, and Shane's heart swelled a little. She didn't forget.

"John was the only one who didn't inquire what the fuss was about in the group text," Vee murmured, glancing at her phone on the counter, which, as if on cue, dinged with additional incoming inquiries from Margaret and George.

"I'll talk to him, but not right now," Shane said, stepping up behind her and taking her waist in his hands. "I think there's a few things I wanted to do with you since we seem to have the house to ourselves," he murmured in her ear, making her shiver a little and close her eyes. The rest of the groceries could wait.

The ground was damp, like it had just rained, but the sky was clear above. Anger so visceral, it felt like it was oozing out of her pores surged through her body, as she looked across the expanse of land she stood on. The trees where her eyes locked were void. Complete blackness. No silhouette or hint of the vegetation behind them, not anything that may be lurking there. The building beside her was familiar, though she couldn't quite place it. A place she had seen before. A place no one was supposed to be.

Somehow, she knew that she only had to wait a few more minutes. Only a few minutes now, and she would have it back. That hole that had been there a moment ago was filling back in, and she would be complete again. But the pain and rage that was consuming her now could not be stopped. She didn't want it to stop. She had had enough.

Her eyes trained on her target just beyond the trees. Eyes appeared within the void, glowing in the darkness, and then she saw the rest of them coming out amongst the trees to her as well. She clenched her fists, letting the fury that ran through her take hold, and with a final glance up at the moon's glow, she let the change take her.

CHAPTER 7

V ee gasped, sitting up in bed. Shane was already sitting up staring at her, his concern evident.

"I'm here, I've got you," he murmured, pulling her into his lap as she shook, still fighting for breath. She clutched him, nails digging into his shoulders. Slowly, her gasps died off, and she began breathing normally, following the pattern Shane was breathing for her. "Are you okay?" Shane asked quietly, running his fingers down her back.

"I ... yes," she said, swallowing as she remembered that hollow feeling. That hole. She had felt that before and knew what it meant. But Shane was right there. He was holding her. She could feel his skin under her fingers, smell his scent, feel his heart beating against her chest. He wasn't gone.

"She okay?" came Patrick's voice from the other side of their bedroom door.

"You can come in," Vee said, her voice still a little hoarse. She didn't move from Shane's lap, but Patrick came in, his steps hesitant as he made his way closer. She felt the urge in him, the instinctual need to protect as he got closer. Shane wordlessly gestured to him, and a moment later, Patrick was climbing into the bed with them and wrapping his arms around Vee and his dad.

"What did you dream?" Shane asked, as Vee relaxed a little more against the two of them.

"I was ... somewhere. I *know* I've been there before. I can't remember what it's called..." She shook her head, remembering the crumbling brick of the towering building. One landmark in front of the vast acreage that her eyes had been trained on. Where it was didn't matter right now, but it still tickled at the back of her mind. "There were trees. Enemies coming from there. I felt this hollow ... *hole* where you were supposed to be," she whispered, whimpering at the memory of when their bond was broken before. Shane's grip tightened on her.

"What enemies?" Shane asked, a slight rumble in his voice.

"I didn't see them. Just their eyes in the forest."

"It was just a dream, Vee," Patrick said, but then he met his father's eyes.

Shane felt that dream as if he was having it with her, but he couldn't see what she saw, only what she felt. The feeling similar to the sensation when Vee had gone into the trance at the Sha. When she had unlocked her spirit. Maybe he couldn't see what happened in her head unless she brought him there, but he knew it was real.

Vee let the tears fall that had been collecting and threatening to escape. She hated that a dream had such an impact. But it had felt so incredibly and powerfully real as she watched those eyes come out of the darkness, surrounding her. Shane and Patrick's arms tightened, holding her close as she began to cry.

Vee was at her shop early the next morning. She had fallen back asleep somehow, surrounded by Shane and Patrick, but when her alarm went off hours before Shane and Patrick's would, she slipped away, taking a travel mug of coffee and immediately going to her safe space to try and understand what she dreamed. She paced the store first for at least thirty minutes. Then she checked that she didn't have any outstanding orders that needed to be filled before she went to the back, grabbing scrap metal and her blow torch. She hadn't had time to make anything from scratch in some time, and to be honest, she still didn't, but she needed the focus it brought her.

Vee felt it when Shane woke up and had been blocking what he could feel from her. She told herself it was only because she wanted him to get his rest, but she knew it was more than that. That dream… No. She couldn't do that again. She couldn't handle that pain. She had already done it once. She already felt what it was like to not be bonded to him anymore.

He nudged her through the bond, and she let her mind open just enough that he called her. She turned the blow torch off and stared at the screen for a moment before picking it up.

"At the shop?"

"I had to do something with my hands," she said, turning the metal over in her gloved fingers.

"Patrick was worried," Shane said, and she heard Patrick's tired grumble in the background as he poured himself some cereal.

"Not to worry. You know I just need space sometimes to think," she said, certain he could hear her. She cringed, knowing her tone was too chipper. Un-Vee-like.

"Are you planning on working all day?"

"I should be," Vee admitted, glancing at the time. She still had a few hours before she would normally open the shop, but it was a Tuesday, and they still had so much unpacking to do. "I just want to finish this up, and I'll head home to unpack some more," Vee said, feeling his sense of relief at her words. The Vee of the past would probably have lingered and ignored anything else that was falling down around her to just stay in her shop, but she wasn't alone now. Neglecting the new house because she had a bad dream meant she was neglecting Shane and Patrick too. She wasn't alone anymore, and even though her heart ached sadly for the Vee of her dream, even that Vee hadn't felt alone.

"I'll see you soon," he murmured before they hung up.

Shane raked his hands through his hair, staring at his phone, as he and Patrick sat in the kitchen. They were both rattled to wake up without Vee in bed between them, as she had been when they had fallen back to sleep, and then more so when Shane realized she had closed down her end of the bond again. Confirming she was at the shop lightened the worry, but only so much.

He wanted to remind her that they had just fought about communication the other day, but this wasn't her not communicating. She had told him what she could last night, and she went to work through it. No matter how much he wanted to smother her with his protectiveness, he knew that wasn't what would help her or make her happy.

"She sounded off," Patrick said, looking at his cereal.

"She hasn't been to the shop much. The move, the Sha gate ... she just needs to work on something. Do something familiar," Shane said, telling that to himself as much as Patrick. Not but a moment later did they hear the front door open and close, and Durran came through, leaning on the doorway. Shane would have to tell her she could use the back door, which was much closer to the apartment over the garage than the front door, but he wasn't sure she was even staying there yet, and now was certainly not the time.

"What happened last night?" she asked, her voice as cold as her eyes. That animosity between them back full force. Shane's ability to keep Vee safe would always be a source of contention between them.

"She had a nightmare," Shane said, turning to the coffee pot to top off his cup. His wolf didn't care for the glare, and there was nothing he could have done to protect her from her own mind.

"That was more than a nightmare,"Durran murmured.

"What do you mean?" Patrick asked, looking over at her, deeper concern lining his face.

"I almost broke through the window," Durran admitted, the coldness gone and a heaviness showing on her shoulders, as she moved to sit at one of the stools.

"What does she mean, Dad?" Patrick asked, whipping his head to look over at Shane.

"It felt like it did when she was unlocking her spirit. Meeting her *zi*," Shane told them.

Vee had told Durran some of that experience, but she hadn't described exactly what went on when she went through it. Patrick had no such explanation. He was given a very short version of events, one that relied heavily on her being brought into the pack.

"A prophetic dream," Durran murmured, her eyes distant as she thought about it. "It makes sense. The type of Fae in her."

"She left before we woke up this morning, so I haven't had a chance to ask her to describe it in more detail. She was too upset for me to pry last night," Shane said tiredly.

"She has prophetic dreams now?"Patrick whispered. Shane looked over at him.

"Not necessarily. I'm not sure what that dream was or meant. I'd rather talk to her first," Shane said, trying to be comforting to Patrick, who was clearly starting to get panicked for Vee.

"Tell me what she said," Durran insisted, eyes intense as she looked over at Shane.

Vee packed up her things after finishing her thera-
peutic piece. She had smiled at herself when she finally
looked down at the completed key and saw what it
was that she made. It now sat snug in her front pocket,
waiting for its new home.

As she was about to move to the showroom to
set the alarm, she felt the buzz of a Were mind. She
paused in the darkened doorway from the inventory
room, feeling it out. Vee wouldn't have been surprised
if Shane sent someone to watch over her until she
came home. It wouldn't have been the first time he
had done something like that, but after what happened
with John the other day and her dream, she decided to
be a little extra cautious.

She felt out, trying to catch some familiarity with
the mind coming closer. Nothing. She decided to test
the pack bonds, which she hadn't experimented with
very much. The only times she had felt for them had
been when she was brought into the pack and during
the protection ritual. From what she could gather, they
were all where they were supposed to be, which was
not near her shop, so this Were was not one of theirs.
She ducked behind the counter when she knew they
were about to cross in front of the window. If there
was a Were that was approved to visit the territory,
Shane would have told her. In fact, that pesky bodyguard detail would have been enforced.

The Were slowed and stopped in front of the windows. She couldn't see them from where she hid, but

she knew they were looking through the glass, trying to see if she was in there. Her heart thudded in her chest, and she clutched her messenger bag at her hip, hoping no one would decide to call her at that moment. But thankfully, they moved on, their mind's vibration falling away as they headed east toward the heart of Westport.

Her phone rang soon after.

"Were in the territory. Not ours," Vee said, her voice still barely above a whisper, even though she knew the threat was gone.

"Come home," Shane growled from the other end.

Vee didn't hesitate. She punched the alarm and moved quickly to the exit, heading to her van while her eyes scanned her surroundings. She was about to get in when she felt Ness approaching. She was in her normal glamour, the old woman wheeling her cart up from the laundromat.

They hadn't seen or talked to one another since they returned from Colorado, though Vee had felt the Fae's presence around the shop a time or two. She still wasn't sure how to handle Ness. The old Fae was supposedly a servant of her mother's, that protection passing down to Vee, but there was no telling how far one could trust a Fae. They may not be able to lie, but they were very skilled at bending the truth.

"Vee," Ness said, a smile spreading across her lips. The kind, twinkling eyes of the old woman flashed with the black of her true form beneath.

"Ness," Vee said, nodding before eyeing the direction the Were went.

"Shop not open today?"

"Not today. I have some other things to take care of," Vee said, unsure why telling Ness they had moved felt like a bad idea, but her instincts were screaming at her that despite this Fae having helped Vee—saved Vee just a month ago—telling her that information would be wrong.

"I heard you moved," Ness said, almost as if she read Vee's mind. Vee nodded, stomach clenching uncomfortably. "You know I'm here for *you*. I'll be here no matter what," Ness continued. The words felt specific and oddly sinister. This Fae woman may have saved her, and Vee may have been part Fae, but Faes were not to be trusted.

"I know. I appreciate the sentiment," Vee said, careful not to thank her. Ness smiled knowingly.

"You're very busy. I'll let you get back to that," Ness said, before scooting her cart back up past Vee's shop.

Once she was past the van, Vee climbed in. Thankfully it was past rush hour, 10:00 a.m., normal opening time for the shop, and she made it home in minutes. She pulled up to the house, taking a deep breath before she got out. Shane, Durran, and Thomas were standing in the driveway as she approached.

"You're sure it wasn't one of ours?" Thomas asked, as she stopped in front of them. The reminder of the Were seemed to dispel Ness from Vee's head. Too many odd occurrences in such a short period of time. Vee would have to tell Shane about it later.

"I felt around on the bonds," she admitted, feeling a little embarrassed by it.

"That explains that weird tug I felt," Thomas said with a smirk. An odd sense of pride came from both him and Shane seemingly any time Vee showed she was using or more comfortable with the magic of the pack. It hummed there now within them, making her cheeks heat a little.

"We don't need this," Durran murmured angrily, looking up at the sky as if the answers would come from there. Shane sighed, rubbing his forehead.

"No, we don't, but we'll have to deal with it. We're getting the Sha's blessing to take care of the Vampire nest. Thomas, I want you and Tommy heading it," Shane told him, rubbing his forehead roughly.

"You're going to need to do something about John. We can't trust him," Thomas said, his voice a rumble as Vee sat on the curb.

"I'll go to his house tonight. They're supposed to be moving tomorrow. I'll use the guise of helping them pack to try to get it out of him," Shane grumbled, pulling out his phone to text Susan with the offer.

"So, I'm just supposed to stay home?" Vee asked, her voice a little more clipped than she would have liked to admit. There were too many things going on around them and though they all knew she had power, she still wasn't sure how to access and use it when needed. It usually came out as a burst in desperation.

"I'll go with you if you need to leave tonight," Durran said, crouching down beside her and placing a hand on her shoulder.

"Patrick won't let you out of his sight when he gets home from school," Shane said, recalling the way his son emphatically detested the idea of going to school for the day when something was clearly about to happen.

"Thomas?" came Cora's voice from the other side of the driveway. "I need you to explain to Toby that thing I told you I wanted last night. I can't remember what it's called."

"Floating, Cora! You wanted floating shelves," Thomas yelled over his shoulder. "I need to get back. I'll make some calls and set up a hunting party once I help Cora remember all the Home and Garden terms she rattled off to me last night," he grumbled, as he rubbed his bald head nervously.

Vee stood, waving at Cora, who was still standing in the doorway glaring at Thomas as he trudged over to her. She stopped her glare when she noticed Vee, waving back happily. Cora had been quite pleased that Vee was going to be living next door. They may have been polar opposites: Cora being very well put-together, her clothes pristine and never a blonde hair out of place, while Vee always threw on whatever worn clothes she managed to scrounge from the closet. The most she ever bothered to do with her hair was a braid, but Vee had always liked the sweet woman, even before Vee was outed to the pack and was just the locksmith they called.

Vee headed back into the house once Thomas and Cora disappeared to go talk to Toby, trailed by Durran and Shane.

"Did you eat this morning?" Shane asked as Vee set her messenger bag on the pile of boxes in the entry.

"Heading to the kitchen now," Vee grumbled, but she pulled her mug from the dishwasher and filled it with lukewarm coffee that she set to reheat in the microwave before she looked in the refrigerator.

"Not just cheese," Durran said, just as Vee was reaching for the cheese slices she bought the day before. She sighed, grabbing her leftover Chinese container instead and started to spread it out on a plate.

"I'm going to get my office set up, then I'll head over to the Meyers' house. If I'm there helping Susan when John gets back from work, it won't seem forced," Shane said.

"I'll try to get as much done while you're gone and stay put," Vee said, though suddenly the thought of him being outside of the pack protection made goosebumps spread across her skin and her need for him to be near increased tenfold.

"You feel that, Vee?" he asked, stepping close to her and touching her chin gently so she looked up into his eyes. "That's how I feel every time I can't keep you safe," he whispered. Vee looked into the softness of his brown eyes, felt the concern and love, and couldn't help the sting of tears that sprang.

"You better be careful, Shane," she whispered.

"I will," he murmured, bending down to give her a kiss.

CHAPTER 8

S hane prepared to leave for John's house, swinging through their bedroom where Vee was trying to put all their clothes away while Durran sat on an armchair she had dragged in from the living room, reading a book.

"I hope you're planning on putting that back," Shane said, raising an eyebrow at Durran. She shrugged, not lifting her eyes from the book as she turned the page.

"Don't you have your own apartment to unpack?" Vee asked, turning to give her a glare.

"Already done," Durran said smugly, smirking at the page.

"I'll be back no later than seven," Shane said to Vee, crouching down so he could kiss the top of her head from where she sat on the floor.

"Six," Vee countered, turning her narrowed eyes at him.

"He won't get home from work until five-thirty. That won't give me much time to drag out of him what he's up to."

"Fine, seven. But text me," she said, turning back to the sock pile that she was sorting. Somehow, all of their socks had been smashed into the same bag, and they were not paired up. She vaguely remembered being the one to do that, and now hated herself for the shortcuts she had taken while packing.

"I will," he said with a chuckle, moving to stand but Vee remembered the weight in her pocket and reached out an arm to stop him.

"Wait," she said, digging into her pocket. She pulled out the key she made at the shop that morning, its head far more intricate than the one she had made previously. It was, again, a wolf, clearly howling. Surrounding the head was a semicircle, depicting a full moon. She pressed it into his palm. "That's what I ended up making this morning," she said, watching how his fingers moved over the metal softly.

"I love you," was all Shane could say, leaning forward again to give her a soft kiss.

"Please go," Durran rumbled from her chair as they parted, garnering another chuckle from Shane, though this one held a hint of malice.

The door to the house closed with a snap, and Vee turned to Durran with narrowed eyes.

"Just going to sit there while I do all the work?" Vee asked, watching one dark eyebrow raise from behind the novel in front of her face.

"You expect me to sort socks?" Durran asked.

"Can't you just grab a box and unpack it?" Vee asked, glancing around at the piles of boxes. She was certain some of them were not meant to go in the primary bedroom, and once again felt the sting of her irritation with herself for not doing a better job of directing the pack on moving day.

Durran simply shook her head as Vee felt her amusement, and she turned back to the pile of socks with a sigh.

Vee had moved on to the closet when she felt Patrick and Lori coming through the front door.

"Vee?" Patrick yelled.

"In my closet," she yelled back. She heard them coming into the room, pausing as they took in that Durran was in there before Lori bounded through the bathroom, leaning on the closet doorframe.

"You always give me the perfect excuse to get out of helping my mom," Lori said with a grin that Vee could see reflected in the mirror.

"How much longer until the house is ready?"

"I mean, we're living there, but I think it's making my mom crazier seeing all the mess she can't clean up," Lori said as she moved closer, peering in a box of Shane's dress shoes that Vee was trying to put away on shelves.

"You playing bodyguard to me with Patrick?" Vee asked, as Lori sat on the bench.

"She wanted to. I didn't force her," Patrick murmured, having come into the bathroom as well.

Vee's phone rang from the other room, and she moved to grab it, but Durran beat her to it.

"Vee's phone," Durran answered.

"Oh, is Vee there?" came Una's voice from the other end. Vee pushed her way past Patrick, reaching Durran and holding out her hand.

"Just a second," Durran said, pulling the phone from her ear and pressing it to her chest.

"Give me the phone, Durran," Vee hissed.

"You shouldn't be taking house calls until we know what's happening," Durran whispered.

"Una is my old neighbor. Just let me talk to her," Vee said, grabbing the phone from Durran's fingers. "Hey, Una. What's going on? Everything okay with the new locks?" Vee asked once she pressed the phone to her ear.

"Yes! I feel so much safer," Una said, though her voice seemed a little strained. "Was that your man?" Una asked, a little hint of mischief in her tone, though the strain was still there.

"No, just my friend, Durran. You remember her?" Vee said, shooting another glare in Durran's direction. It wasn't the first time that someone mistook Durran for a man with her deep voice.

"I think so," Una murmured and paused, as if she was sifting through her memories. "Anyway, why I'm calling you. I know you didn't want me to pay you for the locks you put in, but I wanted to give you something."

"No, Una. It's okay. I wanted to help you," Vee said, the feeling of guilt for leaving this girl who reminded Vee of herself when she was alone.

"I know. But I made you something," Una said. The sound of Midi meowing unhappily in the background could be heard. There was something off about the sound. Midi was usually a rather happy cat, but it could have been she was just hungry or wanted attention.

"Can you bring it to work Friday? I'll take it home then."

"It's too big for me to take to the bar," Una murmured. Something was wrong about this conversation, but Vee wasn't sure what. "Listen, I'm on my break from work. I'll be home about seven. Do you think you could come over, and I can give it to you? I really appreciate you, and I want you to have this."

"Sure," Vee said, her eyes flicking to look at Patrick, who had followed her back into the bedroom. "I'm going to have my stepson with me. We have an errand to run right before that," Vee told her, watching as Patrick nodded in agreement. Coming to Una's apartment with three people seemed like a bit much, but she figured she'd warn Una that she wouldn't be alone.

"Perfect! I'll see you at seven!" And Una hung up the phone.

"There was something off about that," Durran stated, prompting Vee to nod slowly.

"Several things," Vee murmured, looking down at her phone, as if it would answer the questions running through her head.

"We're all coming," Lori said, saddling up next to Patrick.

"I figured," Vee said with a smirk.

[Vee: I'm heading to Una's with Durran, Patrick, and Lori. Something is wrong there.]

Vee had hesitated texting Shane until they were already on their way to the apartment. Something in her gut was telling her things were about to change, and her dream only made her more anxious about him coming with her. She knew she was being irrational. Shane could handle pretty much anything thrown his way, but he needed to have that talk with John, and Vee wanted to do what she could to protect him, even if it was only to keep him from running a simple errand to an old neighbor's home.

But her stomach clenched strangely when they pulled up in front of the apartment, and Shane still hadn't texted her back. Usually, he would text her back almost right away, if not call her. Her admitting something seemed wrong was usually a signal for him to call for more details. She could feel his irritation through their bond, so the conversation with John was most likely still heated. She glanced at the clock on her dash, which read 7:15 p.m. So much for Shane being home at seven.

The sun had set a few minutes before they left the house, and the dark twilight was cast in the sky over the building. She glanced up at Una's second-story window, seeing that the lights were on but the windows were covered. Midi was not outside, nor was she perched in her normal spot, gazing at the neighborhood. The four of them got out of Durran's car, which they had taken since Vee's van only had two seats; the rest of the space in back was for storage of road supplies or hauling safes for installation.

Vee opened the door to climb out until Durran's arm shot out immediately while Patrick and Lori growled in the back seats.

"What?" Vee hissed, feeling around for anything out of the ordinary. She only felt human minds nearby.

"Vampire," Durran said, shutting off the car and moving to climb out. Patrick and Lori did the same. She had only been intending on bringing Patrick up with her. She had told Una to expect him, but she could tell by their demeanor there would be no convincing Lori and Durran to stay put if they scented a Vampire nearby.

Everyone was tense as they made their way to the front of the building. Lori's normally unshakable, chipper attitude was replaced with that of a protective hunter, her eyes glowing blue as she gazed around them. Vee's heart pounded. They all knew something was wrong. Very wrong.

The scent of blood hit Vee's nose immediately when she opened the main door. Patrick's chest rumbled as he pushed past her to go first, taking two steps at a time until he made it to the second floor. Vee ran up behind him, with Durran and Lori a breath behind her.

"Patrick—" Vee started, but she immediately stopped as she looked at Una's door. It was open, but just a crack, and blood seeped out from the bottom, saturating the rainbow welcome mat deep crimson. "Una?" Vee yelled, unable to keep her voice calm as she pushed the door open, stepping through the puddle of blood. It was still warm, as it seeped into her canvas shoes.

The apartment was a disaster. Bookshelves were practically torn from the wall, tapestries sprayed with blood, all of Una's possessions seemed to be scattered across the floor, coated in it. And there on the floor, amidst it all, was Una's body. It was broken, ripped, and torn apart in such a way that had Vee not been familiar with the tattoos on the few places of intact flesh she could see, she was certain Una would be unrecognizable. Vee let out a mournful sob as she got closer, Patrick coming swiftly to her side to catch her and hold her back before she touched the body.

"We need to go, Vee," he whispered in her ear, his own fear washing over her as her breath came out raggedly.

"Una..." Vee croaked. This was not a human attack, and the blood was still warm. This had happened mere minutes before they arrived. Vee couldn't help the hollow feeling of guilt at looking at what remained of the sweet neighbor Vee should have called a friend. If Vee hadn't been part of Una's life, she might still be alive.

"Look at her curtains," Lori said quietly from the doorway.

Vee turned, eyes taking in the bloody mess that Una's curtains were. There, written in blood, was a message.

"'I only want you, Vee,'" Durran read aloud, her voice laced with fury. "Duflanc," she snapped. "We need to go."

A small cry came from somewhere in the room, causing them all to freeze. It was meek. A fearful and distraught noise.

"Midi," Vee whispered, getting down on her hands and knees, despite the blood coating the floor and glancing under the furniture.

"We don't have time for this, Vee," Durran spat, coming forward to try and grab Vee's arm.

"Midi," Vee whispered again, as she locked eyes with the black cat hiding under the couch. "Come here." The cat hesitantly crawled out from under the couch, her paws coated with her owner's blood. Vee scooped her into her arms as soon as she was close enough and stood.

"We need to get rid of that," Lori said, pointing at the curtains, prompting Patrick to go rip it off the rod violently enough to tear it from the wall, along with some plaster. Patrick balled it up, and they left, wiping down the few surfaces that Vee had touched on their way out, as well as their bloody footprints.

"We need to call Margaret," Lori said, pulling out her phone. Margaret was third in the pack hierarchy, but she was also the one who they called to clean up messes. They didn't often have them, at least not ones made by the Weres of this pack, but anything that could be connected to the preternatural community fell within her purview.

"We need to call Shane," Vee said, pulling her phone from her bag once they were back in Durran's car and realizing Una's blood was everywhere, and Midi was getting bloody paw prints all over her pants and shirt. Her hand shook as she dialed, Una's blood smearing over the glass screen. The phone rang and rang and went to voicemail. "Shane ... I know you're talking to John, but I-I need you to call me back. Una ... Dulfanc killed Una," was all Vee could manage to say, before hanging up again.

"Margaret," came her answering voice from Lori's phone in the back seat.

"Margaret. Vee's old apartment. Her neighbor Una—" Lori started.

"The one with the cat?" Margaret asked, a smile in her voice. Everyone knew the story about the cat. They had even joked that Shane should get Vee a cat for her upcoming birthday. Shane had not been eager to have one more thing to take care of, and Vee, though amused by the idea, had to agree with him.

"Yes, the one with the cat. She, um…" Lori glanced up at Vee through the rearview mirror. "We need you to go clean up a situation at her apartment."

"Situation?"

"Looks like Duflanc got to her," Lori said, her voice starting to quake. Patrick reached over and took her hand. She squeezed it tightly, taking a deep breath to hold back the tears. Lori may have been a Werewolf, but her experience with death and destruction was still limited to hunting animals in the wilderness in her wolf form.

"Shit. I'll grab a few others and head over there," Margaret said before she hung up swiftly.

It was only a moment later that Vee was gasping for air. The suddenness of the feeling felt like a punch in the gut. Shane's rage had been building over the last few minutes, but now it came to a fiery head. Vee's eyes glowed of their own accord, the anger pulsing through her as if it were her own. She gripped her seat, her nails tearing into the leather, a roar threatened to rip from her throat, and then, the next moment, nothing.

Nothing.

This wasn't the horribly slow and tortuous pain that it had been when Gwen Tallon ripped the bond away; it was much more instantaneous than that. She went from feeling him, his rage becoming her own, to a piece of her was simply … gone. Shane was gone.

"Vee! What?" Durran shouted, as she drove faster back to the house. The noise she had been making was the most animalistic noise of sorrow that Durran had ever heard come from her lips.

"Shane!" Vee screamed, agony in her voice. Midi jumped out of Vee's lap and into the back seat with Lori and Patrick, while Vee doubled over in the seat.

"What? Vee? What happened?" Patrick said, practically jumping into the front seat with her, grabbing her shoulders.

"He's … gone," she choked out, tearing at her chest.

"What?" Patrick screamed, clutching her shoulders too tight.

"Gone!" she screamed again, this time the glass of the windshield cracked with the sound. Durran's grip on the steering wheel tightened, her eyes glowing red as she punched the gas.

Then Patrick and Lori felt it. The absence so sudden, so great that they both snarled. The pack bonds didn't lie. Their Leader, the one who held them all together, was gone.

CHAPTER 9

Patrick and Durran had to physically pull Vee from the car when they made it back to the house. Her breath was coming out in gasps, her bloody hands clutching at her shirt, as if the weight of it was inhibiting her breathing. Or she could hold her heart in her chest by gripping her shirt tighter. She sat on the cool concrete driveway, trying not to become sick while they watched the cars start filling the cul-de-sac. The pack had arrived.

George and Markus rocketed out of the car they arrived in, running to Vee who was flanked by Durran and Patrick. Lori had taken Midi inside the house and was coming back out with wet kitchen towels.

"What happened?" Markus asked, watching as Lori knelt beside Vee, prying her fingers from her shirt and starting to clean the blood from them. He reached forward to place a hand on Vee's knee, but Patrick snarled at him, not wanting anyone to touch her. She had gone catatonic in the last few minutes, her panicked breathing slowed to even, but her eyes had glazed over. Patrick, still grappling with the fact that his father was gone, didn't need anyone, pack or no, messing with his mom too.

"Has anyone heard from John?" Patrick growled, eyes glowing golden as he stood with clenched fists, glaring out at all the pack members as they came closer.

"John?" Frida asked as she came closer.

"Shane was meeting with him, helping Susan pack all afternoon," Durran said, her voice lower than normal.

"John's been acting suspicious since Shane and Vee got back from Colorado," Lori said quietly, reaching up with the wet towel to rub a bit of blood that had gotten on Vee's chin.

"His phone is off," George said, who had immediately dialed John at Durran's comment, then shoved his phone back in his pocket, raking his hands through his hair, subsequently ruining his perfect waves.

"What do we do?" Emily asked, looking over at the darkened house next door and noticing there were two pack members who were oddly absent. "Where's Thomas?"

Lori stiffened at that, eyes traveling over to her house.

"He was supposed to be putting together a hunting party for the Vampires," Durran said, brow furrowing. A murmur went through the pack members now spread across the lawn. No one had been contacted for such a thing.

Vee seemed to snap out of a trance at that, standing without saying a word and heading over to the darkened house next door. Shane may have been gone, her heart feeling like a hollow shell, but there were still all these people that relied on her. She laced her fingers in Lori's, and the pack behind them followed. Vee began reaching out through the pack bonds, checking to be sure that everyone present was firmly attached. Shane may have been gone and the bonds weak, but they were all still tied together somehow. Thomas and Tommy were gone too, and John felt like a whisper, barely discernible. What did that mean?

As Vee got closer to the front door, she felt the very familiar presence of Cora's mind, though it was clearly unconscious.

"Lori, your key," Vee said after she tried the door, finding it locked. Lori scrambled with the lanyard at her neck, eventually ripping it off and handing it to Vee. Vee carefully unlocked the door and pushed it open.

The scent of fear was overwhelming. Lori whimpered as she was hit with it, followed by the low rumbles of the other Weres as fear poured from the open door and out into the night air. Vee and Lori stepped into the house as a unit, with Patrick and Durran close behind them.

"Where?" Durran asked, their voice changing as they took their true form, drawing their sword from its scabbard at their hip. Vee closed her eyes for a moment to feel for Cora, and then she felt another mind. It was fading.

"Basement," Vee said, pulling Lori with her as they made their way through the construction chaos to the basement stairs.

The door hanging from the hinges and the claw marks gouging the walls and wood were enough indicators of what they were about to see below that all their breath caught. Vee and Lori descended side by side, Lori's grip growing increasingly tighter. The basement was dark. The light had been shattered, but none of them needed the light to see.

Bodies lay across the floor. Werewolves that didn't belong to their pack and humans ... Toby's crew. She could tell by the neon green shirts on some of the torsos that held the crew's logo. No Shane, Thomas, or Tommy amongst them though. In the furthest corner of the room, Vee spotted her. Cora was unconscious, leaning against the wall. Blood was matted in her long blonde hair, a large bruise was forming on the left side of her pale face, and Vee could see the faintest amount of swelling in her wrist.

Lori ran to her, hands hovering, unsure if she should touch her.

"Just unconscious. No brain damage," Vee said, brow furrowing at how she knew that, but everything about Cora's mind activity was normal for sleeping. Nothing felt off, and she knew she had felt that at some point before.

"Toby..." came a gasp from Emily. She had wandered behind the stairs with Frida, the other pack members scanning the rest of the house for dangers and evidence of who had done this.

"What about Toby?" Vee asked, touching Cora's cool cheek before she nodded for Lori to take her. Lori scooped her mother's limp form into her arms as if she was a small child. Lori's tiny frame looked odd as she held her mother of the same size with very little difficulty.

"He's..." Emily's face showed the horror. Patrick moved to where she stood, eyes taking in the sight that made his lip curl with disgust.

"He's not dead," Patrick said, bending down to breathe in his scent. "He's strong. He might fight through it."

The whole pack knew Toby and his feelings for Vee; notwithstanding, they liked him.

"How badly is he hurt?" Vee asked.

"Badly, but we can move him," Patrick said, stooping to sling him over his shoulder. Toby let out a small whimper as Patrick lifted him, but otherwise remained unconscious and limp. Vee fought the cringe that threatened to shake her at looking at him. A deep set of gouges ran from his shoulder all the way down his back, as well as a massive bite mark and missing chunk of flesh on his outer thigh. He was either incredibly lucky or horribly unfortunate that none of his arteries had been nicked, but he had quite a fight ahead of him. Healing and becoming a Werewolf was not painless.

"Take them to our house," Vee said to Patrick, then she glanced at the other pack members in the basement. How was she supposed to keep them all safe when someone had managed to take their three strongest from them? "Everyone's staying. We had two humans associated with us get attacked today. Shane, Thomas, and Tommy are gone. Everyone stays together while we figure this out," Vee said, making sure her voice carried enough for the whole pack upstairs to hear as well. The feeling of agreement from all of them seemed to wash over her forcefully.

Pack is a team.

Pack is a family.

Pack stays together.

Lori and Patrick went upstairs with their cargo, leaving four to look at the bodies that remained.

"Thomas and Tommy did a number on them before they were taken," Durran said, kneeling down and looking at the Were just at the bottom of the stairs, whose jaw and most of their neck was ripped from them. The remainder of the dead man's face was frozen in terror.

"Do you think the crew was trying to help?" Vee asked, glancing at the body parts strewn around the basement floor.

"Probably," Durran said, eyes glowing as she took in more scents. "These Weres are part of Dante's pack." Their voice was so sinister, it made Vee shiver. The pack who was enchanted by Gwen Tallon six months ago was what Durran meant, though they had all been suspicious that perhaps Dante had been in on Gwen's plan the whole time.

"Emily, Frida," Vee said. "Margaret was cleaning up a situation at my old apartment."

"I called her on my way here. She's sealed it off and should be heading this way," Emily said, pulling out her phone.

"Call her again. Tell her about ... this," Vee said, nudging the shoe of a decapitated Were.

"On it," Emily murmured sadly, looking over the bodies of the crew members. Emily wasn't from Kansas City, but she knew most of these men were local. They had families that would wonder where they were soon, and the unfortunate nature of the preternatural world was that they would never know the truth.

As Emily dialed Margaret once more, Vee and Durran moved back up the stairs and outside. Durran had shifted back to her female form, since the threat wasn't imminent, but her sword was still made visible.

George and Markus were standing in the driveway while cars started and left, as various pack members went to gather their families and supplies.

"John's still not answering his phone. Straight to voicemail," George said as Vee approached.

"He won't," Vee said, her voice icy. "They're coming back, right?" Vee asked, glancing at the cars leaving once again.

"Just going to grab their families. I'm glad Shane got the spare rooms set up before the big move," George murmured. The Friday before, Shane had George and Tommy help him assemble all new beds for each of the spare rooms in the house. Four additional upstairs and four more in the basement. They had also gotten several huge new leather sofas to go in the entertainment room for additional sleeping.

Patrick descended the stairs from the garage apartment that was now Durran's.

"We put Cora and Toby in your apartment, Durran. I hope you don't mind."

"Better to keep them separate from the others. Kids will be coming soon," Durran said with a nod. The mention of kids somehow made Vee realize what she had gotten at the grocery store the day before wasn't going to last long with the entire pack in house and their families.

"Food," Vee said, glancing at Markus.

"George and I will go grab supplies. I just didn't want to leave until Margaret got here," he said, sympathy washing over him as he looked at her. She may have been crumbled on the ground when they arrived, but she immediately jumped into action, leading and caring for the pack that remained. This wasn't the Vee that they knew, but it was the Vee they needed right now as they figured out what was going on.

"Durran, go with them?" Vee asked, a wave of exhaustion hitting her suddenly.

"Only if you promise to remain here," Durran said, a warning in her voice.

"I'm not going anywhere."

Vee and Durran explained the situation as they knew it to Margaret when she arrived, and then Vee went with Patrick up to Durran's apartment to look in on Lori, Cora, and Toby. The apartment was sparse. She didn't know which things were brought by Shane or Durran as furnishings, but there was quite literally only a small loveseat that Toby was draped over and, in a separate bedroom, Cora was on the bed. Toby was much worse off, but Cora was one of theirs, and Vee understood the delineation.

Lori was wiping blood off Cora's head as Vee stopped on the bedroom doorway.

"Are you sure there's no brain damage?" Lori asked quietly.

"Her mind feels normal. Just asleep," Vee said, moving closer and placing a hand on Lori's shoulder gently.

"I'll start patching Toby up," Patrick said, his voice shaking only a little with worry. He was trying desperately to stay strong, like Vee. Though Margaret was third in the pack, Vee and Patrick were clearly ones who were looked at for guidance. The only people he would allow, or could afford to let see even that little bit of weakness in his armor, were the two women in this room.

The sudden gasp that came from Cora as she bolted up in the bed immediately made everyone in the room tense.

"Where? Where are they?" she gasped, her blue eyes wide with fear as she stared in front of her, as if she wasn't seeing the room around her.

"We don't know, Mom," Lori said, grasping her hand. Cora's head snapped over to Lori, taking in her appearance. Lori was still dressed in her uniform, but she had blood smudged on her previously crisp white shirt from both Una and Cora.

"Lori!" Cora said, her voice coming out as a sob, pulling her daughter into her arms, fingers digging into her shirt and curling like she never wanted to let her go.

The two simply held each other tightly for a moment, Cora's sobs the only sound in the room.

"Cora, we need to know what happened," Patrick said after several minutes when her crying seemed to die down. She hiccupped lightly, pulling away from Lori and wiping the tears from her daughter's cheeks before she wiped hers.

"This morning, Thomas was helping me tell Toby what I wanted in the basement laundry room when we got a knock at the back door. Tommy was upstairs with some of the crew. I wanted that new banister put in." She shook her head, almost ashamed.

"Your renovations didn't do this, Cora," Vee whispered, sitting on the bed beside her and taking her other hand. Cora nodded, though the tears sprang in her eyes again.

"I don't know if Tommy opened the door for them or what exactly, but he was thrown down the basement stairs. So many people came down after. They were fighting. I-I tried to stay back, but—" She let out a ragged breath, tears streaming down her cheeks. "Last thing I remember was watching them dragging Thomas up the stairs with something around his neck while Tommy kept fighting them."

Patrick growled lightly, his eyes aglow once she dissolved back into sobs. Vee left the room to the mother and daughter, taking Patrick with her out to where Toby still lay unconscious.

"Taken, not killed," Patrick said, staring out the window as more cars started filling the driveway again.

Vee refused to let the spark of hope blossom. The hole was still there, black and cavernous within her, its edges sharp and painful. She couldn't let herself hope because the feeling she got was that he was unequivocally gone. Just torn from her and everyone else.

"We'll need to move Toby to the basement. He'll have to go in the cage," Vee said, glancing down at him.

"The first night of the full moon is tomorrow," Patrick whispered, the realization dawning on him. "We have to bring him into the pack."

"We can't. Sh—" Vee swallowed, her eyes stinging as her heart squeezed in her chest at almost saying Shane's name. "*He* isn't here to bring him into the pack or help his wolf," Vee said. Patrick reached over and took her hand. She glanced over at him, feeling his own sorrow as the first of his tears slid down his face. Vee squeezed his hand, sending him what she could, which was the grim determination that seemed to overtake her. Whatever was going on wasn't over. They were being hit on all sides; their strongest were gone, and it was up to them that remained to figure it out before they were all wiped out. Patrick felt it, his head falling back as he closed his eyes and took in what she gave him. When he opened his eyes, they were rimmed with gold.

"Lori, we're taking Toby and heading to the house to get the pack settled," Patrick said toward the bedroom, before taking his hand from Vee's and pulling Toby back over his shoulder.

CHAPTER 10

Vee quickly changed out of her blood-covered clothes while Patrick and Frida got Toby settled in the cage. Seemingly the moment Vee returned downstairs, the pack members with families started returning.

"We don't need much space," Ceci offered in her small voice. She was the ten-year-old daughter of Roman, one of the pack members Vee rarely spoke to. Roman was quiet and unassuming. While so many of the other Weres in the pack seemed to try to be the biggest and the loudest, Roman always seemed to melt into the background. "Just us two," she said, peering up at Vee as she held her bunny. Roman's wife had died before Vee had met the pack, so he was raising his daughter on his own.

Vee bent down to look in the little girl's big eyes.

"You don't worry about that. There's plenty of space here. That's why we moved," Vee said smiling faintly. She simply couldn't smile more.

"Oh, that makes much more sense," Ceci said, looking at the boxes and chaos. Vee raised an eyebrow at the unconscious insult the little girl made, glancing at Roman, who was fighting a smile.

"Sorry. She certainly has a mind of her own," Roman murmured quietly.

"I don't have a problem with women having their own minds," Vee said, nodding at Ceci, who grinned back. "Most of the other rooms won't be very private, but if you want, Sh—" She froze again as his name nearly slipped from her lips. "The office has a few couches, and I was going to see if you could trace his phone. I don't want to send anyone out of the protection without firm leads," Vee said, trying to keep her voice from trembling. Roman worked in IT and dealt with all the technical aspects of the security company as well as doing independent contract work on the side. And he looked the part too: his lean frame, thin but kind face, and long hair made him look like he spent most of his time behind a computer screen.

"Happy to," Roman said, reaching out to squeeze Vee's shoulder before ushering Ceci with him past the living room to the office.

The flood of people really started after that. Family after family spilled into Vee's home, and she directed them to rooms that would best suit them. The trickle of people seemed to aid in Vee's ability to not feel as overwhelmed, but by the time Durran, Markus, and George got back from Costco and were hauling all the groceries into the house, Vee was slumped on a stool with Patrick at her side. The house was full, and the minds were pulsing.

"I think the kids are all getting settled, but I know the pack members are not going to be in any mood to sleep," Patrick said, though Vee could feel his own exhaustion creeping in.

"Margaret?" Vee said faintly, though she knew Margaret was in the living room after having assessed the scene at Thomas's house. Margaret came into the kitchen a moment later, her face hard, undeniably pained by the two horrific scenes she'd had to seal off less than an hour apart.

"What's up, Vee?"

"Do we have guard duties set up yet?" Vee asked. Margaret's eyes softened at Vee's words. Margaret had never had doubts about Vee, but she knew others in the pack did initially. Any who still held lingering feelings toward the negative would need to deeply rethink that, now that Vee had literally done everything, from the moment she felt Shane's loss, to protect them all. Even now, when it was obvious Vee was well past the point of exhaustion, overwhelmed, and over her head with pain and concern.

"I'll get on it," Margaret said, heading back out the kitchen and immediately barking orders out through the house loud enough for every Were to hear.

"Anything new happen while we were gone?" George asked, eyeing Patrick and Vee.

"Nothing new," Patrick murmured, running his hand through his hair.

"Roman is tracking … *his* phone," Vee whispered.

"We can go check out whatever he comes up with tomorrow," George assured her.

"And Frida," Vee said with a nod.

"The Sha should know what Dante did," Durran said, as she set the massive boxes of cereal on the floor by the pantry. Vee raised her eyebrows, her eyes drifting to the window that looked out at the expansive back yard. Right there, hidden in that thicket of trees, was a gate. The Sha could be there in minutes. She wasn't sure what their enemies were up to. This plot had not fully revealed itself, but she did have one ace up her sleeve.

"I'll text Aho," Vee mumbled, pulling her phone from her pocket.

[Vee: There's a situation. Shane, Thomas, and Tommy have been taken. Based on the scene we found at Thomas's house, it looks like Dante is involved.]

Vee set her phone on the counter before her, her fingers drumming beside it impatiently. Patrick leaned closer to her too, eyes trained on the screen.

[Aho: Shane is not there?]

Vee felt sick.

[Vee: He's gone.]

Her hands shook as she typed the message.

[Vee: Too much to text.]

Patrick's hands clenched as time seemed to slow down waiting for Aho's response.

[Aho: You'll hear from me soon.]

Nothing more.

It wasn't so much Aho's short reply that enraged her, but it was the final tipping point. She hadn't been allowing herself to feel the force of her own emotions over the past few hours since she felt her bond with Shane simply disappear, but now there was no more holding back. The fury that had been building in Vee seemed like a living thing, filling her up and moving from deep in her belly up. She stood abruptly, running out the back door to the stone patio. She didn't care who followed her, who heard, who saw. The rage moved up through her lungs up her throat, and she let out a scream into the night sky. The sound was so loud, so inhuman, and so foreign as it shook the very ground she stood on.

She fell to her knees, hands in her hair, as she fought to regain her breath.

Two sets of strong arms surrounded her. Durran's concern and Patrick's own sorrow surrounded her, but so did their love for her.

"Vee, let's go to bed. There's nothing more we can do now," Patrick said, resting his head on hers. She nodded, her breath hitching as she breathed in again, letting them pull her to her feet.

She let them take her upstairs, Patrick's low warning growl the only sound she heard when various pack members seemed to come out to look at her, the sound that had come from her moments ago shaking them to their core. Vee crawled to the center of the bed, her head falling into Shane's pillow, breathing in his scent and pulling a sob from her aching chest. Patrick curled around her, and Durran set herself in the chair she hadn't brought back to the living room earlier in the day.

Vee was surrounded, encased by those who loved and would protect her, but not by *him*. Sleep only came when her sobs pulled the last shreds of energy from her body.

Durran watched as Vee and Patrick slept. The way Vee clutched the pillow that smelled like Shane made her heart ache uncomfortably in her chest. She loved Vee, but she had already witnessed this anguish. Vee was not meant for Durran; it would always be Shane. Whether Shane was alive or not, Vee had made this pack her family.

Soft footfalls came closer to the room, and the door opened just a crack for Durran to see George's eyes peeking through.

"Is she asleep?" he whispered. It had been a few hours. George, like most of the pack, was running on pure adrenaline and couldn't settle his beast. Durran nodded, standing, and stepping out into the hall. "She left her phone on the counter. I would have just left it there, but a text came through," George said, handing the phone over to Durran.

She looked down, lighting up the screen and seeing the text that would be a worthy reason to wake Vee.

[Unknown: You keep them all close, like you can save them all. Leave the pack. You have no idea what's coming.]

A howl rang out from the front yard. Vee and Patrick were startled awake, and Durran swung the bedroom door open to see Vee frantically crawling from the bed.

"It's the guards in the front yard," she said, shoving past them to rush down the stairs. The front door burst open as Vee jumped the last few steps. Archer, one of the wolves set on guard duty, was still mid-transformation back to his human form, his face more wolf than man as he held out a clawed hand toward Vee.

"Someone drove by and threw this," he said, his voice odd and low as his jaw started going back to normal. Vee held out her hand, letting him drop the object there. It was the new key she had made Shane, covered in his blood. Vee closed her fist around it, fire coursing through her veins.

"You didn't see who?"

"Smells like Werewolf, but I scented Fae on it too," Archer said, now panting with the exertion of changing so quickly.

"Werewolf and Fae," Durran said, taking the last few steps down to stand beside Vee.

Roman came from the office, closing the door carefully behind him.

"I found Shane's phone," he said, holding out a piece of paper to Vee where he had written the address.

"We need to check John's house too," Vee said as she went to take the paper. The address didn't strike her as familiar, but she turned the paper over where Roman had scribbled a bit more text. "Sauer Castle," she read aloud. She had definitely been there before. She remembered being young and her dad, Graham, taking her and Eliza on a ride to the windy road up the hill to see it and listen to the urban legend that went along with it.

"The legends say that the daughter of the original owner, Anton Sauer, hung herself in the tall tower there," Graham had said, pointing up to the very highest part of the structure. "And years later, a man named Igor lived in the house. He went crazy one night, no one knows why, but he decided he needed to rid the world of their family. He walked room to room murdering each of his children and his wife, stringing their organs over the windows for everyone to see, before he hung himself in that same tower," Graham finished, grinning as he peeked at Vee's horrified face in the back seat. They had come just at dusk, the sunset hitting the house, making it appear to be fiery ... bloody.

"Come on, Dad. You know that's not true!" Eliza whined from where she sat beside him in the front seat.

"It could be true," he insisted, still grinning as he winked at Vee.

"Do you know what really happened?" Eliza asked, her tone indifferent, but Vee could tell her sister was intrigued.

"I never really looked into it," Graham said honestly, glancing back at the house. "It's been abandoned since the eighties."

"Creepy," Eliza said as the sun burst its final rays toward the house, casting it even more red.

"I thought you might like to hear the story since it's close to Halloween," Graham said, turning once more to give Vee a reassuring smile before they pulled away and back through the winding neighborhood.

But Vee had done some research since then and read about the history of that house. Built in the 1870s right on the Santa Fe trail. No family was murdered in the years it had existed, but children had died, and a man shot himself after being diagnosed with a terminal illness. The most recent and current owner of the house had lots of hardships trying to get it refurbished to its original glory. Vandals and kids who were intrigued by the urban legends came and destroyed much of the property. A caretaker had even been responsible for a massive amount of destruction, pulling all the copper piping from the house. It seemed bad fortune sprang up for anyone who owned it. Like the very ground the house sat upon was cursed.

Maybe it was.

"Shane's phone is here?" Vee questioned Roman, just to be certain she understood.

"Yes," Roman confirmed, though his confusion was just as equal to hers. That was not their territory; it was in Lieb's territory just on the other side of the state line in Kansas. Vee let out a breath, her fist tightening on the key in her hand for a moment as she thought.

She and Shane had been under the impression that the two pack leaders had come to an understanding after what Vee had done for him the month before. Their meeting at a diner on the way to visit the Sha. The encounter seemed to shift something between them. In fact, Shane had told her in passing one day that Lieb had asked for his counsel on how to change things within his pack, wanting to slowly move away from the brutal way most packs operated to the way Shane lead his Weres. The idea that Lieb had anything to do with this plot was horrendous, but sadly not improbable. She squeezed her eyes shut, trying to rationalize.

Lieb may not have even known. He seemed to spend most of his time in more western parts of Kansas, since his pack was spread through the cities and towns there. But there was always the possibility that Lieb and Dante were working together on this.

"Where's my phone?" Vee asked when she opened her eyes again.

"I've got it. But Vee—" Durran started as she held out the phone, but Vee snatched it, illuminating the screen and looking down at the foreboding message there.

"Dante," was all Vee said, as she looked down at the message. "Sounds like he wants to take over the pack and territory, but there's more than just him at play here," Vee murmured as she read over the words a few more times and then went to her contacts to find Lieb's number. Shane had given it to her, along with a few other pack leaders' numbers, for emergency purposes. She supposed this counted as an emergency.

"Vee, don't call him," Durran said as she hit his contact on her phone. She was about to dial it when she felt the intense presence of a Sha approaching.

"A Sha is here," Vee said, holding off from pressing the call button as the silhouette of the person in the yard grew closer to the house.

"They come now?" Durran hissed, irritation overriding any previous emotions.

"Aho said they'd be in contact," Vee murmured, glancing at Roman and Archer. "We'll handle this. Get some rest, Roman. We might need you tomorrow," Vee said, stuffing the key and the address in her pocket for later.

"Archer, go back out there. Don't change back; you'll be too tired," Patrick said, tossing a pair of sweats he had brought down with him toward the now completely human, but very naked, Archer. Archer snagged the pants in the air, quickly putting them on before heading back out to the front. No question about Patrick's authority, despite his age. Patrick had proven himself to be one of the most powerful and dominant in the pack already, separate from his father's influence.

Vee turned and headed to the back door. The almost full moon was still in the sky, bathing the Sha that approached in her light.

"Vee," Min said as a greeting, pausing on the patio.

CHAPTER 11

Vee brought Min into the kitchen where Patrick, Durran, George, and Margaret were waiting. Vee, with help from the others, broke down the timeline of events that happened in the last few hours, leading all the way until the moment when Vee was about to call Lieb.

"Lieb must not know this is happening in his territory. Him and Dante are famously on bad terms," Min said, rubbing his chin thoughtfully as he stared into the mug of tea Vee had made him. Patrick slid a fresh cup of coffee to Vee, the pot having just finished gurgling minutes before.

"Bad terms?" Durran said incredulously. Fights between Werewolf packs was one of the reasons their population wasn't greater. Their ability to be far more prolific than any other preternatural could have made them the most dominant of them all, but their tempers were such that they warred with themselves about as much as they did any other.

"Dante stole one of Lieb's female Weres a few decades ago. Did not go over well. Shane forbidding them to cross through his territory to fight each other was essentially what's kept them from an all-out war," Min murmured.

"And now Dante's involved with the disappearance of three of our wolves," Margaret said, a growl in her voice.

"I find it hard to believe Dante and a Vampire such as Duflanc would be working together, though the timing is too close for it to be a mere coincidence. It's also very odd that Thomas and Tommy were taken without you hearing anything," Min said, taking up his cup, sipping the tea.

He was right. How did Vee and Durran miss the commotion? And Shane for that matter? He was still home setting up his office when it happened.

"We need to go to Sauer Castle," Vee said, pushing off the counter.

"Not now," Durran said, seeing the way Vee's body tensed. She wanted to bolt and needed to be doing something.

"Now may be the perfect time," Min said, smirking at the way Durran's eyes flashed red as she glared at him. "We don't have time to waste waiting for sunrise. Whatever threatens this pack will still be here." Durran practically snarled at Min as he finished speaking, who raised his eyebrows in challenge. The look was so much like Vee's, it momentarily startled her.

"Has anyone looked on the outside of Thomas's house?" Patrick asked, bringing all their attention to him for a moment.

"No one mentioned anything to me," Vee said, glancing at Margaret and George.

"They all checked the interior," George said, realization dawning on them all.

They moved as a unit, heading out the back door toward Thomas's yard with purpose. Durran split off to round the fenceline, while the Weres and Min were clearly searching for scents. Vee looked at the patio. Cora had gotten the furniture set up first so they'd have a place to eat while the first floor was still in the middle of renovations. Her hope had been that it would be finished before the weather got too cool. As it was, halfway through September, it was still warm. Kansas City usually transitioned from summer to autumn abruptly, one day to the next.

She spotted something odd sitting on the table closest to the back door. At first, she thought it was a cup or a small planter sitting upside down, but as she moved closer, she saw it was a bell. It was made of copper, the exterior dinged and scratched, the green hue of oxidation coating most of the surface. As she approached, she felt the vibration of its magic, without even touching it.

"Fae magic," Vee said, knowing her companions would hear her.

Min and Patrick were immediately at her side, the three of them looking down at the object with distrust.

"I know that Fae scent," Min growled, glancing at Vee. She felt like she knew before he even spoke the words, and the steadily growing stone in the pit of her stomach got heavier. "Ness."

Vee's anger was so close to the surface instantaneously, her eyes immediately blazed amber. She had just seen Ness, spoken to her earlier that morning as she left the shop, and somehow, she was involved in what happened to Thomas and Tommy.

"The deal Shane made, Vee," Durran murmured as she approached.

"What are you talking about?" Vee hissed, turning her molten gaze to Durran.

"Shane told me he made a deal. A very vague deal with Ness to save you," Durran said, moving around her and, with the steadiest hands, picking up the bell and pressing the clapper into the side so it wouldn't make a sound.

"A deal with a Fae," Min said, his voice as horrified as his eyes. The insanity of those words stripped him of his stoicism. There were no good deals to be made with a Fae, no matter how careful you were. A vague deal, much worse.

The air around Vee seemed to ripple as an additional wave of fury moved through her, causing them all to take a step back. She was overcome by it, overwhelmed by it. The hits just kept coming. She closed her eyes, reigning in her emotions, swallowing them down, the ache in her heart, the pit in her stomach, the anger in her veins. She pulled them away. Now wasn't the time.

"Sauer Castle," was all she said before she headed back to the house and directly to her well-worn work

boots that sat in the closet by the front door to put them on. No one said a word of protest.

They took Durran's car again since Patrick and Min were coming. Margaret doubled the patrols around the house, since none of the Weres were sleeping anyway. The sunrise was starting to lighten the sky as the road they drove on changed from Rainbow Boulevard to Seventh Street, and they crossed under the Interstate 39 bridge. Durran turned off onto Shawnee Road, her grip tightening as they got nearer. She did not like this. She didn't want Vee in harm's way, but she also knew there was no way Vee would be staying put and hiding. She was incapable of reason right now, incapable of doing anything but trying to figure out what was really going on, trying to find Shane.

The ride had been silent, the feelings within the car tense. They slowed as they moved through the neighborhood. It was a little patchy. Mostly small one-story buildings: some in fantastic condition with well-maintained yards, while others were boarded up and abandoned. This neighborhood had once been thriving, with a school of its own and small but nice homes. Now it seemed most of it was abandoned, just like the castle itself. They finally saw the chain-link fence that cut the castle, its eleven acres, and its three-story caretaker house off from the rest of the neighborhood, the sun rising behind it, casting the silhouette of the structure in an eerie and imposing light.

The Italiante, German Gothic style home's red brick seemed aflame by the sunrise, and Vee let the eerie feeling take her. Something was wrong with this place. She could feel the magic, but also the anguish pulsing from the very ground. The feeling so strong that for a moment, she could think of nothing else, could feel nothing else, not even those surrounding her. Durran stopped the car, and they all got out. The chain-link would be no issue for her companions, but Vee didn't have super strength to jump over tall things, nor could she fly like Durran.

"I'll carry you," Durran said, as she saw the skepticism in Vee's eyes.

But they didn't get a chance. Seemingly melting out of the large evergreen tree sitting on the lot across from the property, Ness appeared, followed by another Fae.

"I thought you might come here," Ness said, still in her now familiar, old woman glamor. The Fae beside her hadn't hidden much behind her guise. Her spindly true form was mirrored in the thin, lanky woman who stood there, large brown eyes like a doe stared out at them all. She was a forest Fae, Vee assumed, which would also account for them melting from the evergreen tree moments before.

"What have you done, Fae?" Durran snapped, moving to stand slightly in front of Vee. Min and Patrick also seemed to bristle at the Faes' appearances, eyes glowing as they anticipated their change.

"Tsk, Watcher. You may want to tell your dogs to stand down. There are humans who might see," Ness said, gesturing to the house behind her. The one-story house that the evergreen sat snuggly beside suddenly had lights on, as if the humans inside were called by her words.

"Answer the question, Fae," Min growled. She grinned, her false face's wrinkles deepening, though her eyes were sinister.

"I fulfilled a promise." Fae were rarely direct. Questions had to be specific to get specific answers, and they couldn't lie but they could bend the truth to confuse.

"What promise did you fulfill, and what did you do to fulfill it?" Vee asked, glaring past Durran's arm at Ness. Her grin got impossibly broader. Pride in her eyes, as if Vee was a small child in her care. She always seemed so pleased when Vee remembered the rules.

"Queen Kel, like many of our Fae brethren, has diminished. Her gift, her transformation, has hindered her for half a century, and once Fiona abandoned me…" Her features sharpened slightly; a deep resentment began oozing from her. "I tasked myself in her care. She is of my kin, though distantly."

"What promise did you make Queen Kel?" Vee asked when Ness paused a beat too long.

"That I would find someone who could call it forth for her," Ness said, her tone suggesting it was the most logical explanation. Vee's fists clenched.

"Call what forth?" Durran asked.

"Her beast."

"And what did you do to fulfill that promise to Queen Kel?"

"I could find no one powerful enough. In all the years I searched, there were no beast-kind Others who could help her, or who were willing to help her. But once you came out of that Sha realm with your *mate* beside you, I felt the power had changed within him." Ness's smile returned at the shaky intake of air that came through Vee's lips. "He made a deal with me to spare your life."

"She would have saved your life no matter. She is bound by her duty to your mother," the Fae beside her said, her doe-like eyes widening while a smile crept across her thin face. The effect was chilling, inhuman, unnatural.

Vee was barely containing her impulse to leap across the road and rip Ness apart. She felt that rage building in her veins again, and she nearly felt sick tamping it down.

"What did you do to Shane?" Each word that came from Vee's lips was punctuated, forceful. Ness visibly recoiled at it, as if they stung her.

"I saw an opportunity when John Meyers was speaking to another Werewolf pack leader. They so boldly met at a restaurant not far from your shop, but everyone knows you don't go out to eat without someone else. There was no risk of running into you," Ness said, a smirk returning to her lips. Everyone's amusement at Vee's predictability was once mildly annoying, but now was infuriating. "They needed Shane and two others gone; I needed Shane and to get my end of the bargain satisfied, and my promise kept," Ness said, her tone nonchalant, as if what this action meant for not only Vee, but everyone in the preternatural community, was not a terrible act of war. This type of betrayal was so complex and wide-reaching, especially with how inclusive a leader Shane was.

"You've made a grave mistake, Fae," Min said, hand on Patrick's chest. Vee hadn't noticed until this moment but she was not the only one who was about to lose her cool. Patrick's whole body was tensed, hands and forearms shaking and flexing, as if he were trying to keep them in their human shape. He was coiled tight, eyes blazing as if he was about to spring across the road and murder Ness where she stood.

"What about Duflanc?" Durran asked.

"Duflanc? The Vampire?" Ness said, visibly rattled by that question, if not disgusted. "I have nothing to do with whatever he has done." She spit on the ground, as if even the thought of him put a bad taste in her mouth.

"Where are Shane and the others?" Min asked, a rumble in his chest.

"Your questions are for naught, Shifter. There is nothing that can be done until the moon's glow no longer shines. Only then can the gates reopen," the other Fae hissed at Min, before she took Ness's arm, dragging her back into the tree where they came from. Their presence was disappearing along with their visage, as if there were a portal hidden in those branches.

The drive back to the house was just as quiet as when they had left, but now the feelings within the car were far more confused. They had no confirmation that Shane, Thomas, and Tommy were alive, or if they were, that they would live through this. Duflanc's part in all this seemed to be more random than involved in the bigger plot at play. But they did know now that John Meyers was a traitor.

They pulled back into the cul-de-sac, Archer greeting them with a wave as he sat on one of the pillars that flanked the entrance. Lori met them at the door once they all got out and filed through the front door.

"I couldn't stop her. She and Markus just started making breakfast for everyone," Lori said apologetically, looking at the tired faces of Vee and Patrick.

"That's good," Vee said, trying for a weak smile, but it came as more of a grimace.

"Has anyone checked on Toby?" Patrick asked.

"He still hasn't woken up, but Emily is down there with him. She changed his bandages about thirty minutes ago," Lori said quietly. Children's squeals rang out suddenly from the living room just before a gaggle of little ones ran through, bound for the kitchen.

"I'm going to take a shower," Durran mumbled into Vee's ear before making a swift exit out the front door to the apartment over the garage. Vee would have liked a shower. She hadn't showered since the morning before and was certain she still had Una's blood on her somewhere, but she knew there were still things to be done.

"Let's go check on Toby and Emily," she said, moving toward the basement stairs, Patrick and Min following behind her.

The basement housed quite a few rooms. Four bedrooms, a gym, several storage rooms, one of which was where they kept the cage. It was furthest from the living spaces, the door reinforced, and technically so were the walls, but you'd only know that once you stepped inside. Toby hadn't worked on this room yet, so there was nothing that looked finished or polished about it. Silver and steel bars had been secured to all the walls, ceiling, and floor. The floor had been evened out with crude plywood that Shane thought they'd cover with laminate tile at some point, but he wasn't exactly expecting to need to use the room so quickly upon moving in.

Emily sat in a folding chair that she had brought next to the cage. Toby was lying on the floor, a thin mat underneath him. Normally the cage itself would have been enough, but when Todd Downing, a rogue Were, had torn his way out of the cage at Shane's previous house, Shane had envisioned making a more fortified room in the future. And so, he had.

"I hate that we're keeping him in here," Emily whispered as they came in.

"Without Dad here, it was the safest place for him. Tonight's the first night of the full moon, Emily," Patrick reminded, though he felt the same ache she did. Seeing someone they all knew, a man who was kind and thoughtful like Toby, hurt and trapped in the cage, felt wrong.

"His wounds are healing well," she offered, voice still small.

"Then he'll survive," Patrick said. Emily nodded.

"I can help him," Min said suddenly, causing Emily to finally lift her eyes and look at the three of them. "I can help him with his wolf. I can't bring him into your pack, but I can keep him safe outside of this cage. Perhaps not outside of this room," Min said, glancing around at the crude reinforcements. The first change was always difficult. Man and beast had to become one, and that usually meant hunting, but the way things currently were, there was no way they could take anyone outside of the protection, and with Toby not being pack, he couldn't be let loose on the property.

Toby stirred, causing them all to snap their focus on his face. His eyes fluttered for a moment, brow furrowing as the pain in his body fully registered.

"Fuck…" he groaned, trying to lift his arm, but then letting out an even more painful sound at the attempt.

"Toby?" Emily asked, her voice a quiet tremor. He fought to open his lids again, his eyes unseeing at first, but when he focused, he saw the cage surrounding him, panic swiftly setting in.

"Where am I?" he asked, his voice rough, gravelly with pain and semiconsciousness.

"Toby, do you remember what happened to you?" Patrick asked, stepping forward toward the cage. Toby's eyes darted to Patrick's voice, moving past the bars and Emily to look at him. The fear in his eyes creeped in as the scent of it cascaded out of him, filling the room. Both Weres and Min reacted to the scent, their bodies tensing.

"You're at our house, Toby, in the basement," Vee said, stepping forward and crouching beside the chair Emily sat in so she was closer to eye level with him. "Do you remember what happened before you fell asleep?"

She pushed a wave of calm at him and the others in the room. It was difficult, because she felt nowhere near calm. Every calm thought that came to her head was laced with the loss she felt in her chest, in her body.

But it worked. The fear lessened somewhat as Toby's eyes locked with Vee's.

"Shane and Thomas ... they aren't running a mob, are they?" Toby asked, eyes wide with shock, though it was subdued by her influence.

"No, not a mob," Vee said, as a light smile graced her lips.

CHAPTER 12

V ee could see the pieces coming together as Toby stared at her, his mind, though calmed, was racing to fit everything he had witnessed into normal human boxes that didn't fit, and finally letting the truth seep in.

"Men came. Tommy was pushed down the basement stairs. That's when I knew something was off ... different. Cora wanted floating shelves in her laundry area, and I was making notes." His thoughts were disjointed, coming out in spurts as he tried to recall what happened. "I tried to help. I hit one of them when they tried to come near Cora. That one ... his arm..." Toby seemed to shiver at the recollection. "It wasn't an arm anymore. His face..." He gulped, tears spilling from his eyes. "He attacked me and my crew."

Vee nodded solemnly. Looking him deep in the eyes.

"You were attacked by Werewolves and survived," Vee said bluntly, letting that information stay there in the air for a moment. His eyes widened impossibly further, breath coming out in sporadic bursts despite Vee's influence. "Shane and the rest," Vee gestured behind her at Patrick and beside her at Emily. "They are Werewolves."

"And you? Are you a Werewolf too?" Toby asked, watching the way Vee's eyes seemed to swirl between her normal emerald and amber.

"No. I'm something else," she said, glancing at Emily, who had flinched when she outed her. Being a Werewolf was often a sore subject for some of them. They sometimes saw themselves as monsters, knowing how humans would view them if they knew.

"We'll explain everything to you, Toby, but right now, you need to understand why we have you in this room," Patrick said, drawing Toby's gaze to him, then the cage surrounding him. He shifted slightly where he sat, his neck slowly and painfully moving around to take in both the metal surrounding him and the reinforced room beyond.

"I'm in a cage."

"You are going to change. Maybe not tonight, but certainly tomorrow. Until you have control of your wolf, you can't be let free to roam within the city. Even some of our other wolves have trouble in city limits," Patrick told him, though his fist tightened, recalling it was Jonathan Meyers, John's oldest son, who still struggled in the city, even with Shane and John's influence around him. Was John just going to let his son run wild through the city now that they had abandoned and betrayed the pack?

"No," Toby said, his voice quivering as more tears cascaded from his eyes. "I don't want to be a monster!" Emily flinched again, her body shaking a little at the words, blue eyes cast down to her hands in shame.

"You won't be a monster, Toby. We won't let you," Vee murmured, sympathy in her voice.

Lori came to the door hesitantly, her hands filled with plates of food.

"I brought some breakfast," Lori said quietly, catching Toby's eyes. He took in a shaky gasp at her appearance, watching as she came closer, handing Emily one plate, and then, with not even a modicum of fear, opening the cage and coming beside Toby to set the plate next to him.

"Lori. Your mom," Toby whispered.

"She's okay," Lori said with a soft smile. "She made breakfast."

"Is she …?"

"No. She's human."

"And you are …?"

"Werewolf," Lori said, a grin spreading across her face as she let a little of her wolf to the surface, her eyes lightly glowing blue. Toby shivered a little, closing his eyes and gulping again. "You're going to be okay, Toby. I promise," Lori murmured, touching his hand lightly, before she got up and left the cage.

They all stood there for a moment, watching Toby process everything, eyes moving from one face to the other. It was a strange thing to have known these people without having truly understood anything about them. His assumptions that they were all part of a mob sounded so much safer now that he knew the truth. He moved, whining at the pain that shot through his body as he pushed himself into a sitting position, his back pressed firmly into the grating of the cage.

"Can I have a minute?" he whispered with a shuddering breath.

"Just remember you aren't alone," Patrick said quietly, taking Lori's hand as they all filed from the room.

"He will adjust," Min said to Patrick, whose face had become pinched. But Patrick's pain was about more than just Toby. His father would have known just what to do. He would have taken charge. He would have saved all those men on Toby's crew. The feeling was felt throughout the pack, but especially within Vee and Patrick. Without Shane ... without his dad, they were all lost.

Vee was halfway up the stairs when she felt a violent tug at her heart. She stumbled, Min catching her and helping her sit as her eyes stared in the distance, amber swirling through her irises. She gasped as she felt the tug again, her chest moving forward of its own accord with the force of it. It wasn't whole; it wasn't threaded through the fibers of her body, but she knew what that feeling was. She knew who was pulling at her heart.

Shane was alive.

Shane's eyes opened, looking at the red clay wall across from him. It smelled of earth, the air thick with the scent of it and Fae. Shane furrowed his brow as he took in his surroundings. He was lying on a bed, and the rest of the room was sparse, with only a chair sitting in the corner. He tried to recall how he got there, but all he could feel was the heaviness of his chest, the way his body seemed to yearn for something that should have been there but wasn't. He reached out to where his bond should be and found it to be nothing but a threadbare wisp of what it had been. A tiny teasing hint at Vee when she should have been vibrant and strong within him.

He stood suddenly at the panic of that, now reaching out to his other bonds, his pack. They too were barely there, except for Thomas and Tommy. Those connections hummed as he reached out to them, though Tommy was clearly in pain.

"Shane," he heard from somewhere close by through the clay wall.

"Thomas?" Shane asked, keeping his voice low. He didn't know what was beyond this room and clearly, they weren't there of their own choosing.

"I was worried you wouldn't wake up. You've been out for a while."

Shane tried again to recall what had happened, eyes moving around the room as if he would find the answer lying there for him. He recalled going to Susan and John's house. He had spent much of the afternoon helping her pack for their move. She seemed nervous, more nervous than normal. She never did get along well with the pack or its members, preferring to stay a little closed off from them, but he had always thought she at least felt comfortable around *him*.

John had made the mistake of keeping what he was from her far longer than he should have, and thus it backfired horribly when Susan was finally told the truth. And now that two of their three sons would also be Werewolves? She was begrudgingly accepting it, so Shane had made a special effort to make her feel accepted and welcomed.

It wasn't until the time neared for John to get home that she had accidentally let something slip.

"I suppose things will all be different and for the better when we get to St. Louis," she said, after Shane had just assured her that she would feel safer once they moved. Being without the pack protection had been such a devastating blow to all the homes that surrounded Shane, he understood why she would be extra nervous.

"St. Louis?" Shane asked, pausing to look up at her. She froze, realizing her mistake, her gaze fighting to remain straight ahead of her instead of looking into his eyes. Her heart began beating rapidly in her chest, sweat collecting at her hairline, her fear becoming thick within the room.

"I ... I mean. The new house," she said, her excuse as pathetic as her voice.

Shane held himself still, trying to keep his wolf from coming out and frightening this woman. She was not to blame for whatever nonsense was going on. He kept his hands at his sides, trying to keep them loose, even though he wanted to ball them into fists. He needed John to come home now. He'd get the answers out of him, not Susan.

Just as Shane's eyes snapped to the clock on the wall, John, seemingly on cue, called Shane.

"We need to talk," John said, his voice giving a nervous excitement when Shane answered.

"I'm actually at your house. I was helping Susan pack, but I thought we'd talk when you got home," Shane said, eyeing Susan, who had turned, heading toward the kitchen. Her heartbeat was pounding in his ears.

"I'd rather talk away from Susan," John murmured. An understandable request. This was Werewolf business, pack business, and Susan, though married to a Werewolf, didn't need to be involved with what was very possibly going to end in John's expulsion from the pack.

"Where?" Shane asked, a growl in his voice.

"I'll send you the address," John said, before he hung up abruptly.

A car pulled up a moment later, making Shane feel even more on edge. The timing, the cryptic way John was speaking. All of it felt off.

The car turned out to be Jonathan, John's oldest son, who also averted his eyes from his leader as he passed him in the driveway. A part of Shane wanted to stop him and force him to say what his father was up to, but again, Shane considered him innocent. Though Jonathan was a Werewolf and under Shane's leadership, he was John's son first.

Shane followed the instructions to the address. It was on the Kansas side, which made him feel strange. He had considered talking to Lieb about letting John join their pack a month ago, but when John made no moves to do such a thing, seeming to choose to get over his anger about Vee being brought into the pack, Shane had never gone through with it. Now that they were meeting on another pack's territory, however shallow into that territory it was, his heart sank just a little.

His instincts were screaming at him that he was being led into a trap. Shane had thought he and Lieb had come to an understanding recently, but it was very possible that Shane had overestimated how long that truce would last. If John reached out to him with information and ways to weaken Shane, Lieb may have jumped on the opportunity, regardless of what Vee had done to help him protect his daughter, Halima.

As the large Gothic house came into view, the tail end of the sunset was fiery against the brick house. Shane saw no one waiting for him. He turned off his car on the eerily quiet street, looking at the chain-link fence and beyond it to the house, trying to see if he noticed John at all. John's car was parked a little ways down, and there seemed to be a split in the fence there. He slipped through, nose immediately taking in the scent of Fae. And with his pause a few paces closer to the house, he finally saw not John waiting for him, but Ness.

Ness, the Fae who had helped them fight Duflanc. Ness, the Fae who had been charged as Fiona O'Morrigan's servant and protector. Ness, the Fae who Shane had made a deal with to save Vee's life.

His eyes immediately turned gold, burning and on alert. "What is this?" he demanded.

"Shane Keenan, I've come to call in my debt," Ness said, her elderly exterior smiling pleasantly, even though Shane felt the danger in those words. Anger so intense, so unfathomably deep ran through him at that moment. He felt the magic of the deal take hold, snaking around his body, leaving him completely unable to move on his own will.

Each step his body took without his permission inflamed him even more.

"The more you fight it, the harder it takes hold," Ness said, as his wolf called out one final time, invisible claws digging into the flesh of his arms, before a door seemed to open not far from the entrance to the house, a portal, and he was swallowed into its dark depths.

Shane breathed heavily through the memory as it flooded his mind, eyes moving to look at the deep gouges in his arms, but they weren't there. The skin was healed over, but still pink with fresh skin, like he had healed not long ago.

"How long?" Shane growled at Thomas through the wall.

"What?"

"How long was I out?" Shane demanded, fist clenching against the wall as he leaned against it.

"Days, I think. I don't know," Thomas murmured, his voice as confused as Shane felt.

"Is Tommy here?" Shane asked, now casting his gaze around the room for weaknesses. He wasn't bound and though the clay was thick, if it were normal clay, he'd be able to punch through it easily enough.

"He's hurt, but close by," Thomas said, new worry in his voice.

"How did you get here?"

"Dante," Thomas growled, just before the wall Shane had been leaning on shook a little with a hit from Thomas.

"Dante, John, and the Fae," Shane mused, watching the way the wall buckled again as Thomas landed another punch. "Got in my house that morning, right after we had discussed the hunting party for the Vampires."

"How did they manage that without us hearing?" Shane asked, as the wall became convex with a third punch from Thomas. Shane stepped back, watching as the wall move with each of Thomas's hits. He grunted, pausing his assault on the wall. Shane heard him breathing harshly for a moment.

"I don't know. Probably some Fae crap," Thomas rumbled, and then he sighed. "Killed Toby's crew." The way the words came from his mouth were broken. His tone filled with rage and sadness. They had all grown rather fond of Toby and all the guys on the crew. Even if Shane now knew about Toby's feelings for Vee, it didn't diminish how horrifying and sad it was that they had been in the wrong place at the wrong time.

"Cora?" Shane asked, his voice quiet as he stared at the wall, waiting. Silence hung in the air for a moment.

"I don't know," Thomas said again quietly, though his voice sounded broken and filled with agony. Last Thomas saw, Cora was thrown against the wall, the scent of her blood somehow so much more potent in the air than the men he fought around him.

The sound of footfalls from outside the room came to their ears, and they quieted. Shane stood and faced the door, waiting for whatever creature would be coming through. The door opened and a man stood there, or at least he was tall enough to have been a man. His body was lean and boyish, barely any muscle or fat on his frame, but he still seemed to fill the doorway. Dressed in strange, shimmering robes that seemed to float of their own accord around him, his hair was dark, eyes dilated so much they seemed black, though Shane saw the thin ring of blue around them, and he had cuffs on his wrist as well as a silver collar at his throat. He was as much a prisoner as Shane was here.

"The mistress wishes to see you," the boy said quietly, gesturing for Shane to follow.

He hesitated a moment, firming his stiff posture and considering demanding answers from this boy, but ultimately, the blank, expressionless eyes on his face told Shane he'd get no answers from him. With a reluctant sigh, he stepped out from the room into a hallway. It felt like a wholly different place from where he was. The walls were intricate. At first he thought they were carved wood, but then he realized it was complexly interwoven branches and roots, braided and twined together in patterns. The floor beneath his feet was made of soft moss. It was well lit, but not from any discernible fixture.

The clay prison had been an indication, but it was clear now that they were in a Fae realm. Shane followed behind the boy as they moved through the irregular hallways, twisting and turning seemingly with no rhyme or reason, until it opened up to a large throne room. There was menagerie of various creatures and Others sitting around the perimeter, while a small blue woman sat at the center on a throne made of the same branches and roots as the walls.

Her skin was pale blue, eyes black like ink and slanted, as if they belonged more to a creature with monocular vision. Her hair was white, and it seemed to swirl around her as if she was floating in water. Her body was thin, fragile-looking, but her face held a hardness that was only gained with time and having bared witness to things better left in the past.

"Shane Keenan, Leader of the Westport Pack, True Mate of Victoria Malone, do you know why you've been brought here?" the woman seated beside the throned woman asked. This woman was clearly also a Fae, though her true form was much less foreign and alien. Her eyes held the telltale largeness of other Fae, but her skin was deep brown, and her hair black as it curled around her. At her words that he was the leader of the Westport pack, a murmur seemed to float across the room.

"Ness Seeley used our deal to bring me here. That's all I know," Shane said, glancing around at the other faces. There were more collared humans standing around, most of them seemed as vacant as the boy who had led him there. The Others also wore similar collars around their necks, though their eyes were much more alert, albeit broken.

"Yes, you were brought here one day ago your time, four days ours, to this realm," the blue woman said, her voice low and velvety as she spoke, eyes assessing Shane.

"I can't feel my mate through our bond," Shane said, narrowing his eyes in warning, his voice teetering on a growl as he spoke. If they had done something to Vee, he didn't care about any deal or bargain. This place would be coated in blood.

"She lives. No harm has come to her. Your bond cannot work here when the realm is sealed," the dark one said. The relief was brief as it came over him. She was alive, but he couldn't feel her, not truly. He reached out to the thin, lifeless bond within himself and knew it would return to him. He just had to get out of this first.

"Why am I here?"

"Queen Kel is beast-kind. She, though the most powerful of the water Fae, is bound to this realm. Within these walls, she has not once been able to call forth her beast," the dark one said, turning to look at the blue Fae, who stiffened where she sat.

"Our powers are diminishing. Each passing year we lose more and more of what we once had, and there are not enough of us being born to recoup," Queen Kel said, tilting her head as she assessed him. "Your kind does not have that problem."

"No. Werewolves do not have issues creating more of our kind," Shane confirmed, though the mode of the change was sometimes different than it was for the Fae. Having the ability to create Weres from attack *and* from birth gave them an advantage over most other preternaturals.

"My entrapment here was not supposed to hinder my beast, but it seems to have locked her away. I need someone to help me call my beast. Someone who is equal or greater than I in power," Queen Kel admitted.

"And you think I am that?" Shane asked, brows furrowing with skepticism. He had not had much interaction with Fae, but he knew their power, even lesser Fae like Ness far exceeded what any Were could do.

"Ness seemed to think so, but we shall see," she murmured.

"What will happen if I cannot help you?" he asked.

"I'll keep you here as my reward." Her hand gestured out to the Others surrounding her in the room. The various creatures with hollow gazes and collars circling their throats glanced his way. "I have to get something out of this," she continued, with a malicious smirk spreading across her small face. Within that smile that seemed far too wide for its frame, he saw rows upon rows of razor-sharp black teeth. He hesitated to look away from her, but the other animals shifting where they sat around the perimeter made him finally take a better look around.

He realized then that all the exotic animals who sat in the semicircle at her sides were, in fact, other Weres. Tigers, horses, even another Werewolf was sitting there, collared and enslaved to her, and there was no telling how long they had been trapped. The wolf held his focus a moment longer, a warning sitting there in its lightless orbs.

"If it comes to that, Queen Kel, please release my other Weres, Thomas and his son. They have no cause to be here. They made no deals, no offenses to you and yours. They should be set free," he countered. If he had to make yet another deal with a Fae, he was certainly going to be sure it was well-defined. She grinned wider, her black eyes twinkling with amusement.

"As you wish, Shane Keenan, but the realm is sealed until the moon's light shines not in your world. You'll have a month to fulfill your end of our bargain."

CHAPTER 13

Tears were streaming from Vee's eyes as she waited for the tug to happen again. Searching within herself for where she felt it. A very small part of the void inside her seemed to close, but there was nothing for her to grasp onto. The moments ticked by as she searched and dug, but whatever it was that reached out was gone again.

"Vee! What is it?" Min asked, as she seemed to come back to the present. Patrick and Lori were standing a few stairs down from her, both looking at her as they overwhelmed her with their worry.

"I felt Shane. It wasn't all of him, but he reached out to me," she whispered, touching her hand to her chest. She could almost smell him on her skin. Almost. She swallowed the sob that wanted to tear from her, focusing on Min.

"You're still connected, then. Something's just blocking it," Min said, his eyes alight with intrigue. Confirmation of life was one thing, but still having no way to get him back was quite another, and they had no way of doing that before they dealt with Dante and John.

She took a deep breath, moving to stand once again and heading the remaining steps to the first floor. Cora stood in the kitchen, wiping out the now empty pans into the trash. She was wearing some of the sweats that they kept for pack members whose clothes were lost or damaged beyond repair. It was a far cry from her normally much more put-together appearance, but her other clothes had been covered in blood, and she knew better than to try to leave the house to go back to her home when the whole pack was on alert.

"Sit. I'll make you all something to eat," Cora said to the four of them.

"We've fed the rest of them; it's your turn now," Markus said sternly, as he appeared from the pantry with a fresh loaf of bread. Vee and Patrick knew better than to protest.

"I already ate. It's my turn for a shower," Lori said, kissing Patrick on the cheek when Cora's back was turned to the stove, before leaving the room. Patrick and Lori's secret relationship was not going to remain so for much longer with how bold they were becoming. Patrick hadn't even tried to hide the way they held hands in front of most of the pack, and Lori kissing his cheek in the same room as her mother, even if not to her face, was a fairly new development.

Durran made an appearance through the back door as Vee sat, gladly taking the coffee passed to her by Markus. Her exhaustion was digging its claws in deep. Two hours of sleep the night before were not nearly the amount she was accustomed to, but if she was being honest with herself, she wasn't sure she'd be able to sleep if she tried.

"Patrick, I'm sure you don't care in the slightest, but I did call your school and let them know there was a family emergency. Your teachers are sending assignments by email," Cora said as she whisked the bowl of eggs she had just cracked.

"School," Vee groaned, letting her head fall into her hands. Yet another of her responsibilities she had neglected. She felt like a failure as a stepmother. She had completely forgotten that Patrick was in school or what day of the week it was for that matter. Patrick pulled her into a side hug from their seated position on the stools.

"You had other things to think about," he told her reassuringly. It still didn't help the guilt she felt. She may have been new to this parenting thing, but without Shane there, it was her responsibility.

Margaret, Frida, and George all came in carrying empty dishes.

"Roman's got news," Margaret said happily, handing the dishes to Markus.

"Oh?" Vee said, eyeing her as she moved back to where Vee sat and leaned against the counter. Min, who had been leaning on a wall near Vee, let his head pop up at that news.

"He hacked John's phone. He blocked all of us; his phone isn't off," Margaret said smugly, the smirk on her face deepening.

"It's like he didn't pay attention to the members of the pack at all. If I wanted to disappear from Roman, I'd make sure I got a burner phone to use," Patrick said, shaking his head with a similar smirk on his face.

"I suppose 'smart' shouldn't be on the list of descriptors for John Meyers," Roman said as he wandered in, holding dirty dishes of his own. "Ceci loved the pancakes, Cora," he said, gaining a grin.

"Lori and Tommy always loved it when I made faces," Cora said happily, before her eyes filled with tears thinking about her husband and son.

"What did you find?" Vee asked, giving Cora an opportunity to collect herself and bring the topic back where it needed to be.

"He's staying at an Airbnb. Looks like he sent Susan and the kids to St. Louis already," Roman said, pulling out his phone to show Vee the address. She knew exactly where that was. It was in the heart of Waldo, the neighborhood south of Brookside. She did a fair amount of work over there in the past. The only other small-time locksmith in the area had closed some years earlier, and they hadn't made house calls, so when he was open, he used to give his customers her number if it involved travel. They had a mutual hatred for the corporate locksmith companies.

"We need to go," Vee said, moving to stand.

"Go do what?" Min asked, making everyone turn to look at him.

"See what's going on there. Is it just John? Is Dante there with him? Is there anyone else involved?" Vee suggested, her tone unabashedly full of sass.

"When's the last time you ate anything?" Durran asked, crossing her arms over her chest and meeting Vee's attitude-filled eyes with narrowed ones of her own. Vee's face drained at Durran's words, as she wasn't certain. The last thing she remembered eating was the leftover Chinese food she had for breakfast the day before, but the pit of worry had been filling her, and the idea of food made her mouth run dry with distaste.

"You eat, be with your pack. The Watcher and I will go," Min said, pushing off the counter and turning to look at Durran.

"*I* will go. I don't need you," Durran snarled mildly.

"You may be forgiven for killing a Were by Shane when and if he returns, but there's no need if I'm here," Min said, raising an eyebrow in challenge.

"No need," Durran reiterated.

"I can just go, and there won't be an argument," Vee said, trying to stand again.

"No!" Durran and Min both growled at her. She narrowed her eyes but sat back down.

Durran's lip curled and her eyes flashed red, but she walked close to Min, reaching around him to pull Roman's phone close to her face, taking in the address before turning sharply and walking back out the back door to head to her car.

"Don't do anything stupid. Just see what's going on there," Vee hollered after her. Min smirked, walking toward the door.

"I won't let anything stupid happen. You just focus on eating," he said, before closing the door behind him.

Min climbed in the passenger seat of the old black Buick, calmly but slowly, buckling his seatbelt while Durran gritted her teeth. He turned and looked at her, clearly amused by her irritation.

"You didn't need to come," Durran grumbled, as she put her hand on the ignition to start it.

"Vee would have come if I didn't. She's behaving like a Sha or Were, though I don't think she realizes it. She's not eating since she lost her mate. She needs to be forced into it by the pack," Min said, his smile spreading at the clear frustration on Durran's normally cool exterior.

"Vee tends to miss meals in general. It's not necessarily something to do with the Sha in her," Durran countered.

"Either way, this needs to be taken care of, and she requires food. Without us there, the pack will surround her. Like it or not, she's part of them, and a prominent member at that. The pack wants to rally around her, and she needs it," Min said, turning to look out the windshield.

Durran seemed frozen at the thought. For so long it had just been Vee and Durran in the small capacity she let anyone in. She had known Vee better than anyone, and yet when Min, who barely knew her at all, pointed out the very clear reason for this particular behavior in

Vee, at least on this occasion, it made Durran question her place in all of this.

"You may go now," Min said, and suddenly Durran realized they had been sitting there for an awkward length of time. Durran didn't hesitate. She started the car, the engine roaring to life as her eyes flashed red, before she pulled out of the driveway and flew from the cul-de-sac, not bothering to wave at the Weres guarding the entrance.

The ride was silent as Durran turned onto Ward Parkway, heading south. Min simply looked out the window at the large houses as they passed, while Durran alternately seethed and contemplated the future from the driver's seat.

"I'm not sure why you're so hostile, Watcher. It's your presence here that's causing so much trouble," Min said, turning his eyes just in time to see the knuckles on Durran's hand tighten, turning white with her grip. It was like Min had read her mind. She hated him even more for feeding the doubt.

"I belong here. You are merely visiting and will leave eventually. You're not needed," Durran snapped back. Min's deep chuckle seemed to fill the entire car.

"The Westport pack is my charge. Shane my responsibility. Vee my sister," Min said.

"Vee is my ward. I'm bound to her. Bound to her life, and now she's part of this pack, bound to this pack as well, whether I like it or not," Durran countered, snapping her head over to glare at Min once they pulled up to a red light.

Min took her in, the fierceness in her eyes, the way she was so filled with purpose. Durran's duty was to Vee.

His original feeling toward the Watcher, upon meeting them in Breckenridge, was hostility. Shane and Vee had assured Min that Durran was not a threat. That they would uphold the secrets and honor of the Sha. He hadn't believed it, and that coupled with the revelation of Vee being his sister, which had taken some adjustment. It was only recently when Aho was discussing Vee, Shane, and Durran's odd partnership that Min realized he held no animosity to the Watcher. Durran had proven themself formidable, being there to not only protect Vee during Duflanc's attack in the woods the month prior, but even helping the rest of them.

Min may have been hundreds of years old, but he realized he was still immature in the way he viewed other preternaturals. Vee, many, many years his junior, had somehow found a way to find alliances, crossing those borders. He supposed she had an advantage, being not one particular type of preternatural herself, but he had seen for himself that once they proved to her they were good, she would stand with them.

After a lot of meditation and conversation with his father, Min knew he needed to take a different outlook. An outlook against what the Sha had preached for his whole life. Staying separate from others was only hurting them and, in Durran, Min had the perfect opportunity to try to create a bridge.

"We both should be here, then," Min said after several long moments. Durran glanced at him, but his tone and neutral face only showed he was being truthful.

"I suppose so," Durran murmured. At some point during the drive, Durran had transitioned from their female form to their true form. What once was a smaller, softer version of Durran, now sat the androgynous version, wings still glamoured under the black duster, but the jaw was a little stronger, shoulders a little wider.

Durran turned the car onto Seventy-fifth street, the east-to-west thoroughfare in the Waldo neighborhood that was one of the most frequently used paths, and unfortunately the road where the Airbnb sat. They slowed when they got close, Durran rolling down the window so they could catch scents as they passed without stopping. Both bristled as they smelled the variety of preternatural scents coming from the home.

"Dante, some of his men, maybe four," Min said.

"Thomas and Tommy took out at least six before they were able to capture them," Durran said, a little pride coming through their tone. Durran and Tommy had become friends and knowing him, Durran was certain he gave them no mercy. "I also smelled Duflanc."

"We should have hunted him through those woods and killed him that night." Min's voice was cold as ice, his eyes flashing amber with restrained rage.

"Yes," Durran rumbled, pulling off on a side street and turning off the car. "Best vantage point would probably be on top of a roof, but we could be spotted there," Durran said, glancing at the homes directly across from the house. Min saw a small set of red-brick apartments just a block east and across the street from the house.

"There," Min said, pointing at it.

They made their way over to the building, finding an old fire escape that they could use to climb. The day was cloudy, giving them a little shadow to cover them, but not much. They sat, eyes taking in the house. Little activity was happening there. One of Dante's men stepped out on the porch at one point in the morning to have a smoke, but no others were seen patrolling or coming to and from the building for hours.

"I wonder if Dante's even in there," Min said after hours of silence between them.

"Their forces have dwindled, but it could mean there's a second location they're staying at where there are more," Durran said in agreement.

Silently, they both climbed back down the building.

[Vee: Updates?]

Vee's message came to them both, causing them to grab their phones from their pockets once they touched down on the ground again.

[Durran: We're following the scent to see if they have a second location.]

[Min: Not much happening at this one.]

"I'm not sure who would be the least recognizable by John. He's seen me, but infrequently," Min said, trying to determine which of them would be better suited to approach the house to catch the scent. Durran smirked, raising an eyebrow.

"As long as John doesn't come out and smell me, he won't recognize me," Durran said, just as their features began shifting and changing before Min's eyes. Suddenly, in place of the tall, lanky form of Durran, there was a short, unassuming young man. His hair was ashy brown, face boyish and forgettable, with blue jeans under the dark duster that fit perfectly with the cool breeze that was blowing with the cloudy sky. Durran's red-brown eyes hadn't changed though, slightly playful and smug as they took in Min's mildly surprised face. "I'll head the direction of the trail when I get it." And then Durran set off across the busy street.

CHAPTER 14

Three more days had passed for Shane, Thomas, and Tommy. Eventually, they took the walls separating their cells down, allowing them to be together in their strange imprisonment instead of alone. The draw for pack togetherness when they were an island unto themselves was irresistible. Tommy was hurt, but not terribly. He had been given quite a blow to the head in order to subdue him for the transport and was back to normal within days, though no less concerned about those they left behind.

Each day Shane was called to the great hall, he tried a number of techniques to call Kel's beast, but none of them had proven to do much. Though she claimed she felt it reawakening, it still hid inside her, his wolf unable to reach it. Each night, he touched the frayed remnants of his bond to Vee. Kel and the dark Fae, who he discovered was named Azi, may have assured him Vee had taken no harm, but he knew there was far more going on out in the other world. How safe was she when she seemed to constantly be under threat?

They were waiting for the new moon he had deduced, after speculating on the cryptic assurances, and though an end was in sight, his frustration grew as he failed to complete the task he was bound to.

"We can just fight our way out," Tommy suggested as Shane paced the now long room.

"We don't know what these Fae are capable of, and we're outnumbered by a hundred to one from what I've gathered by scent alone. Who knows if there are more that never come through the rooms we do," Thomas said, getting a grunt of agreement from Shane.

"What if you can't get her beast to surface? We're just supposed to leave you here, Shane?" Tommy asked, eyes flashing blue.

"I'll find another way if it comes to that," Shane murmured.

"I wonder how long it's been for them at home," Thomas said to the now silent room. Too many days too long for Shane. They had just moved, and he felt like he finally got Vee back after they had their bonds closed down, but she was immediately ripped from him again. Or, more accurately, he was ripped from her. He touched at the weak bond again, closing his eyes as he sat on the crude bed.

Reaching out in his mind, his fingers barely brushed at the small piece of her that was still there within him. His wolf seemed to whine, aching to get back to her as much as he did. She was their mate. Both parts of him; the man and the beast were hers, and she was theirs. His hand began changing as it reached, the man and the wolf both desperate for one touch, one assurance that she was okay out in the world. His elongated fingers found purchase, delicately wrapping the worn bond around a finger before giving it a quick pull.

Warmth spread throughout his body, the sensation filled him with both joy and pain. He *felt* her. She was there, and she had felt him too. The feeling dissipated, and he couldn't resist the urge to pull once more, feeling her spread throughout him for a moment before she quickly receded back. His eyes snapped open, the gold of his wolf shining as he looked up at the clay ceiling above their heads.

Vee was alive. She was fighting out there, trying to find him, and he would do anything to get back to her.

[Min: Decoy location. They may have met there, but the bulk are still elsewhere. Trail led to State Line Road.]

Vee saw Min's text and let out a breath of frustration. Hours wasted while she was forced to eat and sit at the house with nothing new to go on. Had she been there, she would have easily been able to sense what minds lingered inside the building.

[Vee: I would have determined that in minutes instead of hours.]

She knew her text was laced with malice, but she was hanging on to the weak threads of her civility. Night was on them once again, the first full moon of the next three nights rising in the darkening sky. Vee and Cora were huddled in the theatre room, a movie on the screen with all the kids, while the pack either patrolled or ran through the back yard when Durran and Min returned.

She felt them enter the protection but didn't move from where she sat until she felt them enter the house. Min barely made a sound and didn't say a word as he turned the corner after coming down the stairs, immediately going to the reinforced room where Toby was. Durran stood at the bottom of the stairs as Vee turned to look back at her.

She slipped Ceci's sleeping form from her lap and settled her with a blanket, before walking around the other seats to get to Durran. An odd situation Durran never thought they would ever see Vee in, surrounded by people, and children at that.

"Upstairs," Vee mouthed, glancing at the well-distracted or sleeping children before ascending the stairs first. They stopped in the kitchen, Vee slumping in a chair and looking at her friend with nothing hiding the exhaustion in her eyes.

"I have some ideas I want Roman to look into," Durran said, leaning on the counter. "But it can wait until tomorrow. You need to sleep." Vee's eyes blazed amber, and her fist clenched against the countertop.

"We *can't* wait!" she hissed.

"We can do nothing else tonight, Vee. Min is helping Toby, the Weres are on their run, and you..."

Durran reached out, touching Vee's fist gently. "You are no good to anyone, not even Shane, if you don't sleep," Durran said softly. Something in the concern and sympathy that Durran was feeling seemed to break a dam that she had held back for most of the day. Tears spilled over, running down her face like small rivers of sorrow.

"I'm so tired," Vee let out in a broken whisper, slumping further in the stool. Durran immediately came around the counter, pulling Vee into her arms and straight up the stairs to Vee and Shane's room. Durran set Vee down, watching and prepared to step in and help as Vee pulled the shoes from her feet, not bothering to change out of her jeans before she staggered to the bed and fell into it. Her sobs seemed to increase as her head hit Shane's pillow once again, but they quickly died off as she succumbed to her overwhelming exhaustion.

Patrick sat at the edge of the property, staring above the trees as the moon lessened in the sky, and the sun started turning the curtain of darkness into many shades of red. He had changed back into his human form after letting his wolf out at the moon's call, but his wolf, like him, was not up to this measly run in the back yard. It wanted to hunt; he wanted to kill. There was no joy in running and playing with the others right now, not when his father was gone, and the perpetrators were running amuck in their territory.

He had heard Vee's cries earlier that quieted as she slept. Part of him had wanted to change back then and go to her, but he knew she had been surrounded for these past few days. She had barely had a moment alone since everything happened, and Vee, though much more accustomed to being with the pack than she used to be, needed her space. It was something he and his father had strived to ensure she got, as long as it was safe to do so, since she agreed to share her life with them.

Vee was being so strong for them, stronger than any of them had expected. Not that she wasn't tough before, but he had heard her cries when his father was taken, saw the utter desolation in her eyes as she sat catatonic on the ground. He wasn't certain she would be able to come back from this. She had already lost so much and had already suffered more than he thought a person was capable of; and yet she had pulled herself out of it. She used her own pain to help the pack. He wasn't sure he would have had the same amount of resilience that must have taken her.

He heard the sound of his phone ringing from where he had left it on the patio, pulling him from his thoughts. With a sigh, he stood from the grass, running back to the patio and his clothes to seek out his phone amongst them.

Ethan.

Patrick stiffened at the sight of his brother's missed call. He hadn't mentioned to Ethan what was going on, but that was for good reason. Ethan was being punished, banished from the territory after his involvement with Gwen Tallon, the Witch who had tried to take Vee's power. Ethan's disapproval of their father's relationship with Vee had nearly resulted in not only her death, but the death of many of their pack. Patrick didn't trust Ethan as far as he could throw him, and him calling at the center of all this chaos only made Patrick's wariness of his older brother grow.

Patrick glared at the phone as it rang again, this time answering it.

"What do you want?" Patrick growled.

"I came to the Pleasant Hill property. It's the first full moon in September. We always meet here at this time," Ethan said. It was true. Something about the September moon, bringing in the autumn, the pack had quite a time out at the property every year. Had they not moved the weekend prior, they would have gone this year.

"You aren't even supposed to be in the territory, Ethan," Patrick warned.

"It's been six months," Ethan countered, his voice short. Patrick took in a calming breath. It had been six months, but as far as he knew, his father hadn't given Ethan the go-ahead to return. "I tried calling Dad's phone."

"We're busy."

"Someone else answered." That made Patrick pause. They had tracked Shane's phone to Sauer Castle, but when they encountered the Faes there, they had left without searching for the phone. At the time, it didn't appear that Shane could have been kept there anyway, not with the knowledge they gained from that tense conversation. Now Patrick felt uneasy about having left without searching more thoroughly.

"Who?"

"I don't know. That's why I'm calling you. Where is he?" Ethan asked, his voice sounding slightly panicked.

"What did they sound like?" Patrick insisted.

"I only heard a laugh, but it clearly wasn't Dad's or one of ours. What's going on? Where is Dad?" Ethan demanded this time.

"Busy. He can tell you all about it when he returns," Patrick murmured, glancing at Lori's wolf who approached the patio where he stood. He didn't feel right sharing what was going on when he didn't know if Ethan could be trusted, but the idea that someone else had answered his dad's phone sent a chill down his spine.

"Busy? Busy or not, he will always take our calls, Patrick."

"Not right now," Patrick growled back. It was true. Their dad notoriously went out of his way to be there for his sons, something that had caused issues in the past, especially with Vee. She would never complain about it though. Vee seemed to respect Shane's love for his children in a way many women wouldn't.

"What is going on? Anton told me the master of the nest has been missing, younglings running wild with no one to control them, and when I call, the pack leader, my father, is not the one to answer. Tell me now, Patrick," Ethan ordered, the venom in his voice now alerting all the wolves in the area, causing the pack to filter in from the yard to the patio where Patrick stood.

It took Patrick a moment to sift through the red he was seeing at his brother's tone before he fully registered what Ethan had said.

"Anton? Why are you talking to a Vampire, Ethan?" Patrick asked, eyes locking with Durran's from Vee's bedroom window just above where Patrick stood. The silence lasted a beat, Patrick's temper flaring.

"Anton doesn't truly belong with the nest. She mostly stays on her own. We've run into each other off and on over the years. We keep in touch," Ethan grumbled. "I can explain it better in person. Where is everyone?"

"Just leave it alone, Ethan. You aren't part of the pack, remember?" Patrick reminded briskly, hanging up the phone and letting it fall on the wrought iron table instead of crushing it in his hand.

Lori and Margaret started shifting back to their human forms while Patrick stormed back into the house, meeting Durran at the bottom of the stairs.

"He knows Anton," Patrick said, watching as Durran nodded.

"Do you trust him?" Durran asked.

"He hasn't proven he's trustworthy yet. Six months away, and the first thing we hear from him is that he knows a Vampire we aren't even certain has our best interests in mind?" Patrick asked, growling.

"He said he called Shane's phone," Durran murmured, glancing around as more Weres filed in. Roman stepped forward, phone in his hand.

"Give me a little time. I'll pull the trace up on Shane's phone," Roman murmured, typing away at his little screen.

Vee's fingers dug into the earth, the feel of it wet with rain, soft in her hands. She felt the oppressive weight of it all bearing down on her, filling her. She looked up, eyes drawn to the figures coming from the woods. Her heart pounded within her chest; the men that stood before her she knew, though she couldn't yet see them. She knew the way they felt in her mind and knew what their presence there meant.

They were her enemies, though all for different reasons. A trifecta of hatred, lust for power, or obsession. She was the enigma that stood in all their ways. A reminder of their failings, an obstacle to gain control, or the object of desire.

Her eyes glowed amber, casting the ground before her in its hue. Vee didn't know what to do and felt both powerless and powerful. She had no idea how to direct the energy that flowed through her and no idea how to defeat those that stood before her.

"See the truth and the lies," came a whispering voice, echoing in her head.

The three men before her stepped from the shadow of the trees, revealing themselves. But they were twisted, faces unnaturally shaped, limbs long and grotesque as they drew closer, step by agonizing step. Their minds may have registered as familiar, but these images of them were not. Horror swept through her fiercely as they reached for her.

"You live outside the weave of fate," came the whispering voice again as Vee dug her nails deeper in the moist earth. Somehow, she knew this was only the beginning. That things much bigger, much worse than

this, would soon be coming their way, and she needed to be ready.

And then the images came, flooding her vision as she took them in: blood, death, fire, destruction. The screams of thousands rang in her ears, as well as the roars. She saw the sinister faces, as well as the faces of the dead. She saw the Morrigan in all their glory, standing powerless against the fates that they foretold would come to pass. All this in rapid succession before her eyes, masking the advancement of the enemies before her.

Vee took a deep breath, her lungs filling with the sound, the darkness cascading within her.

"One woman." Vee released the earth from her hands, and what she saw instead were claws. She stood facing her three enemies with her chin held high.

"One pair." Vee felt Shane, his warm heat radiating behind her, his own rage flowing into her and fueling her even more.

"One pack." She felt them, encircling her and Shane as the full moon bathed her in its light.

"One who calls the magic of the white moon." Her head snapped up, the moon's glow filling her as she commanded. Churning together with the pain, fear, and anger within her.

And then she let out a howl.

CHAPTER 15

Vee woke with a gasp, sitting up abruptly in her bed. She was alone, the sunlight flooding the room, indicating it was well into the day. How long had she slept?

She heard the murmur of voices and felt the minds of everyone still safely within the house as she looked around her still-not-fully-unpacked room. She hadn't had a moment alone in days, and she sat there for a few seconds, just looking around, trying to understand what her dream meant. Much like when she unlocked her spirit, the words whispered to Vee in the dream both comforted and frightened her.

There was no pair without Shane, but her dream made her feel certain she would get him back. It was just a matter of how and when.

She moved to the bathroom, realizing it had been far too long since she last showered. Suddenly feeling the residual blood on her skin, Vee shivered thinking of Una, and then she immediately realized since they returned to the house, she hadn't once seen the sweet cat she had brought with her. As if Vee's thoughts summoned her, Midi trotted out of the closet as Vee entered the bathroom.

"I'm so sorry I've been busy and distracted," Vee whispered as she sank to the floor, letting the black cat curl up in her lap. "I'm so sorry about your mom, Midi," Vee said, letting the tears fall as she pet the soft fur she knew so well. She still wasn't certain if Duflanc was connected to everything. Ness seemed disturbed at the notion when they questioned her, but the timing was too coincidental for Vee to think otherwise, and he was very present in her dream.

She gave Midi a soft kiss on the head before moving to stand and get into the shower. However, the shower didn't provide her the solace it normally did, her thoughts too muddled with the confusing puzzle that her life had become. She thought back to the place that had now made a second appearance in her dreams. It was Sauer Castle, she realized. The first dream she hadn't remembered the name, but having been there yesterday, there was no doubt in her mind. The high arched windows and the brick, as well as the open area behind the house, all fit.

She hastily finished her shower, pulling out the first few clean clothes she could find in the closet, faded black jeans and a wrinkled grey top that hadn't made it out of the duffle bag yet, and pulled them on, before racing back out of her room. Patrick tore out of his room at the same time, having heard her quick steps and looked at her frantically as if there was something wrong.

"What is it?"

"My dreams were at Sauer Castle. We have to go back," she said, trying to move past him to descend the stairs.

"Someone has Dad's phone. Roman's working on tracking Dante and the phone to see if it's the same location," Patrick said, causing Vee to freeze on the top stair.

"What do you mean someone has his phone? It was at Sauer Castle, everything is pointing there," Vee insisted. Patrick sighed, seeing her stubbornness snaking around her and coiling her tight.

"I got a call from Ethan last night." Vee fought the cringe she felt come at the mention of Shane's older son. "He said someone answered Dad's phone. I didn't tell him what's going on, but he also mentioned that he knew Anton," Patrick said, watching as Vee's shoulders seemed to deflate with his words.

"Anton," Vee grumbled. Just as she did so, the sound of her phone buzzing with a text message downstairs could be heard. It was rather unheard of for Vee to go too far from her phone, but she had been losing track of it regularly over the last few days.

Vee and Patrick went down the stairs together, heading into the kitchen, which was surprisingly empty. The only people sitting in the room were Min, Durran, and Roman. Vee glanced out the back window, seeing Cora and some of the other human companions happily playing with the kids out in the back yard. Cora looked happy, her eyes twinkling as she watched the little ones play, but Vee felt the stream of pain coming from Cora. It was a consistent hum of agony, despite the calm façade she kept firmly in place. She was missing her mate too, and her age was showing in the lines around her eyes.

Durran handed Vee her phone as she approached. At this point, the only people Vee anticipated contacting her were the people that were in this house, so she was confused until she looked down and saw the message.

[Shane: Your mate is gone. Your pack has no leader. Give in to me.]

Well, clearly this wasn't Shane. The way the message was worded could have been Dante or Duflanc, but despite the fact that it was daylight, the chilling sensation that moved down Vee's spine told her it was definitely Duflanc's words. The insult was far worse when Vee read her last text message to Shane just above it, telling him she was going to Una's.

Vee pushed the phone over to Roman, who stopped his vigorous typing on his laptop to glance at the message.

"Sorry, I've been going back and forth between tracing and trying to look for where Dante might be. I'll trace the location first," Roman said, eyes turning directly back to the screen. Min watched, fully captivated by the way his hands flew over the keys. Vee turned her attention to the coffee pot, which was sadly empty. Patrick, without a word, grabbed the coffee grounds while Vee filled the carafe.

"Once we know both locations, we can decide on a plan," Durran said, noticing the tension in Vee's movements. She was eager for this to be over. Eager to solve the puzzle. Eager to find a way to bring Shane back. The whole pack was, but none more so than the woman who wasn't even one of them.

"How is Toby?" Vee asked, glancing at Min.

"He changed," Min said, seemingly uninterested.

"And?" Vee asked, irritated by his nonchalance. Min looked up at her, taking in her expression.

"He was fine. Perhaps a little wild, but he listened to me well enough to keep him from destroying the room. Once he's brought into the pack, I'm sure he'll do well," Min said with a shrug.

"Where is he now?" Vee asked, looking to Durran instead, who shrugged.

"Still in the room. He said he was too scared to come out with the kids around. Emily is in there with him again," Min murmured, focus clearly on what Roman was doing.

"Vee had another dream," Patrick said, causing Min and Durran to look up from Roman's screen. *That* got their attention.

"*Another* dream?" Min asked, not having been privy to the first dream. Vee sighed, pouring the water into the coffee pot and moving aside so Patrick could fill it with coffee grounds.

"A few nights ago, I had a dream. Seems oddly prophetic looking back," she said bitterly. "And this one just seemed like an extension of the same thing. Both were at Sauer Castle," she said.

"Have you had these sorts of dreams before?" Min asked, narrowing his eyes at her.

"No. They felt similar to when I met my zi," she said, watching the thoughts moving behind Min's eyes.

"You never told us what you saw," Min said, his curiosity suddenly the most prominent emotion Vee could feel from him.

No, Vee hadn't told the Sha, any of them, what she saw when she was in her trance. At the time, the need to get back to the pack was urgent, and the other Sha, mostly Bao, were extremely hostile. Then, once they had returned, her contact with Aho had been fairly minimal in the past month, and she figured she would share the dreams with him, if no one else. That opportunity had yet to come, with this lovely bout of chaos that had been thrown their way.

"And now isn't the time," Durran quipped. Min shifted a glare in Durran's direction and opened his mouth to say something in return but didn't get a chance.

"I got a hit," Roman said excitedly just before his brows furrowed, looking closer at the screen.

"Where is that?" Min asked, his face equally confused.

"It's ... nothing. An empty plot of land."

Vee came around the counter to look. The map that was pulled up clearly showed the Shawnee Heights neighborhood, the same one that Sauer Castle was nestled in. She raised her eyebrow as she made eye contact with Durran, giving her a silent, "I told you so" before moving back around the counter to pour herself a cup of coffee.

George and Markus made their way in through the front door.

"Just had Archer and Michael take over guard duty. Any updates?" Markus asked, moving to the refrigerator to inspect the contents. Somehow Markus and George managed to not look disheveled in the matching grey sweatsuits that they were wearing, but then most Werewolves didn't, seeming to fill them out nicely, like they were heading to the gym.

Markus, having now seemed to embrace his role as the cook of the pack, frowned at how low the supplies were. They had only been there a few days, but a pack of Werewolves and their spouses and children could eat quite a lot. They were swiftly running through the groceries they'd gotten when everything began.

"We have the location of Shane's phone," Vee said sourly from behind her mug. Roman glanced up at her tone, giving her a sympathetic smile before he dove back into trying to find where Dante was.

"We're not splitting the pack until we have all the information," Patrick said, feeling he had to finish what Vee started.

"Dante is clearly smarter than John. He won't make the same mistakes," Min murmured, watching Roman's fingers fly once more.

"Smarter than John, yes. Smarter than me?" Roman's mouth morphed into a cheeky smirk. "Looks like that's a no," he said, turning the computer to show a string of rental houses. They had been leased by a dummy company, the excuse being it was for their traveling employees. Roman had pulled the digital record of all of it. There were receipts, account numbers, contracts, and they all started over eight months previously.

"How long has he been planning this?" George hissed, seeing the dates. "This is before Pleasant Hill. This is *months* before then."

"He must have just been waiting for his opportunity," Roman said with disdain. "Looks like he created the dummy company to hide his plans, but I connected it right back to his accounts. He wired the funds, idiot."

But Vee wasn't looking at any of them as they took in the shock of seeing how long Dante had been renting property on Lieb's territory, right on the cusp of Shane's. She was looking at Min, whose eyes had turned amber with rage. Min stood abruptly from his chair, tearing his pocket as he went for his phone. He dialed violently, his finger cracking the screen with the force before placing it to his ear.

"Min! This is a surprise," came Lieb's voice on the other end after a long series of rings.

"Is it, Lieb?" Min asked, his voice letting on his anger far more than it usually did.

"I-I honestly don't know why you'd be calling. My pack has been doing well," Lieb said, his voice letting on to his unease. That was true. From what Shane had told her in passing, Lieb had made some changes to his pack that fostered a more trusting relationship instead of one run by fear. It was a slow process, given there were old Weres still set in their ways, but Lieb was making it happen.

"Are you aware that Dante has been using property in your territory?" Min asked. Vee's heart seemed to slow as her breath stopped, waiting for the answer to that question. The pause was long.

"What?" Lieb's yell was so filled with rage, Vee could swear she felt it as if he was in the same room.

"I'll take that as a no," Min growled.

"I'm in Wichita. Let me gather a few of mine, and I'll be there in less than three hours," Lieb said, his voice rumbled through the receiver.

"No need. The Westport pack will be handling this, but see this as a warning, Lieb. One more step out of line, and the Sha will step in. You overstepped with Shane six months ago, and now your territory has been unguarded and hiding Dante."

"What's going on over there? Are Vee and Shane okay?" Lieb asked.

"Not another toe out of line," was all Min said before he hung up abruptly.

Everyone remained silent as Min took a few deep breaths and stretched his neck before he moved to sit on his stool once again.

CHAPTER 16

They spent the remainder of the afternoon divvying up the pack. Vee didn't want their non-preternatural members left without muscle, even if they were protected within the pack protection. That wasn't effective against Werewolf threats, which was something they were still dealing with. Emily agreed to stay behind, for protection and for Toby. Vee decided to have Roman stay, as well as a few of the other fathers. She didn't want families separated if she could help it, but none of the others protested. Except for Cora, who was adamant that Lori stay with her at the house.

"There's no need for you to be there, Lori. You stay with me and help keep the children safe. You know this is what your father would say," Cora said, unable to keep the panic from her voice.

"Mom, I'm fast. I need to be with the pack. I need to *do* something to help Dad and Tommy," Lori said, a fierceness in her eyes. She had talked back and had attitude, all the normal things a teenager gave to their mother, but this was different. This wasn't about not going to a party or having her allowance diminished; this was about helping her pack, saving her family. Cora's eyes prickled with tears.

"I can't lose you too, Lori."

Frida came up beside Cora, pulling her against her. Frida was a small woman by nature, her black hair cut short in a sharp, angular bob, making her face a little more dramatic-looking, especially paired with her deep brown eyes.

"She's going to stay with me, Cora. I won't let anything happen to our little one," she murmured, her hint of Puerto Rican accent coming through.

The room quieted when Patrick cleared his throat, making all eyes turn to him and Vee.

"We're going to move as a unit, since we don't know how many to expect. I doubt Dante abandoned his whole territory and brought out the entire pack, but we can't rule anything out," Vee said from where she stood in front of the large projector screen in the basement theatre. It was the best place to have a conversation with the whole pack but having them all around and above her made her feel uneasy. It wasn't just the Werewolves, but spouses and children were also present; whether they were staying or going, everyone was to be included in the plans. Emily stood next to Toby, who was extraordinarily uncomfortable as he looked out at them all.

"We'll go to where we believe Dante is first. We are trying for the element of surprise, but there's a lot of us," she continued.

"Then what?" Archer asked.

"We surround and subdue. Min will be there for Dante," Patrick said, standing beside Vee.

"Once the St. Louis pack members are secured, the first team will head to the location where Roman determined Shane's phone is located. We're not sure what we'll find there. We know he's been taken to a Fae realm, which won't reopen until certain conditions are met, so it may just be that we go and try to determine what we *can* do to help him," Vee said. Though her voice was strong, she couldn't help the nervous fidgeting that she was doing with her hands. So far, she had been rather passive in her dealings with preternaturals. She had never been the active aggressor, going to them for a fight. And a fight this would be.

"We don't know how to get Shane back?" came the voice of one of the pack members Vee didn't know well.

"The Fae said the gate can't open until the moon's glow no longer shines. Does that tell you how to get my father back, Alan?" Patrick asked, his lip curled into a snarl.

"Fae are notorious at being vague or cryptic. Lying without lying. Any clue to where he is or how to get him back is worth looking into, but we have to move as a unit. Not risking anyone in this pack," Vee said, feeling the ache of them all. Each passing day without their leader, the bonds that held them together weakened somewhat. It cried out for a new leader, begged for someone to be the central point.

Thunder rumbled overhead once they were all outside, the air full of electricity as the group got in their cars. Vee's fingers found their way to the chain at her neck that held her talismans and key, the linked gold of the chain Shane gave her soft against her fingers. This chain was supposed to hold her wedding ring once she and Shane got married. There were no plans for a wedding yet, and she didn't have a dress or rings either, but she did have this chain.

Vee's stomach clenched as she gripped the chain more forcefully, her mind whirling. She still didn't have a way of getting him back. This plan only potentially solved one of their problems, and she was trying very hard not to let herself sink into despair's waiting grasp by considering she may never get him back. Fairy tales have held all sorts of stories about people who never returned when they were taken. She had to believe she would find a way.

The sky turned black, blotting out the sunset with the storm that was coming. Ominous lightning illuminated the sky as they drove further north and west to Shawnee Heights. The location of the rental houses was not far from Sauer Castle, which made sense. The castle had eleven acres of property that the Werewolves could run on during the full moon without attracting human attention. It was probably why the location was chosen in the first place. This neighborhood was off the beaten path, with many of the homes left in disrepair.

They had stopped by the security company's headquarters in the Westbottoms to get SUVs to hold the pack and weapons. Fewer cars made for less suspicion, so Vee was smashed in the back seat with Patrick, Lori, and Frida, while Durran drove, and Min sat comfortably in the front seat. Archer and Markus were sitting in the trunk. On Vee's lap was a handgun. She had no idea what kind of gun it was and had only gone to practice at the range with Shane once in the six months they had lived together. The heavy and offensive object felt strange against her legs. Vee didn't want to have to use it, but she wasn't sure what other choice she had. Hopefully Dante's men could be subdued without her even having to point it.

Rain began pelting the car as they took the turn onto Shawnee Road from Seventh Street.

"The rain should mask our scents and help with the ambush," Min murmured as they slowly drove through the neighborhood. They chose a street one block over from the rental houses to park, the houses all dark and boarded up. No humans to witness anything strange that may occur.

Vee felt Min's confidence and tried to drink it in. She wasn't certain she was any help in this situation. She had few combat skills, only having ever taken some kickboxing classes, and was nowhere near as strong as any of her counterparts. Even her gun skills were not up to par. Perhaps she was stronger than the average human, but she didn't even scratch the surface when it came to the strength of any of the people in the car with her.

Once they parked, they all got out, and Frida immediately went through the trees between the houses toward the rental properties. She would go ahead of everyone and report back.

Rain drenched them, the breeze cool and chilling, but Vee's body hummed with adrenaline as they waited. A howl rang out, too far away for it to have been Frida, and they all froze, bodies tensing as they waited.

"Shit," Archer hissed when the second howl made all of them shiver. That one was Frida, her howl a warning.

Everyone bolted through the trees where Frida had disappeared. Vee stopped short as she took in the scene before her: Frida's dark hair was clasped in the large fist of a Were, his beady eyes full of sadistic joy as his other hand wrapped around her throat. A massive man easily larger than even Tommy.

"I knew your pack had women," he rumbled hungrily, tugging a little harder on Frida's hair as he did so, the muscles on his forearms rippling. "I can't wait to have a taste."

"Julian," Min growled. "Dante is in violation of so many of our laws. Put Frida down and surrender." Julian laughed, his wolf in his eyes as his grip tightened around her throat.

"Dante is the only one who makes any sense. We shouldn't be following your rules, Sha. You aren't even one of us," Julian spat as Vee felt the presence of several other Weres coming up on either side of them. They were already changed, which meant they had the advantage over Vee's wolves.

The moment seemed to go in slow motion. Vee turned, her eyes meeting Durran's for a split second, their true form cascading over their body, just as glowing eyes, dozens of them, appeared in the trees around them.

"Run," was all Durran said before they drew their sword, surging forward too fast to see before slashing at Julian's arm that held Frida's hair captive. Min grabbed Vee's hand, pulling her forward, just as the wolves in the woods sprang through, clashing with the still human pack members.

She heard gunshots, screams, and roars as she and Min raced from the back yard they were in toward the front of the house. Vee felt around for more of Dante's men, but there was nothing. No one was inside these homes. The lights were all on, but there wasn't a whisper of a mind in any one of them.

"Empty," Vee said, astonished.

"Trap," Min growled, pulling Vee across the street, through to the next set of houses there. Beyond them were the woods that bordered Sauer Castle's acreage. The ominous trees showing nothing but deep blackness, with the pouring rain around them.

They heard a snarl just as a vibrating Were mind came bounding toward them. Min spun around, releasing Vee's arm to punch it square in the jaw right as it was about to snap its teeth around Vee's other arm. The body of the Were skidded across the road, remaining there for a moment before Vee saw Frida run from between the houses on that side, placing one well aimed shot in its head.

But Dante's wolves kept coming, the fighting moving quickly from the back yards into the street where Min and Vee stood, and Min once again took up her arm, dragging her across the street to the abandoned houses on that side. These were not for rent, dilapidated and boarded up. The smell of wood rot overwhelmed the area as the rain started easing. They tore through one back yard, heading into the trees beyond.

He was breathing through his nose, brows furrowed as he tried to follow a scent, despite the rain. What they thought would work in their favor was actually their downfall, as Min slowed due to the rain washing away whoever he was following.

"It's gone," he rumbled quietly, eyes searching the ground but not seeing anything he wanted. The smells were all too muddled, washed away by the heavy rain they just had.

"A scent?"

"Dante's," he confirmed, his face pinched in frustration and concentration as he ran his hands through his black hair. The leather cords that had held them braided had been lost as they ran, the silky black strands now falling over his back and shoulders, wet from the rain. "I have to take out the head of the operation. The rest will either be put down by your pack or will be reasonable once he's gone," Min told her.

"So much for surround and subdue," Vee murmured, gaining a small smirk from Min.

Both of their heads snapped up at the sudden sound of feet coming their way. It was in all directions, Were minds buzzing more intensely as they got closer. Min pulled Vee close for a moment, the two of them breathing as they tried to take in where their enemies were approaching from. The water still settling from the leaves and branches above them made it harder to distinguish, but Vee felt the minds closing in.

"There," Vee whispered, pointing to the direction they were coming from, closing in on them rapidly. Min started moving, pulling her back toward the house they had just fled from, dragging her to the nearest back door and kicking it in. The rotting stench of the house was much more potent once they were inside and though there were less trees, and the sky had started clearing. It seemed incredibly dark within the room they stood.

"Stay here, Vee," Min said, staring into her eyes, their matching amber glow the only light that could be seen. It took her a moment to realize what he was saying, but as soon as she did, she hit him in the chest.

"This is as much my fight—"

"There's no fight if you're dead," he hissed. "I didn't see it until I spent these last few days with you, and I'm not sure I fully understand, but *you* can't die." He grabbed the hand she used to punch his chest with, pulling her forward and pressing a kiss to the top of her head. "I want to know my sister. Stay here." Without giving her another moment to protest, he left, the door slamming behind him, encasing her in darkness.

Vee stood unmoving for a minute, listening and feeling the activity outside. Gunshots, the sound of fighting, and yells echoed all around her. She imagined the few occupied homes in the area would soon be calling the police. Any additional human presence was *not* what they needed right now. It was bad enough that this type of battle was happening so close to civilization as it was. She glanced at the window, watching the flash of gunfire as the sound rattled her sensitive ears, even within this closed-off space.

This was far more intense than they had been anticipating. They didn't expect so many of Dante's men to have been here and hadn't been thinking a full-on battle would ensue. She was woefully unprepared for this and hated that she was so dependent on the others. If they made it out of this alive, she would at least make herself efficient with a gun. The heavy thing at the back of her jeans felt like a useless paperweight to her at this point.

Her fingers reached up to clutch the talismans around her neck. Her fingers moving over the wolf head and the key, she considered what would happen if she stepped back out of this room. Vee wasn't a coward. She would stand up for herself when she had to, but she also knew when her presence in a situation wasn't helpful. She was good at locks and keys and making things with metal. She was good at solving problems when it came to those areas, but Vee had underprepared herself for a life in the preternatural world.

The feel of the key against her fingertips soothed her a little, her heart not beating quite as erratically with each swipe of her finger against the metal-like bone. She let her fingers glide over the smooth stem to the bit, trying to think of what she could do to help them out there. What could she do that wouldn't make things worse?

This key in her hands could lead her anywhere. This key made of bone, though it looked and felt metal, could open any door and take her wherever she needed to go.

What did she need? Where would she go other than here, where her pack was fighting for their lives?

She needed Shane.

Vee turned, searching the room around her. She was standing in a kitchen. The warped flooring was mildly disorienting with the checkered pattern it held, but she saw a door to a closet or perhaps the basement. It didn't matter. It was a door. She whipped the necklace off her neck, holding the key as she approached. She had to envision it, envision where she wanted this door to go. She had no idea where Shane was, what the realm he was taken to looked like, but she knew *him*.

Vee imagined his face, the strong jaw peppered with stubble after a few days without shaving, the slight salt and pepper by his temples, just making the dark brown of his hair and eyebrows that much more striking against his slightly olive skin. She imagined his eyes, warm brown with just a hint of gold as he looked at her, the way his lips quirked up on one side. She imagined his strong hands and arms as he easily picked her up, knowing he had enough strength to hurt her but would never touch her with anything other than the gentlest of caresses.

Without opening her eyes, Vee let the key draw her in. She placed it in the lock that had formed on the door, turned it, and pulled the door open.

CHAPTER 17

Min hurried out the back door, his heart sinking as he forced himself to walk away from Vee. He was disgusted with himself for leaving her, and also angry. So incredibly angry that his sister had been hidden away for so many years. Not only did she not know her own power, but she was defenseless against all the people that would choose to seek her out in the world. Perhaps that's why the universe sent her a True Mate like Shane, but that was nothing if he was so easily taken from her.

He ran up to where Markus was fighting off two wolves on his own. He was formidable, but the larger brown wolf was getting closer with each swipe of his claws. Min came up behind him, grabbing hold of the opposing wolf's muzzle and pulling him away.

"If you stop fighting, you might live another day in another pack," Min growled in the wolf's ear. It didn't matter; this wolf was practically rabid with rage. Dante had poisoned these wolves into thinking the Sha were the enemy. As he cut off the air from the wolf, hoping to not have to kill as many as they already had, he glanced over to see Durran in all their glory.

Durran was standing in the middle of the street, wings outstretched as if ready to take flight. But they were swinging the long sword in their arms so easily, it looked like they could have been wielding a feather. The swift change in how Min viewed Durran, not as an enemy preternatural, something Min should avoid and hate, to a beautiful warrior who he could trust was like a sucker punch.

He respected Durran. He liked Durran.

And there would be no going back to how Min felt before.

"Where's Vee?" Markus asked, breathless after he managed to knock the other wolf unconscious with the butt of his gun.

"Hidden," Min said, though Durran's ears seemed to perk up at that.

"Where?" Durran yelled, though Min wasn't about to yell out her location for the other enemy Weres to hear.

"Safe," Min hissed, though as soon as the word left his mouth, he knew it wasn't true. She was alone, vulnerable, and simply waiting for one of their adversaries to come find her.

Vee let out a breath, opening her eyes as the door she'd just placed her key in swung open, the key pulling from the door as she clenched her fingers around the chain. Behind the door was a room. The walls, floor, and ceiling were made of mud clay, veiled behind the shimmering wall of magic that was joining the two spaces, the two realms, together. It was dim in the room, but not as dark as where she stood in the abandoned kitchen. The throb of magic that came from that place seemed so much heavier than she had felt before. It was oppressive in its strength. Deep Fae magic pulsing.

And there, lying on a bed right across from her, was Shane. He was wearing the clothes he had on when he left to go help Susan days ago. His face far more bearded than simply the few days he had been gone. He seemed thinner, the shirt a little looser around his torso. It seemed like he was asleep or thinking deeply but seeing him seemed to spark something within Vee, and she gasped at the suddenness of it.

Their bond, though incomplete, came alive, the strength of it rendering Vee immobile for a moment, as it weakly slithered its way back through every facet of her. Shane bolted upright, eyes immediately finding hers.

"Vee," he whispered, immediately standing from the bed and walking to her. The way his eyes burned as they looked at her with relief and need made her heart thump wildly.

She wanted to scream, pull him to her, hold tight, and never let go, but she was speechless looking at him, tears running down her face. He took a step closer, his hand reaching out to her, but he was stopped immediately, the veil that connected the two worlds like a pane of glass between them. His palm spread over the barrier, face pained, and then angry.

"Vee?" came Tommy's voice, and he immediately was in the doorway as well, standing just behind Shane. His eyes were bright with excitement as he looked at her. Vee gave him a weak smile before she turned her eyes back to Shane's, watching as his hand pressed firmly, whole upper body trying to push his way through.

"I thought it would work," Vee whispered, as she watched Shane's fist descend on the invisible wall between them. He let out a roar of frustration, leaning his head against it and looking at her, panting.

"It did," Shane growled, his fingers curling into fists against it. "I just can't get out."

Vee's heart was breaking all over again looking at him, knowing he was just there on the other side of this thin wall of magic, while Shane's rage grew wild. She was there. Just there! Mere inches from him, and he couldn't get to her. It was almost more maddening than feeling the tiny scrap of their bond. Almost.

The rich spicy scent of her, coupled with the thrum of their bond mostly renewed within him, seemed to calm a part of him. Seeing her whole and standing there was enough to keep him from going fully berserk.

"This should have worked," Vee insisted, reaching up her hand to touch her side of the barrier.

She so desperately wanted to feel him again. Seeing him wasn't enough when she needed the touch to know he was real. But as she placed her hand against the veil, her fingers easily slid past the barrier, fingers pushing through enough that Shane's hand immediately found hers. Her eyes widened as she felt his skin on hers, fresh tears of joy welling up. She almost took a step forward, and Shane thought to pull her against him but realized she might not be able to get back out if he did. He kept her hand laced with his but held it so she could come no further, keeping the majority of her body still on her side of the barrier.

"You might get trapped too," he said sadly, bringing her hand to his lips for a light kiss; this would have to be enough for now. Feeling her skin on him had to be enough. He couldn't risk her being trapped too, not when they didn't know what was happening on that side.

"How do we get you out of there? All we were told was—"

"When the moon's light no longer shines in our world," Thomas said, coming behind Tommy now. Vee looked over at the son and father. Thomas's rich dark skin looked almost ashen. They too were thinner than they had been when they were taken. But Tommy's eyes were alight seeing Vee. Ever the optimist, he grinned at her. "We figured it must mean the New Moon."

Vee scoffed at herself. Of course, the New Moon. That made sense, but her brain wasn't processing things the way it normally would have, her emotions having been coursing through her and heightened from the moment she felt their bond suddenly gone from her body.

"I should have thought of that," she grumbled, getting a small smirk from Shane. Then she did the math in her head. This was the second night of the full moon.

"That's weeks from now!" Vee hissed, just before she heard another round of gunshots closer to the house. She flinched, eyes darting to the windows. The shots put all three of the Weres on the other side of the barrier on alert, Shane's fingers tightening against Vee's.

"What's going on out there?" Shane asked, drawing her attention back to him with a tug on her hand.

"A lot of things," she whispered, her gaze drifting to some other point in the room, as if she could see the battle waging around her. "Right now, we're fighting with Dante and his pack." All three growled, eyes aglow with their wolves on the surface, and then they heard it. The chaos outside the building she stood in suddenly seemed to come to a head. "I don't know if we can win this without you," Vee admitted, her voice barely a whisper, eyes searching his.

So many things passed from her to him in that gaze. Her exhaustion and feeling of inadequacy, her grief and rage, but also her determination. She always had a way of sticking to something and figuring it out. Sure, she had a history of running away from things when she was younger, but once she put down roots, they went deep. She wouldn't shy away from danger, because she knew all of them would lay down their lives for her, just as she would for them.

Shane gripped her hand in his harder, his own eyes pleading with her. She had him now, though he was trapped in this Fae realm. He would not leave her. She didn't have to sacrifice anything. He wouldn't allow it.

"Look at me," he mumbled, pressing her fingers to his lips again. "I will get out of here."

"It might be too late." Her voice broke, tears springing there. What had happened out there?

"I will find a way to get back out there to you. I will. But right now, you—"

But Shane was cut off when Vee was suddenly ripped from him, gone in a blur of activity. The scent of Vampire reeked in his nostrils and his fingers stung from the force of her hand being torn from his, heart aching at the loss. Their bond now even weaker than it was just a moment earlier, but he could still feel her immediate fear, the venom of it poisoning him with rage.

"Vee!" he roared, fists hitting the barrier as if he could break it.

"It was Duflanc," Thomas growled, a ripple moving over his body, as if he was ready to change right then and there. Shane's hands turned to claws, desperately trying to dig them through the layer of magic that was keeping him from helping her.

Tommy reared back too, two fists over his head as he gathered all his strength to try to rip the magic that separated their world from the realm they were trapped in. But instead of hitting the invisible wall, he fell through, the whole force of his strength taking him into the opposite wall of the broken-down kitchen. The counters gave way in a loud crash, and they all stood for a moment, shocked at what had just occurred.

"I..." Tommy muttered, surprised as he turned to look at Shane and his father, bewildered from the wreckage of the splintered wood he now sat in.

"You can pass through," Shane rumbled, realizing it was only he that was trapped there. "I'm stuck here because of the bargain."

"But we aren't," Thomas said, stepping beside him. He hesitated, looking at his son, and then glancing at Shane beside him. "I don't want to leave you."

"I'll find a way. Go help them," Shane said, practically shoving his best friend and second through the veil.

"You'd better find a way. I don't want to be leader," Thomas said, giving him a smirk, though it didn't meet his blazing blue eyes. With a final and solemn nod, Thomas stepped through. They both turned to look at Tommy, who had immediately started changing into his wolf when he realized he was free, the adrenaline and call of the moon helping him push through it faster than he ever had before. Shane watched, feeling rage and helplessness as Thomas waited only a beat before sprinting out the direction Vee was taken, out of sight, Tommy's wolf behind him only a moment later.

Min was trying to make his way back to where he left Vee, but the fighting was chaotic. Enemy Weres were everywhere, and there were far more of the St. Louis pack in this territory than he would have anticipated. He was nearly back and could see the house from where he stood in the road, ripping the jaw from a wolf that had clamped down on Archer's arm.

The Westport pack had scattered: some shooting, though their ammunition was getting low, while most were trying hand to hand, but still others began trying to run and find a place where they could change into their beast forms to better fight. He paused outside of the house next to where he was certain Vee still waited, starting to let his transformation take him, just as a massive hand descended on his head, tearing at his hair as he was thrown against a brick wall.

"Stupid Sha. You sit in your domain, far away from all of us, and have the gall to try and dictate what we can and can't do," Julian said, as Min braced himself against the crumbling brick he had been thrown into. The wall was weakened more than Min was, easily pulling himself up to face down the mountain of a man that Julian was. Min may have been smaller in stature, but the power coursing through his veins was far greater.

"The fact that your pack and leader are stupid enough to try this and not expect some sort of retaliation or consequences shows exactly why you need our guidance," Min snarled back, eyes glowing amber. He was going to kill this one and take pleasure in it. Julian had been a stain for a while, a recurring issue at keeping the preternatural world safe from human eyes. There were many times he had implored the other Sha to let him just kill the bastard outright, especially when he kept narrowly escaping prison after murdering women. Julian was not a gentle man. With so few female Weres—not that many Were women would want anything to do with the likes of him—he had a tendency to get a bit too rough with the human women he took to his bed.

Min saw the tendons of the arm Durran had severed moving, as if he still had a fist there, just before he was poised to attack again. Min easily dodged Julian's attack, coming around and climbing atop the giant man's back, his hands elongating into claws as he began digging them into Julian's shoulders.

"We should have put you down when you killed your fifth human wife. You've been a danger to us all," Min growled, tearing at his flesh as Julian roared in pain and anger. The giant tried in vain to grasp Min, who only sank his claws deeper with each movement. He knew he just needed to get the job done and get back to Vee, but he grinned as he felt the muscles beneath his fingers clench with pain, the scent of Julian's fear and rage filling his nostrils. He would remember and relish this kill.

Patrick's wolf came flying at them, clearly having been thrown. His wolfen body hit the wall where Min had just been thrown, going through the already weakened brick and into the house. Durran came down on the wolf pursuing him, easily cutting their head from its body, before glancing at Min, approval in their eyes at the state of the monster beneath him before turning their gaze to the hole Patrick had disappeared into.

"Patrick!" Durran yelled, clearly trying to make sure he was alright, getting a yelp in return. Hurt but not badly, the sound conveyed. Lori came running over a moment later, still human and holding a gun in both hands. She had blood coating one side of her body, her eyes wide and wild as she approached. She may have been a teenager, and only a little over a year into her change, but she looked formidable and experienced.

"Where is he?" she growled, eyes blue and shining.

"Through the wall," Durran said, glancing around to see Markus running into the woods behind the set of houses, tearing at his clothes as he went, clearly preparing to change into his wolf. "Where's Vee?" they asked, turning to Min.

"Just there," Min said, nodding his chin toward the next house over. Durran started to head there, gripping their sword as they moved swiftly closer. However, there was a flurry of movement that caused her to pause.

As Lori pulled Patrick from the rubble, the chilling sound of Vee's surprised yell filled the air for a brief moment, and then there was silence. The sound seemed to make them all freeze, the intensity shifting. Surprise and fear had been in her voice. Vee was in danger.

Min tore his claw from Julian's shoulder, taking it to his throat and ripping the entire meaty mass from his spine. A faster death than the creature deserved, but he didn't have time to waste on worthlessness like him. The body toppled to the ground, and Min broke into a sprint toward the house to catch Vee's scent.

"Vee," Durran breathed, eyes glowing bright red before immediately taking to the air.

Patrick, Lori, and Min immediately took to the trees once Min caught it, racing through the thick, untamed vegetation. This section of forest was large, the lack of a path hindering them moving at full speed. Branches whipped at their faces and arms. Everything was slick with the rain that had finally ended, but her scent trail was strong as they pursued.

A wolf streaked ahead of them, pushing between Patrick and Lori, the sight of which caused Lori to stumble momentarily. There was no mistaking that coat, the glowing blue of those eyes, or the familiar scent.

"Tommy?" she gasped. She had to be sure she didn't imagine it, slowing only slightly to feel through the bonds where her brother should have been these last few days. He was there, vibrant and strong, and so was her father. Tommy's wolf didn't pause to look at her, continuing to push ahead of them through the trees on a mission and onto Vee's scent.

A hand grabbed hers, pulling her from where she had slowed. She knew this hand, having felt these callouses all her life.

"Vee got us out," Thomas said, grinning down at his daughter's questioning face as she looked up at him. The distinct sound of a grunt, as someone was thrown to the ground, seemed to stand out amongst the growls through the trees. Weres were still fighting and transforming, having just moved to the forest. Everything was pushing them onto the Sauer property. "Let's keep moving," Thomas rumbled, eyes ahead at the darkness that seemed to shroud them.

"Shane?" Min asked, coming up beside them, their pace fast but cautious as they took in the sounds around them.

"Not yet," Thomas growled. "The bargain he made …"

"Fae," Min hissed like it was a curse word.

CHAPTER 18

Vee's breath was stolen from her lungs at the force with which she was grabbed. One minute she was staring at Shane, holding his hand and their bond was weak but filling her once again, and the next moment it was all torn away. The hollow hole in her chest returned, and the void of a mind and cold arms were wrapped around her.

The tree branches whipped at her face and hair, stinging as they made small cuts in her skin. The rain had stopped, but the coolness of autumn air hissed against her wounds as the Vampire who held her ran at breakneck speeds through the forest. She struggled against him, but the cold limbs wrapped around her were like steel vices, not allowing her to move an inch. It didn't help that she was fully disoriented.

Duflanc didn't need to breathe, but she could still hear the raspy sounds of him breathing in her scent, pressing her closer to his body with each step. She felt the ghost of his lips on her skin and shivered in revulsion. She tried again to pull free from his grasp, but with each attempt, he only held on tighter, holding firm to her diaphragm so she couldn't take in the air she so desperately needed.

"I told you, you would be mine," he whispered, his voice cruel against her ear before he licked one of the cuts, slowing his pace as a shiver went through his body.

The momentary loosening of his hold gave Vee the opportunity she needed. She tore at his arm, slipping through and tumbling to the ground. The impact was hard, pain searing through her shoulder and hip, but she didn't hesitate, ripping through the trees and gasping as she stumbled out into a clearing. He had taken her all the way through the wooded acreage, back to Sauer Castle.

She only had that one moment to process the empty expanse of grass and the towering backside of the building before Duflanc slammed into her, her body sprawling several feet forward into the grass.

"You smell so good. Taste like *paradis. Je te désire*," he rumbled as his mouth descended on her neck, his hands ripping away the fabric of her shirt so her shoulder was fully exposed.

Vee's throat restricted to the all-too-familiar sensation. The weight of Duflanc's body at her back, pressing her front into the ground, his coldness, his lips defiling her skin as his void of a mind made her entire body shake at the direct contact. Her fingers sank into the rain-softened ground beneath her as she felt the first graze of his fangs against her skin, the same place he ripped into her before.

But before, in Colorado, she was still in the throes of her vision from the Sha ritual.

Before, she was weakened by the crashed ATV.

Before, she let the pain of those around her take a toll.

Now, she was fueled by undeniable rage. White-hot fury pumped through her veins, only inflamed by the hole where Shane should have been. Instead of sucking the oxygen, it ate everything else, making the fire only burn brighter within her. His fangs broke the skin, and she felt the distinct sensation of her blood being pulled from her. For a moment, she let the added pain enrage her even more. This man, this *creature* that was stealing her blood, stealing her life. He didn't deserve it. He was nothing. Or he would be nothing.

Vee didn't know where the strength came from, but her rage seemed to turn a key within her, unlocking something she had never dared touch on before. She let her fingers sink further into the earth beneath her, her back arching as she threw his body with force off and over her, his fangs tearing away from the flesh at her neck painfully.

He growled, scrambling back to his feet, his eyes glowing as he stared at her from the tree line.

"Duflanc! You'll have her all to yourself soon enough," came a voice from the trees behind him.

"I just—" Duflanc started.

"Not now," the man in the shadow barked, as Duflanc pulled himself from where he crouched.

Vee's eyes never strayed from Duflanc. She was feeling everything so intensely. Now on her hands and knees, she felt the trickle of blood from her shoulder down onto her chest, the hum of despair in the ground beneath her, the cool metal of her chain wrapped around her wrist, and the pounding of her heartbeat. Her breath came out as ragged gasps, eyes illuminating the ground before her, fingers clenching into the earth. The scent of her rage, the damp earth, her blood, and the Others that were around her filled her nose. The rain had stopped, the sounds of battle in the trees circling the clearing no longer muffled by the thundering rain.

She could feel all their pain, their anger, their fear. She could feel it and smell it in the air, just as potently as she could smell the blood saturating the earth, even a distance away. Vee could feel the full moon at her back as the clouds finally parted, the clearing basking in its eerie rays.

"Why do you fight, little one? You know you're going to lose," came the voice. She looked up, the trees some yards before her in darkness, save for the glowing eyes behind Duflanc.

"She's a nuisance," came John's voice.

"She'll be mine and cause you no more trouble soon enough," Duflanc rasped, his French accent thick and drunk off the blood he just stole from her.

They stepped from the shadow of the trees. John's eyes were alight, slightly crazed as he took in the blood now coating her chest and the way her breath heaved from her body. As if seeing her in pain, with evidence of her wounds soaking her clothes, gave him a sense of joy. She didn't realize John hated her so much, but that eagerness and pleasure she both felt from him and saw in his face made her lip curl with disgust. Somehow, he seemed unperturbed by the fire behind her eyes.

"So weak that you had to find another pack leader to do your work for you, John," she said, pushing herself from the ground. Her legs shook, not from the pain but from the adrenaline pumping through her. Her body wanting to do something. To fight for what was hers.

"Shut up, you mixed-breed bitch!" John snapped. "Shane's gone. You're going to become this Vampire's whore, and Dante, a *real* pack leader, will rule all of Missouri. With the full power of both packs, he'll easily take out Lieb, and the Sha will be useless to stop him," John growled.

"I doubt even three packs deep that Dante would stand a chance against the Sha," Vee said, watching as John's body twitched. His wolf was so close to the surface, the moon above them now screaming for him to submit to the change.

"Duflanc, do what you need to do to sever the pack bond she holds," Dante growled, clearly wishing he could be the one to take her out. Duflanc's eyes seemed to become more vibrant with need as he took a step closer, his body coiling as he prepared to spring on her.

"She just needs to make a bond with me," Duflanc said, his voice low and husky with lust. Vee's stomach clenched at the idea. Of course, a blood bond with another preternatural would sever the one she had in place with the pack. It probably wouldn't take much, either, since it had become so much weaker when Shane was stolen into the Fae realm.

"Then do it," John snapped at Duflanc. Dante stiffened beside him, clearly irritated by John giving any direction. Duflanc didn't seem to care either way, his eyes glowing but pupils blown, high off the small bit of blood he had gotten from Vee. He took a slow step toward Vee, pulling back the sleeve of his dress shirt and letting his fangs sink deep into his own flesh.

"You won't come near me again," Vee rumbled in warning, her fists clenching.

"You will be nothing but a memory of how weak this pack was with you in it," Dante said, a menacing glimmer in his eyes as he looked at her.

"I think you underestimate me," Vee said, letting her eyes drift from Duflanc and the two Weres behind him to the moon above.

Vee could hear it, heard the cry of the moon. She hadn't ever realized it before, but it was there, singing at her through the pack bonds, echoing through the void in her heart. Shane was alive, even if she couldn't feel him. The pack was there with her. Durran, as they had vowed, was again fighting for her somewhere in these woods. Even Min was not leaving her side. She wasn't alone.

Vee could feel her anger building. Anger at these men. Anger at Una's unnecessary death. Anger for Toby's crew. Anger for Toby. Anger for Shane.

Her heart was thumping rapidly and hard with it, pulsing with the moon's call. Or was the moon pulsing with her anger?

She let everything she was feeling draw together within her, the sensation now easier. Each time she had done this, it got easier. Instead of being frightened by the power she was collecting, she relished it. It was fueling the fire, centering her focus.

Her eyes homed in on Duflanc, who had come closer but not by much, blood dripped slowly and languidly from the wound on his wrist. He was trying to hold her gaze, trying to lure her, but the reality was it was her drawing him in. Her blood still soaking her shirt from her shoulder was calling him closer. Her scent, her blood, was the drug he simply could not resist.

She let the feeling build, coalescing within her, and her eyes glowed bright, casting his pale skin in an amber hue just as she let a scream burst forth from her lips. Like before, the ear- splitting, inhuman voice burst from Vee's lips, rippling the air outward. She focused the scream solely on Duflanc. He had done so much to destroy her life. He had abandoned his nest, letting the younglings run wild on the city, killing innocent humans. He had murdered Una. He had hunted her mother and had nearly killed Vee. It was time for him to end.

Duflanc seemed to freeze for a moment before the force of her scream brought him into the air. His body lifted, floating and writhing in pain, as Vee's voice shredded him from the inside out. Vee felt the way her power moved within him and felt the void of his mind fighting against it, but it didn't matter. Vee's magic snaked through his body, ripping the magic that animated him, the magic that gave him his undead life and power, from where it nestled.

Duflanc's screams of horror and agony cut through her scream, but it wasn't enough to overpower the ethereal resonance that was tearing from Vee's lips.

Duflanc's body started to disintegrate before her eyes, the magic leaving him and returning him to dust slowly as it moved through his body. Dante and John watched on in horror as the Vampire's face froze, distorted in terror and pain, his torso arched back, eyes burning brightly as his face was trapped in a now silent scream.

And then he was no more.

The light died in his eyes, the irises going dull white, before his face seemed to crumble around his skull. Vee's scream died in her throat once he was gone, dust floating down to the earth where he was once suspended in the air. She fell back to her knees, shaking from the power.

Dante looked across the open space to where she sat. He had vague, hazy memories of what came to pass on the Pleasant Hill property, but seeing her power fully, with no enchantment covering his view, was bone-chilling. He had never seen anyone, not Fae, Witch, or any preternatural, wield power like that. Power to strip another of their magic. This small, human-like, and weak creature held more within her than anything or anyone he had ever known.

But she was spent. He saw the way her body slumped, heard her ragged breath as it came from her lips. She had given it all, and only to reduce one foe to ashes.

"Stupid girl," Dante said, letting his sneer return to his face as he stared at her. "Wasted all that on one Vampire." But a wolf burst through the trees behind Vee, slowly trotting over to stand beside her, hackles raised as he growled furiously across the grassy clearing toward the two Weres.

"Wasted?" came Thomas's voice as he broke through the trees a moment later, followed by Min, Patrick, and Lori, with Durran descending from the sky to stand beside Vee with their sword outstretched. "Oh, but you can't feel what we do anymore, John. If you were still one with the pack, you'd know Vee hasn't wasted anything."

"Look at her! She can't even stand!" John yelled, looking at Vee more intensely now to see if he had missed something.

"That weak excuse for a preternatural is spent. She's shaking like a new Were after their first change," Dante said, disregarding Thomas's words with ease.

The fighting seemed to cease from around them. The woods quieting, as all the Weres came closer to the clearing, pushing through the trees until the Westport pack, both changed and still human, crowded behind Vee. Dante's wolves also seemed to gravitate toward him, emerging from the trees to have his back as well. There were a lot of them, as he had brought most of his pack there for this fight. Most of them growling menacingly from where they stood, eager to continue what they had started.

Meanwhile, Vee was vibrating with power. Something clicked. Something released. The pack surrounded her, and their bonds were no longer weak. It was as if Shane was there with them, but her mate bond was still cold and empty. They were sending her their power, like they would send Shane. Her body shook with the surge, the pulse of the moon matching Vee's own heartbeat in her chest. She dug her nails into the damp earth once again, letting her head whip up to the sky. The moon's rays cascaded over her, as if she had forced it to only shine on her.

"This isn't your territory, Dante," she growled, her voice low, but it still carried all the way to his ears.

"And what will you do about it? Your pack is no match for me. You're falling apart without Shane here," Dante spat back, but John shook beside him.

The pack was breathing with her. John could see the way the moon seemed to focus on her, barely feel the whisper of the power she was taking in with each breath. The whisper of the bond he once shared with the pack pulsed. How could someone who wasn't even a Were pull on the strength of a pack like their leader? Was a True Mate bond that strong? How could she do this without Shane?

"You can either back down, Dante, or you'll lose everything," Vee said, her voice sounding foreign and not her own. Cold. Deadly.

"She's given you a final warning," Min said, his eyes glowing amber like Vee's as he stood beside her. "But don't think the Sha will forgive you," he spat.

Dante laughed, the sound booming over the empty space between them.

"This little girl doesn't scare me, Min. And neither do the Sha," his voice a growl at the end of his malicious chuckle.

Then the air seemed to fill with electricity. Vee's eyes blazed brighter, like two flaming orbs, sucking all the light within them so the darkness from the trees seemed to get impossibly blacker. Vee threw her head back even further, and a howl ripped from her throat. The sensation was so instantaneous and intense, vibrating in the air like her scream before did as it tore Duflanc apart. Every Were that was still in human form fell to their knees, except Dante. The moon's call that they had been fighting against was one thing to resist, but this ... there was no resisting this call.

Vee's voice was forcing their change. Dante, being a leader himself, was fighting so hard to resist, his face turning red, sweat dripping from the force to keep himself from heeding her call. But he couldn't hold out. Dante kept fighting, even as his knees buckled finally, clawing at the earth, foam coming from his mouth. His skin started to stretch and tear, bones growing around and rearranging roughly and painfully, as if this were his first change. He let out a pained sound, as so many of his other wolves were doing as well, fighting against her irresistible demand.

Vee felt the pack bonds strengthen. She felt the power, her own power, surging through her. The moon's call from her own body. They all had to obey. Every Were in her vicinity had to change at her command. She knew when Thomas succumbed, at first uneasy from the feeling, but then his wolf agreeing. She felt when Patrick's wolf bristled beside her, pressing his body against hers in comfort and pride. Lori made no move to resist, almost sighing as the change took her.

Once their transformations were complete, Vee's song didn't end. The Westport pack threw up their own heads toward the moon, a mighty song of howls ripping from their throats into the night air. Even Durran let out a battle cry from their throat. Vee's anger had not abated. Her hole where her mate should have been, not filled. Her eyes at the moon, her voice changed, the

sound more of a ringing than any howl as her amber eyes bore into the light of the moon.

It was as if her eyes were stealing the moon's light. Darkness started taking over, so much more complete than it had been. As if the moon was being eclipsed, a dark shadow began moving in front of it, slowly encasing its white light in darkness, until there was nothing but the eyes of all the preternaturals glowing like burning lanterns through the pitch.

CHAPTER 19

S hane had felt her call. He had been dragged back to the throne room shortly after Thomas and Tommy chased after Vee. He was so enraged his wolf was very clearly at the surface. Queen Kel said nothing when he was thrown before her, watching with eager eyes as he breathed heavily, only barely holding onto control. Wolves were not animals that could be easily caged. And not only was he trapped there, his mate, his son, and his pack were in danger.

"Your friends have left us," Queen Kel said, after several long, silent moments.

"A door was opened," Shane said, his voice gravelly.

"They are not important, though I do not take kindly to people slipping through my fingers."

He barely fought the growl in his chest from becoming more at her words.

"Your mate is quite something if she can open doors into my realm. Maybe I should have brought her with you," Kel said, grinning as she watched Shane stiffen at the thought.

"You'll not go near her," he warned, his eyes flashing slightly brighter gold as he glared at her. Her smile only widened.

"Have you thought of any new ways you might bring out my beast?" she asked, changing the subject as if bored with the previous one, though her smile was unchanging.

Shane had tried so many things over these weeks they had been trapped down there. He had his wolf come close to the surface, trying to use his power as a leader to pull her beast forward too. He had tried directly commanding her and howling, creating a call that later he realized had made it such that Thomas and Tommy barely managed to get their clothes off intact before the change took them. But one thing he hadn't tried was changing into *his* wolf for anything of these.

His wolf was so close to the surface already, the man and beast's combined rage boiling over. Shane wasn't sure what he'd do if he succumbed to it, and what would happen if he did, but he couldn't wait anymore. He looked into her eyes, letting his wolf take hold over his body.

Bones shifted, fur sliding over skin, as each part of him shifted and changed to his second skin. The black fur painted over him beautifully, his fingers elongating and changing into sharp claws, and his teeth snapping as they became sharp within his snarling mouth.

Within minutes, the beautiful black form of Shane's wolf stood before her, making Kel's eyes sparkle as she watched.

Shane shook himself once he finished changing, but then he felt everything shift. His hackles rose with an increase in the electricity in the air, the scent of magic somehow growing even heavier. The queen seemed to feel it as well, eyes tearing away from Shane's wolf and all its glory as she felt the magic surge.

"You! Go to his room and see this *gate* that opened," Kel hissed, pointing toward two collared beasts that stood closest to the hallways where Shane always was brought through. A wolf and a tiger, which never ceased to amaze him each time he came to this room. He didn't think there were many Weretigers left.

The two beasts seemed to slither from the room, but it was only a moment later that a shockwave of magic seemed to ripple through the space. Shane felt Vee's power, her call.

This wasn't the call of the moon, or even the same call that he gave to his wolves. This was purely Vee. She was calling, forcing the beasts out. *She* was the moon call.

He turned to stare at Kel, watching as her body shook, eyes wide open suddenly as her own beast responded to the way Vee demanded. The magic rippled around her. His wolf responded to the call too, but more to the feeling of his mate's magic. Shane's soul seemed to sing as he embraced what Vee was offering, his own magic swelling within him.

And then he was overcome. It was like a hold that he hadn't realized was there was breaking. His golden eyes glanced toward Kel, who was no longer the slight blue Fae he had grown accustomed to seeing. Her body was changing, limbs having grown impossibly long and deformed, wings at her back seeming to have sprouted from her like spidery legs. Her beast transformation was distracting her. Their deal was done, and somehow he knew that whatever had broken inside of him meant that he could go.

Without a second thought, he dug his claws into the moss floor beneath him, his muscles bunching before he turned and sprinted through the twisted halls, away from the throne room, and back to the cell he and the others were kept in. The door was still open, but it was not unguarded. The wolf and the tiger snarled at him, the open doorway behind them, blocking his way.

Shane snarled right back, letting his golden eyes burn as he dared them to keep him there. The bargain was completed. Their queen, unwittingly or not, had changed into her beast once more. And almost as if he said the words out loud, or perhaps because her change was finally complete, the collars that were trapped around their necks fell away.

The two Were-creatures before the door let their snarls drop as their eyes fell to the metal that had been released from their throats. When they looked back at Shane, he gave the briefest of nods, letting them know that he had fulfilled his bargain. And apparently, he'd fulfilled theirs too. He briefly wondered what else and who else he'd released, but couldn't dwell on that. He had to get through this door and to Vee.

The guards both parted so he could pass. Pausing briefly, he stared at the veil that didn't want to release him, hesitating. But the feel of Vee's power thrumming around them prompted him. He pushed his nose through the veil that had previously eluded him, the feel of it tickling as his muzzle broke through to the other side.

As soon as he knew he could go through, he burst into a sprint, the mate bond with Vee rushing through him, thrumming and alive within each part of his body as it should have been. He knew exactly where she was, felt the rage within her, the determination, the magic pulsing. It didn't matter that the sky was black as pitch, and he couldn't see anything. It was like an invisible tether was pulling him through the thick trees, bringing him where he most needed to be, by Vee's side.

Shane slowed as he got to the edge of the trees, watching his pack just before him, and beyond that, Dante and his wolves finishing their change. A snarl came from Dante, before he bristled, his large wolf form coiling as it prepared to sprint across to Vee. Shane glanced at her, her head still snapped up at the sky. Her olive skin somehow seeming to illuminate amber, as if she had stolen the moon's glow straight from above.

Dante's wolf snapped, his pace brutal and unnatural in its speed, as he barreled across the clearing to where Vee stood. But Shane burst from the trees before he could get to her, knocking Dante to the side and toward the dilapidated castle. Dante's body hit a brick-and-stone wall, the force crumbling it and leaving the interior open to the elements. Dante scrambled within the debris, trying with flailing limbs to turn and right himself. Shane's attack seemed to break the tension between the two packs. Wolves from the St. Louis pack sprang forward, so on edge and ready to attack once they saw their leader get thrown. Tearing across the clearing, they clashed against the Westport pack. The sudden sound of them struck, echoing against the trees that surrounded the clearing space. Growling, roaring, the sound of fur and flesh tearing, bones breaking ... the cacophony of wolves at war were all that could be heard.

Shane tore his eyes away from Dante, still within the hole he had created with his body. He moved toward Vee, coming up to her side. Her fingers slid through his fur, his body shivering at the sensation of her touch, coupled with the renewed bond. They felt whole, the bond and the magic flowing through both was wide open. He turned and looked at her, unable to keep his eyes anywhere else. And as he did so, the change started to take her.

It wasn't like a Were transformation. The air seemed to ripple around her, and as it did so, the human form dissolved away, making way for her white wolf to emerge. Shane had only seen it for a second when she unlocked her spirit with the Sha, but now, she stood right beside him. Her white coat like a beacon, brilliant against the blackness surrounding them.

Vee felt the change take her. It wasn't a conscious thing she thought about or forced: it was just one moment she felt Shane beside her, felt their bond returned, making all the pack bonds even stronger, whole, and she just knew it was time. Shane had told her numerous times that he knew she could change. When they placed the pack protection, Vee had felt a pull and urge to shift into her wolf, but it was something she could easily resist. And that ease apparently transferred to how the change took her.

It wasn't the bone-breaking pain that it was for many Weres but simply one moment she was Vee the woman and the next Vee the white wolf. But as a wolf, she felt both herself and different. She could see Shane differently, understand the subtleties of his movements, and know what he was telling her by simply the look in his eye.

And when their mutual gaze flicked over to where Dante stood, having regained his footing after stumbling over the loose bricks that had cascaded around him and getting ready to attack them, the muscles in his back tensing and rolling over his shoulders to spring, they were ready.

Vee bristled, baring her teeth and letting a growl rumble in her throat before she launched herself across the grass, lithely dodging clashing Weres. Shane shot after her. As Vee got closer, Dante pounced, crashing into her in midair. Shane caught him by the leg, ripping him away from where he was poised to bite at her throat, just as another Were seemed to take Dante's place, lunging to snap at Vee. But Shane couldn't go to her now; Dante's focus was now trained on him, deviousness oozing from him.

Durran was cutting their way through the throng of enemy Weres, disabling them so the Westport pack could move on. The injured Weres were piling up around them when the Watcher let their eyes fall on the glowing white wolf, struggling a bit to fight off the viscous attacks of the massive red wolf that had taken

Dante's place. Vee had managed to get back on her feet, dodging the attacks while trying to get a swipe or two in herself, but she was not used to this wolf body, let alone used to fighting in it.

Durran took to the air, moving swiftly over top of the battle to aid Vee when they were suddenly hit with a jolt of magic, the salty scent of ocean water burning in their nose. The hit caused Durran to fall abruptly from the air, their body landing roughly against the grey wolf that was Min.

"Are you okay?" Durran asked, scrambling up and looking down at the wolf. Min's amber eyes took in Durran's appearance, the splattering of mud and blood across them as they glanced around to find the source of the magic that just pushed them from the sky, before looking back down into the amber depths.

Min gave a short nod of his head, before turning to take a wolf that had gotten ahold of Lori's back, biting down hard enough on a front paw that it tore from the limb, while Patrick's wolf bit roughly at the top of its head, bones crushing beneath the force of his jaws.

Durran took back to the sky, watching as Vee overtook the wolf that had been plaguing her, getting beneath him and tearing out his throat. She shook her head, the lump of flesh still bloody and dangling from her jaws as the wolf fell dead before her. But she didn't pause, she dropped the lump of flesh, tearing back across the clearing to where Shane and Dante had moved, their dance pulling them from the chaos of the main battle.

Dante's eyes burned with rage and determination, despite the blood soaking his coat from the various tears Shane had made at his flesh. With Vee slowing as she approached them, he snapped his teeth angrily, eyes darting between them. There was no going back, no way for him to live through this, and he had felt the Weres of his pack dying, pulling his strength away as each of them fell beneath the Westport pack's claws and sharp teeth.

Vee stayed back as Shane advanced. This was his fight. His victory. This leader stepped onto his and Lieb's territories. This leader had conspired against him. Dante couldn't be allowed to live after this. But in the trees, just a few yards from them, John's wolf broke through, leaping out and tackling Vee. That simple action managed to shift Shane's focus long enough for Dante to attack, taking Shane's scruff between his teeth and shaking, trying to tear deeper into his flesh.

John's wolf snapped his teeth mere inches from Vee's muzzle, her paws barely keeping him out of reach by pressing against his chest. She growled, trying to turn to get away from him or roll them over, but he kept her pinned firmly, his body so much broader and stronger than hers.

You control your own fate.

The words echoed through Vee's mind as time seemed to slow. Her eyes glanced at her bloodstained fur of her paws, pressed firmly and deeply against John's chest. Her claws were pressing, but not hard. She remembered what Shane, Min, and Aho had told her, that she had changed into three different forms. She was not locked into any one form. Not unless she wanted to be. Without another thought, her claws lengthened, becoming more like sharp talons, pushing slowly but steadily through John's flesh.

At first he didn't seem to notice, even when his blood started running down her paws, simply continuing his endless attempt to tear out her throat. Then the pain became too much, once the claws seemed to push further, slipping between ribs. She felt his body tense when they breached one of his lungs, feeling it collapse within his chest cavity, his mouth stilled, breath coming out like short, pained pants. He tore away from her, struggling to breathe as she quickly got back to her feet. Her human feet.

At some point during that altercation, her body had returned to her regular form, now naked and covered in blood. The clothes she had on before she changed seemed to have simply disappeared, but the blood was still soaking her. Her face from her mouth down was soaked in deep crimson, her chain with her talismans firmly wrapped around her wrist.

"You chose wrong, John," she said, staring down with her burning eyes as he faltered, struggling for breath that would not come.

Shane overtook the injured Dante a moment later, taking his lower jaw between his teeth and savagely tearing it from his face. Vee's focus turned to him, watching as the once powerful leader lay dead on the grass, his blood soaking into the earth, feeding the despair that already plagued the ground.

When her gaze turned back to where John had been, he was gone, a rustle in the trees beyond the only indication of where he went. Her lips curled, body tensing to chase after him, but Durran came down to stand beside Vee, placing a hand on her shoulder.

"He won't make it far. He's injured," Durran said quietly.

The cacophony of fighting sounds finally started to die off. Vee looked up at the sky where the moon should have been, listening to the quieting of the clearing before the moon's light slowly came back. As if a cover had been lifted from over top of it, light began flooding the space that had been so black, back in the pale shine of the full moon.

CHAPTER 20

"It's not over," Durran rumbled, as Shane finally turned his gaze away from the still body of Dante, eyes landing only on Vee, whose head was still tilted up toward the sky. "A Fae attacked me." Vee's head snapped over to Durran.

"Ness," she hissed. Though her anger had somewhat subsided with Duflanc and Dante being gone, there was still the pesky Fae situation, which she didn't fully understand. If Ness was bound to protect her mother, and therefore Vee, would that not put her on *their* side in all of this?

"Where?" Vee asked as Shane came up to her, pushing himself against her body as if to shield her nudity from others. The little flicker of possessiveness warmed Vee and amused her at the same time. Werewolves were notoriously not shy about their

bodies, having to bare themselves on a regular basis before and after their change, but Vee was not accustomed to that yet. Shane wanting to cover her was for her comfort, though his wolf form could do little to hide her nakedness from the others around them.

"It came from the side of the house, but she could very well have disappeared by now," Durran said, gesturing toward where they indicated.

Min turned back into his human form as he strode across the clearing to where the three of them stood. He had somehow managed to grab pants, though they were severely torn and soaked in blood as they hung from his hips.

"I don't know how many of yours were killed, but Thomas and Tommy have the injured St. Louis members in one location," Min said to Shane.

"There's still a Fae to deal with," Durran grumbled, glancing over at Min and quickly away.

"I'll go," Vee said, turning abruptly and heading toward the side of the house Durran had indicated. Shane stopped her by putting himself in her path, growling in his chest and locking eyes with her. They weren't separating again, not for a long while yet. "*We'll* go," Vee corrected with a light smirk, coming up beside him and letting her fingers lace through his fur again.

Durran and Min followed behind, moving around the abandoned building, the building's shadows harsh against the darkened landscape. Vee could feel a bit of residual Fae magic, but there was no accompanying mind. Ness or her mysterious Fae friend were long gone by now. Vee glared darkly toward the front gate, through to the evergreen tree Ness had disappeared into when they met with her on that very street before.

"She's gone," Vee said, turning toward the three who had followed behind.

It was in that moment that the exhaustion finally caught up with Vee. Perhaps it was the fact that their current threats were mostly taken care of, or that she had used so much more magic than she even knew she could, but she fell to her knees beside Shane, her eyes closing before opening, with hooded lids, to reveal their amber had simmered back to her brilliant emerald green.

"She needs to get home," Durran said, stooping down as if they were going to pick her up, but Shane snarled, pulling what strength he had left through him and forcing the change back to his human form. He needed to be human now anyway, to talk and organize his pack, but he would be damned if he was going to let anyone take Vee from his side. For him, it had been weeks without her, but it felt so much longer.

Once he was panting naked beside her several moments later, he pulled her against him. Both were horribly covered in mud and blood, but neither of them cared as their skin touched. Vee sighed, relaxing against his body, his warmth, as Shane pulled her against his chest, standing and striding between Durran and Min, back toward the clearing.

A few pack members went back to the cars to fetch more vehicles to transport all the injured Weres,

Westport and St. Louis pack alike, back to the house. Once everyone was packed up, and Margaret was organizing a clean-up of the area, they headed back through the city, out of Lieb's territory, and back home, passing the blaring police cars that were headed where they had just left.

The house was immediately teaming with activity when everyone returned. Thomas and Tommy scrambled with the others to pull wounded Weres from the cars and get them on surfaces. Some wounds were already almost fully healed, a change back to their human forms being nearly all they needed to set the magic healing them; others were in much worse shape, struggling and whining with pain.

Vee would have happily helped, but Shane not only had her firmly against his chest, his emotions somewhere between protective and desperate, but she wasn't sure she could have stood on her own to do anyone any good. On the ride over, they had put on pack sweats that were stored in the back of the SUV, so they were decent but still coated in grime.

"Set up the cage with tables and cots for the St. Louis pack members," Shane said to Frida, who was tying off a still bleeding leg wound on Archer.

"Toby," Vee said.

"Toby?" Shane asked harshly, his eyes darting down to Vee's face.

Something about Vee mentioning the man gave him two very differing emotions. Thomas had said that Toby and his crew were there when he and Tommy were taken, most likely killed. But on the other hand, the last time he saw Toby, it was plain as day that he wanted Vee, that her presence in Shane's home in a state of undress had shocked him and filled him with jealousy and lust.

"He's been staying there. Attacked by Dante's men and changed. He made it through the first night with Min, but he's down there now," Frida said, filling in the blanks for Vee.

"Shit," Shane said, his voice gravel by now, but his eyes were drawn to Vee, realizing what kind of chaos she had to endure that she had taken up the mantle of leader in his absence.

"Most of Dante's Weres aren't going anywhere. Ours are in better shape," Frida said, glancing around as the wounded were being tended to. "As long as we're watching."

"I'll watch," Durran said, still in their true form, their sword pressed before them with both of their hands resting lightly on the hilt. Their face showed nothing, but Vee felt their tension. Watchers were naturally alone. They had their ward, and perhaps another Watcher, but they rarely were surrounded so much as Durran had been over these last few days. Only now was Vee realizing what a strain that must have been on her friend, who was still not slinking away. Durran was accepting their place here as one of them.

Somehow Durran's declaration that they would keep their eyes on the rival pack members seemed to be enough for Shane.

"Take her and get cleaned up. She deserves a break," Min said, having popped Archer's arm back into its joint before strolling over to them. Archer looked incredulously toward the Sha but managed to stifle the groan of pain before moving to help others.

Min wasn't wrong. Vee was so tired; she was completely incapable of blocking the pain and fear filling the house. Patrick, sporting a sling made from a sheet over his heavily bandaged arm, came up, pressing a kiss to Vee's hair before wrapping his good arm around his dad.

"Go rest. We have it, Dad," Patrick said, trying to keep the emotion of having his dad back, safe, from overwhelming him.

"Thomas!" Cora's voice rang through the house, high and desperate, as she raced through the crowds and crashed into him. They were completely opposite. He was deep, dark, tall, and broad, where she was pale, blonde, short, and thin, but somehow, they fit together perfectly. She sobbed against his chest while he held her tightly, Tommy and Lori coming to encircle their mom in a group hug.

Shane's face tightened, understanding the feeling of being reunited entirely, letting his gaze linger over his son for a moment before he looked back down at Vee. He finally nodded, kissing the side of Patrick's head before relenting and moving up the stairs to their bedroom. No one said a word to them, mostly watching as they pressed through the chaos to their own little sanctuary.

When they entered, Shane was immediately hit with a wave of surprise as it smelled like Vee, Patrick, and Durran. It made sense that they would hover over her in this time. Though he and Durran had harbored jealousy, Durran also understood and respected honor.

Vee had chosen him, and Durran would honor that as long as Vee wanted him.

What did surprise Shane was that his scent still lingered there as if he hadn't been gone for weeks. He knew the days passed differently in the realm with Queen Kel. She had said as much when he first woke up, but there was no way for him to trace the passage of time back home.

Carefully, he set Vee on the counter in the bathroom, starting the shower, before returning to her and gently peeling off the oversized sweats she was wearing. He took note of all the injuries across her skin. She was littered with bruises, coated in blood, both hers and others, and mud caked her hands and was mixed with the blood across her skin. She was horrifying and breathtaking at the same time.

"I'm disgusting," Vee murmured, as Shane's hands traveled over her body, touching each scratch and bruise he could see under the filth.

"You're perfect," he whispered, bringing his eyes back to hers. She visibly shivered at the look he gave her. His wolf was angry at her injuries, horrified that she had to fight for her life again, but was enamored with her resilience and unwavering strength. He pressed his lips to hers before he stepped away to begin pulling his own sweatshirt off.

"How long was I gone?" Shane asked, as Vee slid from the counter to help him out of his own sweats. She was tired, but she couldn't stand the distance from him, needing to feel his skin and know he was really there before her. She let her fingers travel over his body, seeing the way there were more dips and bone revealed from the weight he'd lost. No less muscle, but now there was no give, nothing soft left.

"It's only been a few days," Vee said thickly, letting him pull her against him as he steered her to the shower stall. The steam of the water seemed to swirl in the air, making it appear they were stepping into a mist. Like they were stepping into another world, their own bubble where it was only the two of them.

Vee felt a strange twinge from the bond that didn't show on his face, but she studied it closer then. There was that beard growth that couldn't have happened so quickly, as well as the strained and haunted look he had in his eyes when she first saw him across the veil when she opened the door. And of course, the weight loss.

She reached up, touching his cheek just below his eyes, and letting her fingers run down to feel the coarse hair of the short beard on his face.

"How long has it been for you?" she whispered, trying and failing to keep the tremor from her voice as she asked the question.

He stared at her for a long moment, his eyes filling with a deep sadness Vee hadn't seen there before. It was as if he both wanted to tell her but was horrified that the words would be true as soon as he let them slip from his lips. His hands at her waist gripped harder as if he was afraid if he loosened it, she would slip away as she had when she opened the door with her key.

"Weeks," his voice breaking slightly as he let the words free. "We were there for weeks."

Tears sprang in Vee's eyes again, her fingers tightening slightly against his face, before he pulled her against his chest again, pressing his cheek to the top of her head.

"I don't know how it was for you. I could tell the bond was there ... just broken and weak," he whispered.

"I felt you when you tugged," she said, letting a sad smile grace her lips.

"But you felt nothing?" he asked, searching her eyes.

"It was like you were suddenly gone. Not the torture when the bond was broken by Gwen. This time it was sudden, an instantaneous void where you should have been. The pain and the hollow feeling always there, for days."

Shane shivered. Even the memory of the way it felt after their bond was broken by Gwen was enough to make him sick. At least he had the frayed, weak bond there, not completely gone. Its presence within him gave him enough comfort that she was alive and that he would get out of the Fae realm somehow.

"Never again," Vee whispered, her fingers threading through the hair at the back of his head, keeping him firmly against her as they were.

"Never again," he said in agreement, pushing forward to press a gentle kiss to her lips.

They washed each other, more out of love and need to care for one another than out of lust, washing away the physical and mental filth that they had accumulated. Their touches were soft, reverent, and not rushed.

"I can't lose you again," Vee whispered, as Shane rinsed the shampoo from her hair, pushing his fingers through the silky, wet strands. Her head was tilted back into the stream of the water, but she was still facing him, holding onto his shoulders as he massaged the suds away.

"You won't," Shane murmured, as Vee's hands clenched against his shoulders.

"You can't promise that," she whispered, eyes closed as she tried not to feel overwhelmed with despair. She would have never thought it was possible for him to be taken from her, then her dream came true. The echo of how the void within her felt was like a searing pain. A reminder it could happen again. He was there with her. She felt their bond, his skin pressed to hers, but the fear that it had happened twice made an uncontrollable sob burst from her chest.

"Look at me," Shane rumbled. Vee's eyes opened, tears falling against her already wet cheeks. "I promise you. Your dream warned us, and we didn't pay enough attention." He kissed her tears, as if he were taking her fears into himself, then her nose, resting his forehead against hers before he continued, "You are mine. I am yours. I promise it will never happen again, Vee."

Vee's breath hitched, and she wound her fingers through the hair at the base of Shane's neck, tilting her head up to press her lips to his. There was never a time that their kisses didn't feel electric, the simmering spark never dulled from the first time they gave in, but this, this kiss with the promise of never again, and the unspoken *forever*.

Shane's grip on her hair tightened, deepening the kiss. It took no time at all for it to become frantic. Teeth scraping against lips, the force bruising as they cling to one another. Their need to be together, connected, outweighed any other pain or exhaustion they may have been feeling. A growl in his throat, Shane dipped down, taking Vee by the thighs and lifting her. She immediately responded, wrapping her legs around his waist, before he pressed her roughly against the shower wall, pinning her with his body.

She gasped as her back pressed against the cool tile of the shower wall. The difference of temperature between it and Shane's hot body was shocking to her sensitive system. Shane broke their kiss, only to trail his lips over the skin of her neck and shoulder. There was still torn skin there, no longer bleeding, but still angry and tinged with residual blood from where Duflanc bit her. Another growl rumbled in Shane's chest at the wound, his tongue gently swiping over it, healing it for her. She shivered at the sensation, the Were magic tingling as it began closing the wound and spreading to all the other aches in her body as well.

Shane was doing more than healing her; he was erasing Duflanc's touch. Taking away the pain he inflicted and making sure the only magic that touched her, that flowed within her other than her own, was his.

His mate.

His Vee.

Their lips met again, Vee clinging to him, trying to draw him close and needing him closer. Their bond fully opened, Shane knew exactly what she needed, and he needed it too. This was more than lust, more than desire. This was needing to be home.

Shane didn't hesitate. A simple tilt of his hips brought them together again.

Whole.

They were one once more.

But there was nothing else slow about this. They couldn't contain themselves. Their moans filled the bathroom, barely drowned out by the sound of the water. Vee's nails dug into Shane's back, unable to contain herself at the pleasure they both felt, the rightness of this reunion, the passion. Their promised words became so much more solid, strengthening their bond as their combined ecstasy burned within them. A zinging sensation traveled through them as their movements became more frenzied, even the tiles at Vee's back began cracking with the force of Shane's wild thrusts.

And then they hit that impossibly high peak, where both were unable to hold back their cries as it crashed over them. Blinding white, purse bliss, shared together, lingering seemingly forever as they lost themselves in each other.

It didn't matter that the house was full, or that neither of them had slept well. They simply stood there, still connected, staring into each other's glowing eyes as their breathing came back to normal, pressing soft, sweet kisses to each other's lips.

Vee wasn't sure how they made it to the bed, let alone how the shower was turned off. They fell against the bed sheets in a heap, limbs tangled, unwilling, and too tired to move. She pressed her face to his damp chest, breathing in his scent, as he did the same to her hair. She fell asleep, feeling more *right* than she had in days, just as the sun broke over the horizon.

CHAPTER 21

Vee woke up to the hesitant sound of knocking at the bedroom door. Shane's arms were still wrapped around her, her body pressed firmly against his. She took a deep inhale, her breath hitching at the relief she felt as her fingers laced through his at her hip. She could feel the minds of the pack and their families buzzing around on the levels below, the thrum of their combined minds giving her a feeling of rightness, having everyone there under one roof and safe. The Vee of two years ago would have been distraught at even the idea of being in a house like this, while this Vee felt more relaxed. They were all together. Pack. Family.

"Dad?" came Patrick from the other side of the door. Shane didn't move, but Vee could tell he was awake, his hold around her body tightening.

"What is it?" Shane rumbled, his voice sending a shiver over her body.

"Ethan's on the phone."

Ethan.

Too many things had happened in such a short time. She had Shane back for a matter of hours, and they didn't have time or energy to go over everything. There was a lot to discuss. Ethan's phone call to Patrick had slipped from her mind amidst everything else, but now it was rearing its ugly head. The timing had been too coincidental.

"I'll have him call back," Patrick said quietly when Shane said nothing.

"We'll be down in a minute," Vee said, listening as Patrick turned and walked back down the hall.

Vee reluctantly sat up. Her body was stiff and achy, but not in pain as she expected it to be. She looked down at her body, which she assumed would be littered with bruises, and saw nothing but her normal skin, seemingly unblemished. She turned to look down at Shane when he hadn't moved. He was watching her, eyes sparked with a desire they both knew they couldn't do anything about right now.

"You're beautiful," he murmured, letting his hand drift up to rub over her shoulder; the spot where Duflanc bit her, now nothing but a slight red spot. She turned away, hiding her smile from him.

"And you need to be filled in on everything you missed," she said, slipping from the bed to head to the closet. She wasn't used to sleeping naked. Nudity was something she was comfortable with for others, being that she was surrounded by Werewolves on a regular basis, but for herself? Not so much. She pulled out the first few things she saw, a worn pair of jean shorts and a faded band T-shirt, pulling them on. She caught her reflection in the large mirror on the wall of the closet. For some reason, it caught her off guard.

She didn't look particularly different. Her face was the same, dark hair falling over her shoulders, perhaps a little more frazzled than it usually was from sleeping with wet hair. Her bangs still came down her forehead, providing the curtain for her eyes. Her body showed no discernible change. No horrible scars, except for the ones that she knew still graced her stomach. The first wounds Shane had ever healed for her.

She looked back up at her eyes. The emerald of her irises seemed ... brighter.

She had been so absorbed in the defeat of the St. Louis pack and Shane returning to her that she hadn't even mentally grasped what *she* had done the night before.

She wielded her power. She controlled it. She forced the moon to shadow and the Weres to change. She had dominated them all. She had the control. This wasn't a burst of power as a defense mechanism. She somehow just *knew* how to do it, and she made it happen. And the feel of the pack bonds blossoming, strengthening under her command. She wasn't sure what had happened in that clearing behind Sauer Castle, but now, as she felt and really paid attention to the bonds within herself, she realized that something was different.

Shane came to the closet door, having pulled on some sweats from one of the duffle bags that hadn't yet been sorted through.

"Something's different," Vee murmured, glancing away from her own reflection to look him over.

"Different, but not bad," he said, nodding his head as he came up behind her. He didn't say a word as he let her necklace drop from his hand, her eyes catching the talismans that were dangling from the chain in his fingers. Without a word, he put it around her neck, kissing the still slightly sensitive shoulder with his lips before he pulled away to look at her once more.

They made their way down to the kitchen; it seemed like most of the families were outside. The rain the night before cooled the temperature, so the kids were happy playing in the expansive yard. Patrick sat in the kitchen, a fresh pot of coffee waiting for them.

"Where's Min?" Shane asked as he stepped forward, filling a mug for Vee and handing it to her to add cream to before filling his own.

"Still downstairs guarding the room with Durran," Patrick said, staring into his own cup.

"How's Toby?" Vee asked, after putting the cream back in the refrigerator.

"He's managing okay. He opted to stay in the cage when he changed, which was for the better once the St. Louis pack members were put in that room. Min said he looked like he wanted to tear them to shreds as soon as he smelled some of them."

"Wouldn't be shocked if a few of his attackers are in there with him," Vee murmured, raising her eyebrows at the thought of Toby in wolf form viciously killing everything that was trapped in that room with him. It would be quite a mess to clean up, but not one she would regret too terribly.

"How many are in there?" Shane asked, glancing toward the basement door.

"Ten. A few others died in the night. Min couldn't help them," Patrick murmured sadly.

"And ours?" Shane asked, taking a moment to feel through the bonds.

"We haven't lost any," Patrick said, his eyes brimming with relief-filled tears for a moment before he cleared his throat. They had been ambushed, their members cut in half so some could stay and protect their families, and were leaderless, and yet they somehow lost no one in that bloody, horrific battle.

"So … Ethan," Shane prompted, getting a flinch out of Patrick at the mention.

"He called while you were gone. Came to the Pleasant Hill property, thinking we'd be there for the September Run," Patrick started. Shane's eyes narrowed. He was surprised Ethan felt he could just waltz back into their lives after his banishment. Six months had passed, but the wounds of his betrayal still felt fresh, and in the limited communication they had during that time, Ethan made no mention of changing how he felt about Vee.

"The timing seemed too perfect," Vee muttered, glancing between the two of them.

"He said he knew Anton," Patrick told Shane, finally meeting his eyes.

"Anton," Shane growled. He hadn't liked the mention of the lone Vampire when Vee and Durran told him about her approaching them. He had yet to meet her, but he couldn't help his wariness. So far, she had done nothing but provide them with information, but nothing that could be seen as actually helpful. Stark warnings were not the same as concrete information.

The mention of her also reminded Shane that they still had the Vampire problem to contend with, something that was never handled, since Thomas had been taken before a hunting party could be assembled. Shane reached up, rubbing his forehead roughly.

"I'll call him once I talk to Min," Shane rumbled, as Durran and Toby came up the stairs.

Toby froze as soon as he saw Shane and Vee, his eyes wide with fear. He was fully healed from his attack, dressed in the standard sweats that they kept around the house, since his clothes had long been thrown away. His fear was understandable. A lone wolf, and a new one at that, in the presence of a pack leader as powerful as Shane would normally cower, but there was an additional twinge of guilt. The last time they interacted, Shane had very nearly had to stake his claim before this man. Now there was additional magics, making Toby's feelings for Vee even more nerve-wracking.

"You look good, Toby," Vee said, pleased that he seemed recovered. The scars from his attack would fade over time but never really go away, marking him as a changed wolf.

"Toby, here, thinks he should go home," Durran said, moving around him with a flash of irritation, since he stopped awkwardly in the doorway.

"There are still a lot of things that we need to do for you before we can let you go home," Vee said apologetically. She wasn't sure how much time Margaret had had in the midst of everything to get a believable story for the bodies of his crew. They had friends and family that deserved to know what happened to them, but perhaps not the complete truth, and he would have to be briefed so that his story lined up. Toby would also need to be brought into the pack.

Emily came bounding into the room a moment later, stopping short when she saw Toby there.

"You came out!" she said excitedly, rushing over to him and placing a hand on his arm. He seemed to visibly relax at her touch. "Come, the showers in one of the guest rooms upstairs is clear," she said, dragging him through the kitchen and toward the stairs in the main hall. Vee grinned toward Patrick while they shared a knowing glance. Emily had been *quite* attentive to Toby since he was changed.

"Min will be up in a minute. Archer took over guarding the room for us, but Min wanted to be sure the surviving ones knew they would suffer his wrath if they moved," Durran murmured, taking up a stool at the furthest end of the island, closest to Vee. She glanced out the window to the back yard, watching as the cluster of trees where the Sha gate was nestled shimmered a little. Min would go back soon. The idea that he wouldn't be around anymore was odd, as Vee had grown used to her brother's presence in the last few days. They still didn't know each other well, but his words during the battle the night before resounded through her head.

"I want to know my sister."

She had felt it would take him more time than Aho to get used to the idea of her existence, and that perhaps he never would, but something changed over these few days. He was no longer quite the angry, brooding Sha that he was when she had first met him. He had shown her a few different sides to who he was, and she knew when he went back home, she was going to miss him.

But before anyone could say anything more, a roar resounded from the front of the house, the sound ripping through all of them with its agony and rage. The mugs Shane and Vee held immediately crashed on the stone floor of the kitchen as they all raced through the house and out the door. The whole pack seemed to flood out into the front yard, with Vee and Shane at the front.

There, standing in the middle of the cul-de-sac, was a very naked and bloody John Meyers, his hand wrapped around Ethan's throat, lifting him into the air.

"You've taken everything from me!" John screamed, his face distorted with rage, breathing coming shallow and uneven at his still partially collapsed lung struggled to give him enough oxygen.

"I took nothing from you, John," Shane growled, hands clenching as he watched his son struggle against the other Were's hold. Ethan was strong, almost as strong as his father, but the pure, adrenaline-filled rage that John was in, he was no match for.

"Susan will never take me back now! Never!" John roared, his grip tightening on Ethan's throat, causing his eyes to bug a little.

"Put Ethan down, John. He has nothing to do with this!" Shane snarled, teeth snapping together as he watched Ethan's face grow steadily redder with the lack of air.

"You deserve to lose everything too, Shane. You were supposed to lose to Dante! *She* was supposed to die by the Vampire, and the pack should have been his!"

"He said put Ethan down," Vee growled, her body tensing, ready to spring. With her voice, John's eyes immediately snapped to her. With no warning, he dropped Ethan, sprinting over to where Vee stood, his eyes wild with rage and hatred. But before he got to her, Min seemed to appear out of nowhere, landing a bone-breaking punch directly to his ribs on the side he was still favoring.

John's body skittered across the pavement of the cul-de-sac, and everyone was still for a moment. His body shook as if he was going to force the change, muscles rippling over his body roughly, his breath coming out as wheezing gasps.

"Why did you do it, John? I've done nothing to you," Shane said, his voice still rough with anger, but his wolf was no longer fighting to come out.

"You really don't know, do you, Shane?" John said, his voice not but a harsh whisper, but they all still heard it.

"Enlighten me," Shane growled.

"I should have been the leader," John rumbled but then wheezed again, finally managing to pull himself up to a sitting position, his body hunched with defeat, more blood covering his body with the road rash that now littered his arms and legs. "But beyond that ... it was Patricia."

"Patricia?" Shane whispered, eyes wide with shock. John had known Patricia well, Susan and Patricia got along well; and beyond that, he wasn't sure what his dead wife had to do with anything, but like John's hatred of Vee, Shane quickly realized it was a similar sentiment with Patricia.

"You ... you always get everything, Shane. All your children have been Weres. Even your human wife wasn't afraid. How did you get her to be that way? How did you convince her we weren't monsters?" John asked, tears falling freely down his dirty cheeks.

Patricia had been loving, gentle, and kind. From what Shane and a few of the others had told Vee, she had embraced the life with the pack so thoroughly that everyone adored her. It was hard for Vee not to feel a spark of jealousy sometimes in the way they reminisced. Patricia had been loved within the pack, but she had never been truly one of them. Patricia couldn't have stood up with the pack against their enemies like Vee did, but she certainly embraced the pack, unlike Susan Meyers.

"I didn't have to convince her of anything," Shane rumbled.

"They're always scared of me. Every wife I've ever had ... Susan is no different."

Susan was always fearful, and it was a miracle that two of their sons were born with the Werewolf trait. Margaret had told Vee that none of the children he had ever fathered before had been born with the trait, nor did they want to change to be like their father. John had loved and had families many times over in his long life, but he'd watched them all die.

"But your boys, John," Vee whispered, feeling his agony, the years of pain and sorrow far worse than the physical pain he was in.

"She was going to leave us when the youngest turned. She told me she would. Unless I could guarantee that she would never be harmed, she was going to leave me," John said, letting a sob break from his lips as he spoke.

"How would Dante being the leader make things safer for her, John? Do you know what kind of leader he was?" Min snapped, his anger still palpable in the air.

"I don't know. I don't know!" he screamed, clutching either side of his head. Vee took a step forward hesitantly before moving slowly closer to John. Shane, Min, and Durran followed close behind, but didn't crowd her as she crouched a few feet from where he sat so she was eye level with him.

"You just wanted to show her that you were serious. You had to do something to make her believe she was safe," Vee said quietly. John looked up into her eyes. The fire was gone from his, the rage having melted away for his own torment.

"I didn't want to lose her too." His voice was broken, weak. There before them sat the hazards of living an impossibly long life. This man was tortured by his past, by the family he watched fear him and die before they would agree to stay with him forever.

"I'm sorry, John. If I had known, I would have helped," Vee said, her voice sincere, eyes swimming with unshed tears as she looked at him. She wouldn't have been able to change Susan's mind, but she would have made an effort to get to know Susan better, encouraged others to do the same. There was no fixing what he had done now. He had committed too many offenses, spilt too much blood with who he sided with.

CHAPTER 21

"Will you help her?" he cried, glancing at Min, who had stepped forward a bit more.

"I'll do what I can for Susan and the boys, John. We won't leave them unless that's what they want," Vee promised. He nodded, taking in a short, ragged breath before moving to kneel before her.

"I won't ask for mercy. I should have died a long time ago, when my Rosie, my first love, died," John said, giving a small smile as more tears fell down his cheeks at the memory of her.

Min stepped forward beside Vee as she stood from her crouch, Shane following and taking her hand in his.

"John Meyers. For your crimes against your pack and the Sha, you are sentenced to death," Min said, his face blank of emotion, though Vee could still feel the anger and sadness brewing under the surface.

"Make it quick," Shane growled as Min stepped closer to John, taking his head in both his hands, and with a quick, but powerful jerk, snapped his neck, letting his body fall limply against the pavement.

251

CHAPTER 22

"What the fuck?" came Ethan's voice once John's body stilled, eyes vacant, his mind no longer a buzz in Vee's skull, and the weak tether that still held John within the pack gave a painful tug before it was nothing.

"Are you alright?" Shane asked, turning to where Ethan kneeled, hand at his neck and face contorted with confusion and shock.

"I want to know what's happening here!" Ethan yelled, eyes moving over all the pack members who were still assembled in the front yard.

"You really think you deserve to know?" Patrick growled from where he stood beside Tommy.

"I really think a lot of messed-up shit has been happening around here the last few months," Ethan said, standing and glaring at his brother.

"You'll need to calm down if you want any answers," Shane said, his voice full of warning as he pulled away from Ethan, after having confirmed nothing physically was wrong with him, at least nothing that wouldn't heal shortly. He immediately pulled Vee with him back toward the house, away from Ethan, while Margaret set about grabbing John's body with the help of Michael and Archer. "Take a minute to breathe, and then you can come inside," Shane finally said, before completely turning them to head into the house.

The pack went back in, Thomas stopping Vee for a moment before she went inside after Shane to give her a kiss on the head.

"You didn't have to be so kind to him. But I thank you for it," Thomas said quietly when she looked up at him. Thomas was also a very old Werewolf, Vee knew, and she imagined he had also faced his fair share of loss. The sincerity in his eyes, along with adoration, made her blush.

"He was hurting. It doesn't make what he did right, but Susan and the boys deserve to be happy and safe." He smiled down at her for a moment, her blush deepening, before she turned away, heading in after Shane.

Shane and Durran were cleaning up the broken coffee mugs and spillage from the floor while Patrick paced uneasily. Vee never expected to see the two of them cooperating, let alone in something so domestic as cleaning up a spill, but neither of them said a word, working seamlessly to get the job done. Ethan stormed through as Vee took a seat at a stool.

"What is this?" Ethan demanded.

"Not as calm as I would have liked, but I suppose it's better," Shane grumbled, as he dumped the wet shards of ceramic into the trashcan. "This is our new house."

"Not just this *place*. What is going on here?" Ethan growled, getting a snarl from Patrick as his eyes darted to Vee.

"Vee and I bought this house. There was a plot to take over the pack. John got involved with Dante," Shane said simply, stooping to wipe the remaining coffee residue from the floor.

"So, he deserved to die for it?" Ethan hissed.

"He plotted against his own leader, caused the unnecessary deaths of both Were and humankind, collaborated with two other preternaturals to abduct Shane, and attempted to abduct Vee. Not to mention this whole thing teetered on potential exposure to humans," Min said, having come in behind him. Ethan nearly jumped out of his skin at the sound of his voice.

"Is that why you weren't answering your phone?" Ethan asked, after a moment of contemplating everything Min had said.

"I was trapped in a Fae realm, so yes," Shane said simply, grabbing two more mugs from the cabinet for him and Vee.

"Who answered your phone the other night, then?"

"That was Duflanc. He tried to steal me," Vee said, as she noticed the clock on the oven only read 10:00 a.m. They had only gotten a few hours of sleep. She groaned and put her head down on the cool marble of the countertop as Shane poured cream in her mug and slid it into her hands.

"There's always someone after you, isn't there?" Ethan said, glaring as Vee raised her head to take a sip. She shifted her eyes to him, her irises turning amber, her magic pulsing out from her for just a moment. Just a slight warning, but one that made him physically step back.

"Did you not just see her?" Patrick hissed, stopping, and turning toward his brother with a look of pure fury. "And you haven't even been here the last few days to see what she's done for this pack while Dad was gone. She lost a friend. Murdered in the most horrifying, bloody way to send Vee a message. As she was wracked with that guilt, she felt Dad get taken. Thought he was dead. And the moment it became clear, literally *minutes* after she felt their bond gone, that something had gone wrong at Thomas's house, do you know what she did?" Patrick had crossed the room, pressing his chest to his brother's, eyes burning with such intensity that Ethan's face practically glowed. "She got up and *lead* us in there. She found Cora and Toby, organized us, brought the humans and children here. She made sure this pack was safe and protected."

"I just—"

"Then, with no idea what we were facing, she went into *battle* with us. She's barely shot a gun before, hasn't been well trained in hand to hand, let alone against the strength of a Werewolf, but it didn't matter. She was right there beside us. And it was *her!* It was *Vee* who brought the pack whole, who saved Dad! Vee!"

"Patrick... I—"

"I don't want to ever hear another word! Not another opinion about Vee! You don't get an opinion. She's one of us, and it's not changing!" Patrick screamed. His body was shaking with rage. Ethan had tried to step back away from Patrick, but he followed him until Ethan's back was pressed to the wall.

"Patrick," Vee murmured after a moment. He tore away from Ethan, turning to Vee and pressing a kiss to her cheek before storming from the room.

The whole house had gone silent, the pack bonds humming with agreement. Shane hadn't known all of that; there hadn't been time to hear everything that had taken place since he was taken, but he didn't doubt a word of what Patrick said. When he came out of the Fae realm, he realized that the pack had, indeed, changed. There wasn't one leader of this pack anymore. There was two.

One Woman.

One Pair.

One Pack.

Vee cast her eyes down to her mug, embarrassed at the amount of pride that she felt from everyone else in the room. Pride for her.

"I didn't know," Ethan murmured, still pressed against the wall.

"How could you? You aren't part of their pack," Min said coldly, crossing his arms over his chest.

"Leave him be," Vee said, glancing up at Min, whose face was hard. She looked at Shane, who only had eyes for her. Her heartbeat hastened, her body growing hot with the way he looked at her. "We have other things to go over. So, unless you plan on staying while we decide on a hunting party, Ethan, I suggest you leave. John was the last loose thread with the St. Louis pack we didn't have contained," Vee said, managing to tear her eyes from Shane's and keep her voice even, despite the way his gaze made her want to crawl across the island to him.

"I can help," Ethan said quietly, glancing around the room. Durran narrowed their eyes at Ethan, Min turned away to look through the refrigerator for something to eat, and Shane merely kept looking at Vee. He knew what she said was true, and it was prudent that they get the Vampire problem taken care of, especially now that Duflanc was dead, and there was no one to take his place as Master of the nest, but he couldn't be bothered to hide his need for her. She simply continued to amaze him, and he would never get enough. There was never enough of her for him.

"You can come help my crew clean up Thomas's basement," Margaret said as she entered the kitchen. "Just came to grab the paper towels George said he stashed in the pantry. Figured we'd kill two birds with one stone, since we need to deal with John," she said. Her strong body was covered by a white hazmat suit, blood dotted lightly on the surface. She had clearly used shoe covers, since her boots were clean and not leaving marks on the floor, but she reeked of blood, death, and the strong scent of cleaning products.

Ethan took in her appearance, a grimace coming over his face at the scents that came off her, before turning his eyes back to Shane, who simply gave him a smug smirk, raising his eyebrows as if to dare Ethan to refuse.

"I—" He shot a glare his father's way. "Fine. Where do you want me?" Ethan asked, pushing from the wall

just as Margaret shoved the package of paper towels into his hands.

"Follow me," she said with a grin.

A short meeting was called between the higher-level members out on the patio. Margaret opted out to continue cleaning, though Vee sensed a bit of disquiet in her. Perhaps the feeling of the power structure changing in the pack wasn't good for everyone involved. For the longest time, Margaret had been the highest woman in the pack, being only under Shane and Thomas. Now that had drastically changed with Vee's magic. Patrick was absent, having chosen to go work on missed schoolwork with Lori, and subsequently keeping an ear out for Ethan in her house. Vee felt slightly guilty for the distrust Patrick had for his older brother, but she couldn't do anything to defuse that situation. That was for them to work out, and for Ethan to come to grips with.

Shane, Thomas, and Tommy sat silently as Min, Durran, and Vee explained the events that happened in their absence. Though Patrick had given the cliff notes version in the kitchen earlier, Durran and Min gave much more details, especially with what they'd found out about Dante having planted himself in that neighborhood for no less than eight months. When the conversation seemed to die down, Thomas and Tommy agreed to take up the hunting party effort, dismissing themselves to go gather volunteers.

Once Min brought up the St. Louis pack members, Durran decided to excuse themself to take a shower. They were the only person still covered in blood and filth from the battle the night before, and Vee could see the strain in their eyes at the effort to not be completely disgusted.

"Not sure what we should do about them," Shane murmured, thinking about how they could possibly deal with the St. Louis pack members sequestered in the basement, and the remnants of the St. Louis pack who had stayed behind in their city.

"You could always take it over," Min suggested from the patio table where they sat. Markus had shooed them from the kitchen as he and Cora started making dinner for the pack. Midi sat quietly on Vee's lap, purring as Vee's fingers ran through the fur on her back, while Vee leaned against Shane on the rattan loveseat they sat on. Shane stiffened a little behind her. "Lead all of Missouri," Min continued.

"I'll not have pack members who don't want to be with us," Shane said quietly, though his mind was racing, his emotions conflicted.

The idea of more Weres under their leadership was enticing. Each additional pack member meant they were stronger, and the more territory they claimed as theirs meant more control. If he had the whole of Missouri, they would be a force not only against rival packs, but also against other preternaturals. But Shane was not a leader by force. His pack members chose to stay with him; they were family, and Dante's pack had been far from that for a very long time.

"Maybe you should talk to them," Vee suggested, feeling his inner turmoil.

"*We* should," Shane corrected. It made her squirm a little, the strange knowledge that the power dynamic within the pack had shifted. Shane was still the leader, but so was she. Vee, who had thought she would be alone forever, isolated, was now not only mated and engaged, but the joint leader of a Werewolf pack. Vee was about to protest, but her attention was stolen away as the gate between the trees behind Min shimmered, and the vibration of Aho's presence tickled her mind as she watched him step through.

"Aho," Shane said as he reached the patio. His white hair was undone from its normal braids, hands clasped behind his back. He was wearing what he normally did in the Sha domain, a loose T-shirt and worn jeans, but instead of barefoot, he wore the worn boots Vee had seen beside the door at his little house when they visited last month.

"Papa," Min said, nodding to his father in greeting, gaining a slight widening of the eyes from Vee. She hadn't heard Min call Aho anything other than his name in the time she had spent with them.

"I thought I'd come and see how things were going with the remaining St. Louis pack members," Aho said, glancing toward the house just as Durran came around from the apartment, hair still damp from their shower. Oddly, they seemed to be opting to stay in their true form instead of changing back into the female version Vee had known for most of their relationship. She wasn't sure what that meant, exactly. Was it that Durran was more comfortable to be themself?

"Funny, we were just discussing that," Min grumbled, moving to stand from where he sat as he eyed Durran's approach.

"We haven't gone down to see them yet. I wanted a better idea of what happened while I was gone first," Shane said as Vee sat up, watching Midi jump from her lap to rub against Aho's leg before trotting back toward the house. They were going to have to install a kitty door for her so she could come in and out, Vee realized, standing to make her way over to the kitchen door and open it for her.

"Well, now's as good a time as any," Aho said, raising his eyebrows expectantly. Aho never seemed to say or do anything without purpose, and they all knew that when he made a "suggestion," it was more of an order.

They shuffled through, all of them heading to the basement, passing the children as they watched a movie on the projector screen, before heading back to the secured room. As Shane opened the door, the scent of blood and fear permeated the air. Pain and anxiety burned in Vee's mind, making her stomach roll uncomfortably. The room was much like it had been when Vee was last in there to talk to Toby, though now there was no less than twelve people in this room. They all had grey sweats on, but they were still coated in mud and blood. Dishes were strewn about on the floor, and they were all either sitting against the wall, or lying on the cots and tables that had been placed there for them.

Vee's eyes were immediately drawn to a set of blue eyes in the corner of the room. His face was covered in filth, his body too thin, she could tell even with the sweats covering him, but she would know him anywhere.

"Jack?" Vee whispered, freezing in place. Jack had been one of the kids she had spent her teenage years with. A Were who she had trusted and confided in about her secrets before she'd learned to trust anyone else. She never knew what had come of any of her friends until she learned Talia, the white Witch of their group, had been killed by her own mother.

"Vee," he said, letting out a breath as a small smile came to his lips. He stood slowly, wincing a little, before he moved closer toward the center of the room to look at her.

"You went back to the pack?" she asked, her hands going to her necklace to fiddle nervously. Emotions from years ago came surging back. The fear of the pack that ruled St. Louis creeping through her body. Dante was very dead; she wasn't a teenager anymore; and she was in her city, in their territory, but something about seeing Jack there, thin and broken, the sadness and regret in his mind and flowing through to her, shook her.

"I had to so Bea could get away," Jack said quietly, but his comment brought out a sinister chuckle from one of the other Weres. Jack flinched at the sound, eyes closing as a wave of embarrassment washed over him.

"Why are you here, Jack?" Vee asked as Shane moved closer, pressing his chest to her back, while his hands gently ran down her shoulders and arms. Vee released one hand from the key at her neck, letting their fingers lace together, grounding her from the past that was still shaking her.

"Dante had plans," came a gruff voice from one of the cots. Vee and Shane turned their gaze to him. The man was stretched out, his leg in a splint, clearly having sustained a substantial break. That sort of break would take a day or two to heal on its own, easily mending incorrectly if it hadn't been treated by their pack. He looked a lot like Dante, Vee realized, as her eyes moved over his partially shadowed face. Similar strong jaw, long nose, and dark hair. Even his voice had a hint of an Italian accent.

"For some time, it seems. How long have you all been in Shawnee pack territory?" Shane growled.

"We didn't go back after we woke up in Pleasant Hill. Dante had us staying here while he moved between," Jack said, earning a growl from a number of Weres.

"Dante is dead, you idiots. We're lucky we haven't joined him yet," came the dark one on the cot.

"Adrian, you and these wolves have a decision to make," Min said, stepping forward through the doorway further so they could all see him, Aho coming close behind. The room of St, Louis Weres seemed to stiffen at the realization that not one but two Sha were present. "Do you want to become part of the Westport pack, or do you want to pay the price for what your dead leader did?"

"We were just following orders!" one man snapped, standing abruptly from where he sat against the wall and rushing forward. He kept his distance from Jack, as if he was afraid that getting too close would infect him, but he stopped with the same amount of distance between him and those standing in the door. His body outwardly showed rage, red face, clenched fists, but Vee felt his guilt, woven in with his fear.

"I believe many of you had means to get ahold of us," Min said, his voice sharp and ice cold. "We have clearly let some of these packs have a far longer leash than they deserve."

"You think the Sha could ever dream to overpower all the packs that run like ours? Do you know how many want to take you out like Dante did?" another said; this one was the Were who had chuckled. Vee looked over toward the corner where he sat, a stump where his leg should have been. Vee had no idea how long it took a Were to regrow a limb, but she was certain it had to be excruciating.

"I think you've all been brainwashed by your former leader. You have no idea what goes on within the other packs. Especially not this one," Min said, gesturing to Vee and Shane. "And *not one* of you knows what goes on within the Sha."

CHAPTER 23

Adrian moved to sit up, his face not showing the pain that shot through him when his leg was shifted, but Vee felt it. He let out a breath once he was sitting, gaze roaming over the four of them in the doorway briefly before he turned to look at Jack.

"This is the one, huh? The girl you all sacrificed yourselves for all those years ago?" Adrian asked, eyes narrowing as Jack flinched.

"We couldn't let any of you get your hands on her," Jack said with a quivering voice, eyes downcast. Vee's breath caught, brows furrowing as she looked at the tortured look on her old friend's face. Vee had thought they all ran when Talia went missing, but at those words, she realized how wrong she had been. They *sacrificed* themselves so she could get away.

Adrian turned back to Vee and then let his eyes fall on Shane.

"What makes you think we'd choose to join your pack?" Adrian asked. He was clearly the second in the pack, now the leader, though their bonds were weak until he officially took the mantle.

"I haven't decided what to do with you if you choose not to, but know this," Shane said, his hold on Vee tightening slightly. "Those that join this pack aren't simply soldiers or slaves. We don't pay dues, and no one is left to starve. What is good for one in my pack is good for everyone. This pack is more than just Werewolves, more than just the whim of a leader. If you can't get behind that ideology, you won't be accepted here."

"I thought it was our choice," the legless man in the corner sneered.

"I may be offering, but that doesn't mean I won't make you leave if you don't fit with the family we have here," Shane said, his voice a rumble in his chest, vibrating against Vee's back.

"Who runs the pack when Dante is away?" Min asked Adrian.

"Our brother, Gio," Adrian said, gaining another mutinous rumble from a few Weres for his freely giving up information. "How long until our decision is made for us?"

"Three days. Time to give you all to heal. Time for me to send people to St. Louis. After three days, I'll determine what I'll do with those of you who make the wrong choice," Shane said, turning and pulling Vee with him out the door.

The next day, Margaret, Ethan, and her clean-up crew moved on to Una's apartment, leaving Thomas's house ready to be lived in again. Cora seemed so relieved to be able to go back home, while simultaneously feeling anxious to step back into the place that had been so traumatizing.

"We're right here," Vee whispered to her, as they hugged at the entry to the house.

"I know," Cora whispered back, swiping the tears from her cheeks when they pulled apart.

"Come on, Toby. I'll show you your room," Cora said, looking over Vee's shoulder to the nervous man just outside the door.

Toby, though still shaken from the very huge change in his life, had opted to join the pack. Once Shane had explained it would help him control his wolf, he had been eager to get it over with. It was happening later that night, and with the knowledge he would be in better control, though still wanting to be close by, Cora extended an invitation for him to stay with them until they got the rest of his life sorted. It would also make it easy for him to keep working on her house, a distraction he would most likely lean on heavily for some time as he came to grips with his new reality.

Vee had never seen a real pack-bonding ritual; hers had been rushed, and she had still been partially in a trance from meeting her zi, so when they had gone out into the yard later that night, the final night of the full moon shining above them, she was just as intrigued as Toby.

The pack circled around them, Min and Durran staying below with the St. Louis pack members who had not yet made their final decision on whether they would be joining the pack. The only ones in the center were Vee, Shane, Toby, and Jack.

"Tobias Curtis," Shane said, eyes locking on Toby, who had previously been shaking with nerves. "With this is a promise, an oath that we become more than just two men living in this world, but we walk together. All of us, a family."

Toby nodded, though he was nervous about this. He was more eager to feel certain he wasn't a monster. Monsters had attacked him, killed his crew, and he was one of them now. The promise of the pack was safety and protection, even from himself.

Vee began stepping back, knowing what part would be coming next. It was the blood exchange, and only the Leader could bring a new member into the pack, so she should be back in the circle with the rest of them. But Shane reached beside him, grasping Vee's hand and halting her before she could get any further from him.

She glanced up at him questioningly, not sure why he would be keeping her at the center. He looked down at her, wordlessly showing her through their bond and the pack bonds what she already knew was true. The pack hummed with agreement; she was their Leader too.

Shane reached his other hand up, fingers changing partially to have sharp clawed ends, easily parting the skin at their wrists, blood hitting the air and making the glowing eyes of all the Weres in the circle burn a bit more vibrantly. He then reached across the short distance, waiting for Toby to extend his own arms.

Toby's blue eyes, filled with concern and hunger, as he stared at the blood dripping down Vee and Shane's arms. This was not a pretty ritual: it was grotesque, animalistic, and true to the reality of Werewolves.

"Toby," Shane said, causing Toby to tear his eyes away from the blood and at Shane, who once again gestured with his partially changed hand to Toby's arms. His arms shook as he reached forward, palms to the sky. He hissed when Shane slashed Toby's wrists, his own blood welling and pooling before it began dribbling.

"Our blood becomes yours. Our pack, your pack. Do you take it freely?" Shane asked, his words stirring with magic as they snaked like smoke from his lips, spreading so it surrounded both him and Vee. It tickled a little as it touched her skin, thrumming like the feel of his mind over her body. It seemed to reach out toward Toby, inviting him but waiting for his response.

With a slow swallow, Toby looked down at his bloodied wrists, his glowing blue eyes flashing as they then looked back up and darted between Shane and Vee's.

"I take it freely," Toby finally said, and Vee watched as the magic moved to surround him too. The three of them stepped forward, closing the distance between them. Shane took one of Toby's arms as Vee took the other, both pushing their joined hands and bloodied wrists forward for Toby to take, and they closed their mouths around the wounds. Toby's blood hit Vee's tongue, and she felt the magic pulse through her. His wolf and his own power joined them, creating connections with both her and Shane before spreading out and connecting to each of the other pack members too.

They disconnected with a growl from both men, Toby stumbling back and gasping as the magic of the pack took hold. It was Emily who stepped forward from the circle, hands coming to his shoulders and steering him back to stand with her. He seemed a bit dazed, clearly overwhelmed while taking in everything the pack was giving him, but it was all good. Everyone was pleased, joy and acceptance pulsing through their bonds.

"Jack," Shane said, nodding his head toward the thin, broken man that was once the vibrant boy Vee had been friends with years ago. He shivered as he approached. He was the first, and the only one of the St. Louis pack thus far, who had immediately wanted to join their pack, but Vee knew why. Jack had never wanted to be part of the St. Louis pack. He knew what went on there when they were teenagers, had actively tried to hide and escape the fate he knew would come if he joined them, and yet it had happened anyway.

Breaking away from that pack would hopefully be a clean slate for him.

Shane's wrist wound had already closed, so he once again sliced his skin, with fresh blood hitting the air once more, before he did the same to Jack. Somehow when the cut was made, Jack's trembling seemed to stop. Pain was something he knew intimately, and it calmed him more than the anticipation had.

"Jack Williams, our blood becomes yours. Our pack, your pack. Do you take it freely?"

"I take it freely," Jack said, not hesitating a moment as he stepped forward, taking up Shane and Vee's blood as they took his.

The bonds came alive, power surging through as they took on yet another member. Acceptance, concern, and happiness coming through slots of the bonds, and they added yet another new member, which made tears spring in Jack's eyes. With the new connection, Vee could almost see how awe-inspiring those feelings toward him were. He had only ever felt animosity, disappointment, and disgust from his old pack, but here he was being welcomed.

Vee never wanted him to feel that way again. She hated that Dante and the rest had done this to him, but more so was flooded with the pleasure of the pack as Jack stepped away and was enveloped into the circle like he'd belonged all along. The now bigger circle all looked toward Vee and Shane, their leaders, the heads of this family.

"Welcome," Shane said to the two new members, watching happily as they both let smiles break over their faces before he turned to the moon above them, leading them in their first howl together at the moon.

A few days passed, the weekend had turned back into Monday, and Vee was filling her travel mug with coffee at the bright and early 6:00 a.m. when she usually headed out to her shop. She had decided to get out of the house, despite how heart-wrenching the idea of being more than a few rooms away from Shane was. George, Vee had discovered, was a morning person and was sitting at the island, sipping his own coffee and glancing at the newspaper. Some pack members made their way home, but a number of them, mostly those without children, opted to stay and help guard the St. Louis pack members that were still in the basement.

This evening, a convoy of pack members and a few Sha would be heading back to St. Louis where, with Shane's instruction, they would be dismantling the structures Dante had in place there for years, assisting the Weres who weren't joining their pack with getting their new lives set up as lone wolves, and officially being sentenced by the Sha. Shane had opted to leave the punishment in the Sha's hands, with the only caveat being that he didn't want any of them in the whole of the state, which was now their territory, after the sentencing.

Knowing their basement would soon no longer be a prison certainly helped Vee's mood as she imagined coming home later this evening to see Margaret, Tommy, Archer, and George off.

"Happy birthday," George said, eyes still on the headline. Vee cringed, hoping everyone had forgotten it was her birthday. She had practically neglected her shop for a week, her attention not focused on it for more than that time with the move, and now she was trying to get back on track. If they decided to do something for her birthday and disrupted her plans of digging into some locks, they were sorely mistaken.

"Thank you," she said stiffly, snapping the lid on the mug and turning to watch the smirk pull at the corner of his mouth.

"Off to the shop today?" he asked, glancing up to watch as Vee let her gaze slide toward the back window at the thicket of trees where the Sha gate was.

Min had gone back, but not for long. There seemed to be a revolving door of Sha coming and going to help guard the St. Louis pack members. Yona was the one currently in the basement, snoozing on one of the couches in the theatre room, Vee thought, based on the way her mind felt. She would be going with them to St. Louis, along with Hurin.

Somehow the reminder of Vee's birthday made her wish Aho and Min were there, but she quickly shoved that away. She was going to *work* today. Not get swept up on birthday feelings. Besides, everyone was plenty busy. On this day, in the past, she would usually just buy herself her favorite ice cream and pick a good comfort movie to put on. Much had changed since the last time she celebrated her birthday in her tiny apartment, cuddled against her worn futon as *The Mummy* played on her small television.

"Yes. I have a lot to catch up on, and my employees are back in school, so it's all on me," she said, turning back to him.

"I'd say have a good day, but that honestly sounds terrible," he murmured, turning back to the newspaper. Vee gave him a smirk of her own before heading out to the front door to the cul-de-sac where her van was parked in front.

The morning felt so oddly normal. She had slipped out of the bed, unable to resist giving Shane a kiss on the cheek, which roused him just enough to tell him she was going to the shop. Then she took a shower, dressed, got her coffee, and was now on her way to her locks and keys. The normalcy was both comforting and put her on edge. Nothing was *normal*. It would never be normal. And if she was honest with herself, it never had been.

While her life was full of preternaturals, chaos, and so many people that she now cared about so much, she had been prepared to lay her life down for them more than once, what she had called living before had been a shadow of a life. She had been a prisoner of her own making, isolating herself for safety when she was far safer with Shane. With their family.

She pulled up to her shop, quickly going in and sighing as she tried to decide where to begin. The voicemail light, blinking on the counter like an angry alarm, made her want to hurl it against the wall instead of listen to them. How much business had she missed? She may have been happier with the way her life was now, but that didn't mean she didn't pride herself in what she had accomplished doing on her own.

The morning passed quickly. She finished up some repairs and custom pieces that were due to be picked up the following day and got the paperwork sorted out that she had been neglecting since the move. Her eyes reluctantly went to the blinking red light of the voice-mail, and she picked it up, going through the messages. Several were inquiries, one about safes and two about custom keys that they had seen on the website Patrick and Lori had built for her. Two were late-night house calls that happened over the weekend. She wasn't too sad about missing those. Her cell phone buzzed in her pocket just as she was about to get to the last message, so she put it down, figuring it was just another house call she could listen to and delete later.

[Shane: Come home for lunch.]

Somehow the command in that text message made her instantly want to rebel against it, but she hesitated, only because despite how much she truly enjoyed fighting with Shane, she had just gotten him back.

[Shane: I felt that.]

She smirked, knowing he felt her immediate reaction to his message.

[Vee: Maybe I had other plans.]

[Shane: I think what I have planned for your birthday lunch is much better than anything you had in mind.]

A wash of promising lust spread over her from the bond.

[Shane: Patrick has a half day. Some teacher meeting. He's heading to the shop now.]

She glanced at the clock; it was later than her usual lunchtime, but she had decided to work until she felt she needed the break. She was about to text Shane back when a small group of women walked through the door, and right behind them a package delivery person.

[Vee: Customers. I'll come home when Patrick gets here.]

[Shane: I'll wait as long as I need to.]

Somehow the sincerity in that text made her shiver more than the other text had. He would wait for her forever. He would wait for anything, as long as she was with him.

"Victoria Malone?" the package handler asked as he approached the counter where she stood.

"That's me," she said, shoving her phone in her pocket and looking up at him quizzically.

"Package for you. I just need a signature," he said, setting the box down before her and scrambling to grab his device from his belt so that she could sign. He scanned the barcode on the label, holding out the little keypad for her to run her finger over with her signature.

"Who is it from?" Vee asked, confused.

"Don't know. Doesn't say on the label. There's no return address," he said before making a few additional clicks on the gadget. "Have a good rest of your day," he said before quickly leaving the store to her and the women who had entered before him. One woman came up to her while the others perused.

"Hi. I just wanted to get some keys made," she said, holding out a key for Vee to take. "You're my last hope. No other places said they could make copies for me."

Vee knew why; it was an old-fashioned skeleton key. The long circular shaft was made of thick brass, the bow an intricate floral design, and the bit was even quite complex. Vee let the key rest in her hands as she looked it over.

"I won't be able to do this today. I could have keys made that work on the lock in a few days, but if you want this design," Vee said, holding up the key so the bow was prominent in the girl's view, "that will probably take a week or more, depending on how many keys you need."

The girl turned, glancing at her three companions, before turning back to Vee.

"I need three more. Maybe four, depending on the price," she admitted, wringing her hands in front of her nervously. Vee wasn't sure what this was about, but she had a strange feeling come over her with the amount of nervousness flowing from the girl.

Vee went over pricing for custom keys like this, all the while searching for signs of what could possibly be the reason these girls, all of them, were giving off such strange feelings. Like they were afraid they'd be caught.

"I think we can manage that amount," the girl said once Vee had finished, gaining a nod from the other three.

She tried not to narrow her eyes at them, instead keeping her eyes firmly on the tablet while she typed up the order with the quoted price, getting the girl's information and credit card for the deposit.

"Late next week would be the earliest since I'm making four keys, but I'll call to give you an update on Thursday," Vee said, as she handed the girl the quote sheet.

Patrick came through the door at that moment, still dressed in his uniform for school with his backpack over his shoulder. It made the hair raise over Vee's skin, the back of her neck prickling when all four girls tensed at his presence. She felt an odd thrum in place of their normal human vibrations. These were not simply four human women, but they weren't fully Witch either. Patrick's eyes lightened slightly as he strode behind the counter to stand beside Vee.

"I'll just wait to hear from you," the girl Vee had learned was named Tilda said abruptly, glancing toward Patrick as she backed closer to where the other three stood.

"Yes. Thank you, Tilda," Vee said, being sure the half-Witch understood Vee knew what was going on now, or at least enough to know these women were up to something.

The four of them hurried out, the door of the shop closing with a definitive snap.

"What was that?" Patrick growled from where he stood behind her protectively.

"Half-Witches wanting copies of this key made," Vee said, holding it up for him to see.

"What's so special about this key?"

"I guess I'll have to find out," Vee said, slipping it and the quote sheet into a bag, before taking it back to the shelf where she kept projects.

"I'll do some research. See if there's anything special about it ... or them," he said, still facing the direction they went when they left. Vee nodded, pulling her bag over her shoulder and walking past him toward the front door.

"I don't know how long I'll be," Vee said as she grabbed the door handle.

"I'll close the shop down. You just go enjoy your birthday lunch," Patrick said, his entire face and mood changing from suspicion to excitement. Vee gave him a quizzical quirk of the eyebrow.

"What do you know?" she asked with narrowed eyes. He grinned.

"Can't reveal our secrets. I only wish I was there to see the look on your face," Patrick said, as he let his backpack drop to the floor by the counter.

"Fine," Vee said with a roll of her eyes. "See you at home."

Vee pulled up in front of the house. The cul-de-sac seemed rather quiet now that there were fewer pack members staying with them. In fact ... the house seemed far more vacant than it should have, she realized, as she approached. At least ten of their pack had been in the house that morning, and Yona had been there to watch over the St. Louis members. Now there was only one mind in the house: Shane's.

It was far too early for the convoy to have left already. The emptiness and the timing setting her nervousness off. Confused, she hurried in, trying to sense where he was.

"Shane? Where is everyone?" Vee called out, putting her bag on the little entry table and tossing her keys in her teal planter. He didn't answer, though she could feel his amusement. That eased her just slightly. If he was amused, then nothing was truly amiss. "Where are you, Shane?" she asked more quietly this time, eyes darting in all the possible directions she could choose to find him.

Still, he didn't make a sound. She closed her eyes, feeling him, letting that subtle pull she always felt to be near him spur her steps forward. She knew, after a moment or two, he was in the basement. Her eyes snapped open as she moved with purpose through to the kitchen and down the basement stairs, but once at the bottom, facing the theatre room, she realized she had no idea where she was going next. Once again, she closed her eyes, the feeling of Shane's eager anticipation pulsed through her. He was excited.

She smiled a little, letting her feet guide her with closed eyes to the right, toward the rooms on that side. The further she walked, her worn work boots making plenty of sound on the carpet as she moved through the hallway, the more excited he became until she simply *knew* she had arrived at the right door.

CHAPTER 24

When she opened her eyes, she was standing in an open doorway. It was one of the storage rooms Vee hadn't explored. Mostly she hadn't explored these rooms because she simply didn't care. She wasn't storing anything; there was still so little she considered hers, and most of what was being put in these rooms belonged to Patrick, Shane, and the pack as a whole.

Standing in the middle of the room, leaning against a massive table that was bolted to the floor, was Shane. He was wearing the suit he had, presumably, worn while he met with clients that morning, but the jacket was gone, the top few buttons unbuttoned, and the sleeves rolled up. His hair was tussled like he had been running his hands through it nervously. He hadn't shaved the beard growth from his time in the Fae realm, instead opting to trim it and keep it combed.

A bit of the salt and pepper was flaked through the dark hair.

"Hi," Vee said quietly, gaining a smirk from him.

"Happy birthday," he said, pushing himself off the table and taking two long strides to stand right in front of her. Once her eyes had fallen on him, she lost whatever purpose she was down there for.

"Thank you," she said awkwardly, still mesmerized by him. He chuckled, moving around to stand behind her, threading his arms around her waist. "*This* is your surprise."

Shane being removed from her field of view made her actually look around at the space. It was like a dream come true. There were massive floor-to-ceiling shelves with bins and rolling ladders attached so she would always be able to reach. Most of the bins were empty, but several were filled with various types of metals. The massive table at the center of the room was covered with a pristine sheet of stainless steel. It had lights that clamped onto the sides so she could move them wherever she needed them for various projects. There were four smaller additional tables on wheels so she could move them around.

And then there were the tools. Oh, the tools. Every possible thing she would need to create custom pieces was there. And safety gear hung from hooks right by the door.

"I know it's been hard since you moved in with me to change your routine. You used to spend a lot more time at your shop than you do now. I also know you need a space of your own to work through things, and *work* seems to be how you do that," Shane said, tightening his hands at her hips and pressing a kiss to her hair.

"You did all this … for me?" she asked, staring in awe at the space. Shane gently pressed her, turning her back toward him and tilting her chin up so she looked into his eyes.

"I love you, Victoria Malone. Everything about you, even when you frustrate me with your stubbornness, you make me in awe of your strength. You may think sometimes that we don't fit together, but those overalls you wear are the cutest thing I've ever seen." Vee felt the heat rise to her cheeks, and she tried to avert her eyes in embarrassment, but he caught them again. "*You* make me happy. And if *this room* makes you happy to stay with me, I'd do it a thousand times over," he murmured, every word clear and sincere.

"I love you," was all Vee could say, as she twined her hands around his neck, standing on her tiptoes to reach his mouth. His lips crashed into hers: the kiss was fiery, passionate, electric. Vee's fingers raked through his hair, needing him as close as they could possibly get. Shane growled, nipping at her bottom lip hungrily, as his hands trailed over the hem of her shirt, lifting it up so his hands could grasp at her bare skin.

Vee couldn't handle it. His fingers were so strong on only the skin of her back, she broke the kiss to suck in a ragged breath. His lips didn't stop, traveling down her neck as Vee's fingers shakily tried undoing the remaining buttons on Shane's shirt. With a frustrated snarl, she tore the shirt apart, buttons flying in all directions. She didn't care. He had plenty of shirts. She *needed* to touch his skin, to caress; the skin rippling over his muscles as they clenched at the feel of her fingers.

When her fingers slipped beneath the waistband of his slacks, Shane stooped low, grabbing her and pulling her in the air against him.

"It's *your* birthday, Vee," Shane admonished, as he brought her over to the bolted table. Setting her there as he began to unfasten her jeans.

"I thought I was getting lunch," Vee said a little breathily, bracing herself against the table as he tugged roughly to pull her pants from her body. He smirked as he removed her boots, the last thing keeping her pants in place, before everything was suddenly gone, and her lower half was bare to him. He leaned forward, pressing his hips into hers before his mouth came to her ear.

"You'll eat. But I'm eating first," he rumbled, sending shivers of anticipation throughout her. His lips trailed down her body from her ear, slowly, torturously, before he was exactly where he intended to be, hands holding her hips firmly in place.

Vee opened her eyes, watching the light filter in through the windows of their bedroom as she rested her cheek on Shane's chest. They had somehow made their way upstairs to their room. The thought had been that they would take a quick shower and have some lunch, but they didn't quite make it to the shower. Now the two of them were sprawled on the floor, as several yet unpacked boxes were toppled over and spilling their

CHAPTER 24

contents across the carpet, but neither of them could be bothered to move or care.

This was the best birthday Vee could remember.

Somehow the previously nagging feeling of guilt at leaving the shop so early on the day when she had already missed so much work was whisked away. Shane seemed to have that effect on her. His fingers brushed up and down her back lazily.

"We need to pick a date," Shane said suddenly, making Vee furrow her brow.

"Hm?" she murmured, turning her head to look up at his face. He smirked a little at her confusion, amusement flickering in his eyes.

"A wedding date."

Vee hadn't thought much about it. He had proposed, which she had essentially asked for, but too many things had happened in the intervening time. First, her adjustment to simply living with him had been enough, but they'd also had the pressures of finding out what she was. That mystery was solved, but not the scope of her abilities. What her mother was, other than the Fae in her, was vague. Witch was all Aho had known, but depending on the Witch, the powers that came along with that could vary greatly.

But then the chaos seemed to pile on. She had completely pushed their search for Fiona out of her mind in favor of the more pressing issues that fell at their feet, but Vee realized they still needed to work that out.

"We could elope," Vee offered weakly. Her small but hopeful voice only made a chuckle rumble in his chest.

"We'd never get away with it."

"Lori and Cora would kill us," Vee said in agreement, cringing at the image of the two women finding out they had gotten married with Vee in her work boots. Then she smiled a little; that actually wasn't a bad idea. "Ugh! I don't know! I can't imagine planning something like that after all this," Vee grumbled, flipping on her back and, therefore, off of Shane's chest, waving her arm weakly around their room. The house still needed to be unpacked fully, and there were baby Vampires running loose in their city. Adding a wedding and all the stress that came with it to her plate sounded dreadful.

Shane moved too quickly for Vee to catch, shifting to be on top of her and grasping her hands in his, effectively pinning her to the floor.

"I won't let it get too big. Any decisions you don't think you can handle, I'll take over. But Vee…" He released one hand to bring it to her face, brushing her cheek lightly, his eyes glowing. "I don't want to go much more time where I can't call you mine in all ways."

Vee's breath caught, as it normally did when his words and the emotion she felt behind them were so powerful, so honest, so full of love for her that she was amazed by it. She had no trepidation about marrying him; it was all the steps, all the planning that went into it.

"Pick a date," Vee said, her voice breathier than she thought it would be.

"Mid-October?" he suggested, brushing his lips over her clavicle.

"That's only a month."

"I think Lori and Cora can handle it," Shane said, pulling her up with him as he stood and walking her to the bathroom.

"They're going to throw fits." Shane chuckled as his fingers dug into her skin briefly, before he quickly started the shower, letting it warm up before striding over to the closet and rifling through the side pocket of a bag that sat on one of his shelves.

"They'll get over it once they realize we're actually going to be married," Shane said.

"What are you doing?" Vee asked, mesmerized by his odd search through the bag. It wasn't a bad view, especially since he was unabashedly naked, muscles rippling as his arms searched inside the bag's contents. He apparently found whatever it was, pulling up straight, and turning his eyes to her with satisfaction moving through him.

"Getting your last present," he said, walking back to her, a swagger in his step. When he returned to the counter where he left her leaning, he held up a small black box before her.

"You already spent enough on me," Vee said, narrowing her eyes at the little box.

"Just open it," he said, only barely holding back his laugh. She took it from his hand, slowly popping the lid up to reveal two stones and his key. Not the new one she had made when they moved in, but the first one she had made for him before they had decided they were anything more than begrudging acquaintances to one another. "It's not much of a present, since you'll have to do some work, but I thought you might like to make our rings."

Vee's eyes sparkled as she looked up at him, tearing her gaze from the contents of the box to look at the gold-rimmed eyes of her mate. She would have to add some additional metal to the key, and probably make it unrecognizable, but that didn't matter. *They* would know what the rings were made of. They would understand what made these rings special. She would relish this task. She wasn't one to make things or get things for herself, but the idea of making a ring to mate with Shane's, which shared everything with its other half, its pair, was too perfect to pass up.

"I got us both emerald stones. They represent true love, and your eyes."

Vee slowly closed the box, setting it on the counter beside her before she wrapped her arms around Shane's neck and gazed up at him. He wasn't sure for a moment if she was unhappy or not. Their bond was overwhelmed by his own feelings to the point that he was struggling to understand which were his and which were hers.

"Yes, I'm happy. Now kiss me," she whispered. He didn't hesitate, pressing his lips to hers, hands threading through her hair. He pulled her against him, her legs circling his waist, before he moved them into the shower, letting the steam fill the room.

Far after lunch time, Vee sat happily in the kitchen watching as Shane inspected what food they had available. Apparently, his planning only went as far as the room in the basement and the emeralds, not that Vee minded. She had a perfect view of him, still slightly damp from the shower, shirtless, with a look of concentration on his face.

"You don't have to make anything. We can just order something," she offered, amused.

"The sounds your stomach is making tell me there's no way you can wait for a delivery to get here," he said, glancing at her from the open refrigerator door with an eyebrow raised. As if on cue, her stomach growled loudly, making her pinch her lips together. His smirk only made her narrow her eyes, but she didn't say more, as her phone pinged with an incoming text message.

[Aho: I have something for you if you aren't busy.]

The sudden realization that Aho, her real father, was going to bring her something on her birthday was mildly overwhelming. She had a father for the first ten years of her life, one that she still thought of fondly, but after twenty years of being fatherless, it felt strange to have the warm sensation settle in her chest of paternal care. Perhaps it was that she had come to terms with the fact that Sarah Malone had not been her real mother for a longer time, because for months she had solidly known the name of her real mother, Fiona, even if she had yet to meet her.

In those months, her real father had been such a mystery still that the revelation still hadn't quite hit her.

[Vee: We're just preparing dinner. You're welcome to join us.]

"Aho is coming by," Vee murmured once she sent the text message off.

"We have plenty of steak," Shane offered, pulling out four butcher packets of KC Strip Steak from the meat drawer.

"Is this more of a, 'you want steak' situation?" Vee asked with a knowing smile.

"If we're feeding more than us and Patrick, it would make sense," Shane offered, though the little buzz of his white lie sat behind her eyes.

CHAPTER 25

P atrick closed down the shop. The first day open in a week and in the last five hours of being open, he had quite a bit of business. He smiled to himself that he would have good news for Vee on her birthday of all days, as he locked the display cases after reconciling the register. But as he closed the inventory door, he finally noticed the package Vee had left under the counter and the blinking light of a voicemail. He had answered all the calls that came in since he arrived, having taken plenty of notes for Vee on a house call that wanted her to come the next day, but he didn't think he had missed any, even with the push in business that afternoon.

He pressed the button to listen to the message, his body immediately going rigid before he dug his phone from his pocket to record it. It was definitely something

Vee and his dad would listen to before tomorrow. He listened to it a third time, finally leaving it saved, even though he recorded it already. Somehow, he knew Vee would want to hear it straight from the recording before he picked up the package, set the alarm, and headed home.

There was definitely something off about the box. He could smell the delivery driver and all the humans who had handled it, but nothing more. Like whatever was inside that box had a sort of seal on it. Beyond the clear lack of scent, having it near him, sitting in his passenger seat, was making the hair rise on his arms unpleasantly.

He pulled up in the driveway, waiting as the garage door opened so he could park beside his dad's car. The feeling of unease began growing more intensely when he picked it up, carrying the package into the house. His backpack hit the floor in the entry, the murmuring voices of his dad and Vee were coming from the kitchen. She was laughing, a sound that made Patrick smile. Her laugh was not a frequent occurrence. Sure, she would smile more often than when he had first met her, but a laugh? He almost hated to interrupt whatever his dad had done to bring that sound out of her. Especially since he knew between the message he had recorded on his phone and the strange box in his hands, he wasn't going to be hearing it anymore tonight.

Vee was sitting on the stool closest to the refrigerator, which had apparently become her spot. Her dark hair was damp and in braids down her back. Her feet dangled, swinging happily as she watched Shane

CHAPTER 25

make the finishing touches to whatever dinner he was cooking up.

"Just in time, Patrick," Shane said, turning to glance at his son.

"What's for dinner?" Patrick asked, setting the box on the counter as far from Vee as he could before moving to sit next to her.

"Vee wanted steak," Shane said, a hint of surprise in his voice as he glanced at her.

"Your dad wanted steak," Vee corrected. "I didn't care either way."

"Love steak," Patrick said, grinning. "Did you like your surprise?" he asked, watching as Vee's face grew even brighter before a tinge of red found its way on her cheeks.

"How long had you all been planning this?" Vee asked, a playful glare on her face as she saw Shane's mouth spread into a wide smile.

"Before Colorado. Had to change plans with the new house," Patrick admitted.

"I'm assuming Lori was in on it too?" Vee asked.

"Oh of course. She was disappointed when she couldn't be here for the reveal," Patrick said, unable to keep the hint of his own disappointment from his voice, but he imagined, based on the strange glow and the fact that they had both recently showered, it was for the best that he and Lori hadn't been here for whatever transpired after. He had no qualms about hearing them, but he imagined if he went into her workroom now, there would be quite a scent permeating the air.

He kept smiling, though, and trying his hardest to keep his discomfort from the surface. The box was there, just a reach away. His phone and the recorded message were hot in his pocket. But Vee felt his unease. She turned her gaze away from Shane, eyes narrowing.

"What's wrong?" she asked, turning to look at his face. He cast his eyes down, then toward his dad, who had turned to look at Patrick with the pan of steaks set to the side of the stove.

"I don't really want to do this now. Not on your birthday," he said quietly, pleading with her to let it go.

"Is it something that can wait?" Shane asked, noticing the box on the counter.

"Just spill it," Vee said, feeling his growing anxiety. He pulled out his phone, setting it on the counter between them all, just as Durran walked through the back door.

"Good timing," Shane said to the Watcher, watching as Patrick navigated his phone, finally getting to the recording.

"Timing for what?" Durran asked, pausing just inside the door and taking in the scene.

"We don't know yet," Shane grumbled, as Patrick's finger hesitated over the play button.

"Something weird happening on Vee's birthday? How am I not surprised?" Durran said, lips pinching as they moved closer to the island.

"Play it, Patrick," Shane murmured.

Patrick hit the button and the robotic voice of the voicemail box said, *"Replaying saved message,"* before a strange, muffled thrumming came over. The sound made Vee's stomach drop and her breath hitch as she listened to it. She knew that sound. She didn't know from where or what it was, but she *knew* it nonetheless.

Then came the voice, a female.

"Vee. I just wanted you to know I've taken care of our Fae problem. You shouldn't worry about Ness and her interferences anymore." The voice didn't belong to anyone Vee knew, but somehow the sound resonated within her. She couldn't place a face to the voice, but she knew she heard it before. Somewhere deep in her mind, that voice seemed to blossom from a long-forgotten memory. Her fingers clenched against the counter, eyes wide, as she stared at Patrick's phone.

"I have waited so long to talk to you, but alas it wasn't meant to be this time. Soon," the woman's voice said, maybe a hint of sadness in her tone.

"I do hope you enjoy this present I sent to you." Vee's eyes shot to the package on the counter, eyes scanning over it with suspicion. Shane leaned over it to reach the nonexistent return address.

"Soon, little one," the woman finally said before the strange thrumming sound took over once more for a few seconds, and then the message ended.

Everyone was staring intently at the box.

"It doesn't smell like anything, but I felt dread the whole way home," Patrick told them, eyeing it warily. Vee stiffened, now tentatively moving her hand to pull the box closer.

"Not a bomb," Shane said quietly, watching as Vee slid it closer. She picked up one of the steak knives Shane had set on the counter earlier. The intention had been to eat at the dining room table, but neither of them had bothered to set it. She made quick work of the tape securing the box closed.

As soon as the first two flaps of the cardboard were lifted, a rush of magic filled the air, as well as the pungent mixture of Fae and rotting flesh. Vee's hands stilled, eyes glancing up at Shane, who was clearly eager to remove the box from her.

"Let's do this outside," Vee said, pushing her stool back as Shane snatched the box from the counter.

The four of them moved quickly out to the patio. Thomas and his family were out in theirs, enjoying their own dinner, when they saw them.

"Happy birthday, Vee!" Lori called, getting a strained smile and wave from her. Thomas stood from where he sat next to Cora.

"What is it?" he asked, not raising his voice higher than normal volume. Everyone on the other side could hear him just fine.

"Someone sent Vee a…" Patrick started but was unsure how to finish that sentence. They had yet to completely open it, still only the two flaps raised as they set it on the wrought iron patio table.

"Stay there, in case something happens," Shane said when he saw Thomas begin to step forward, Tommy hunching to stand from his seat. They both froze, but their eyes glowed ominous blue as they watched.

Vee flipped the other two flaps up to reveal a dirty, rumpled piece of cloth. It was stained with a bluish-black substance, and the scent only intensified.

"Don't touch it," Durran hissed, causing Vee to halt just as her hand was reaching toward the cloth. Durran pulled a knife from their pocket, flicking it open in one fluid movement, before gingerly finding an end of the fabric and pulling it up and over.

They all held their breath as they looked down at the contents of the now uncovered object.

"Ness…" Vee said in a whisper. The unglamored face was unmistakable, even with the horrified expression frozen on her face. The black, unblinking eyes were dull, mouth locked in a lopsided scream. Her head was ripped off, it appeared. The skin torn raggedly, and the bones of her neck were shattered. It was raw and horrible. Vee's throat and stomach knotted violently.

"She pissed someone off other than us," Shane said, his lip curling with disgust.

"Who sent it?" Durran asked, their face also unable to hide their disgust as they wiped the blade against the box to rid it of any Fae blood before pocketing it once more.

"Well, given the person who left the voicemail message mentioned Ness, I'd say the mysterious caller did," Vee murmured, tearing her eyes away from the box in time to see the thicket of trees the Sha gate sat in shimmer just before Aho and Min stepped through. Shane's head snapped up to look at the two approaching Sha once he felt Vee's surprise.

"But who left the message?" Patrick asked, as he pushed the nearest box flap to him back down, partially obscuring Ness's nightmare-inducing face.

"I think I might know," Vee said quietly, watching her father step closer through the grass.

Fiona.

AUTHOR BIO

Chelsea Burton Dunn is a Kansas City native—the Missouri side, not the Kansas side. That matters to locals. Where is that, you might ask? Right smack-dab in the middle of the country. She has two beautiful children and is married to a superb partner, but let's not forget their two snuggly cats and eager-eater of a dog.

Having always been a little strange herself, Chelsea instantly fell in love with paranormal, supernatural, and fantasy books, movies and TV shows as a child. Did everyone think it was a phase? Absolutely. Was it? Absolutely not. Being weird is a blessing, not a curse. She's always embraced that part of herself and those around her.

She started writing from a very early age, initially starting and completing one of the *Deadman's*

Handbooks in high school. She is a lover of music, having her other love and talent be singing. She performed on main stage operas in the children's chorus from grade school to high school.

Chelsea loves to delve into the difficulties of life, love, and loss, while spicing it up with a little magic and monsters. As she liked to say when she was younger, "The monsters in my head need to come out to play every once in a while," so giving them life on the page seemed appropriate.

You can see more about Chelsea, her projects, and find her social medias by going to www.chelseaburtondunn.com.

SNEAK PEEK AT
CITY OF BLOOD AND MOONLIGHT
BOOK 5 OF THE BY MOONLIGHT SERIES

The sound of the blow torch was drowning out every other sound. Vee sat in her basement workroom, delicately welding small pieces of metal to the bow of a key, trying to match it to the ornate design from one a customer brought in nearly two weeks prior. She had not put much work into this set of keys, mainly because it was her first big project since she, Shane, and Patrick had moved into their new house, and absolute chaos followed directly after. These past few weeks had not been much better, but she was determined to get this order fulfilled.

The loudness of the welding served the purpose of getting her work done, while also drowning out the incessant buzzing of Vee's phone that was sitting on one of her rolling worktables behind her. She may not have been able to hear it behind the gear she had on, nor could she see it illuminating with each new call and text notification, but she could feel the vibration, rumbling against the wooden tabletop, down its legs, and across the concrete floor to her waiting socked feet.

This was an effort in purposeful ignorance. She had no desire to answer those calls and texts, because if she did, that would mean she would have to acknowledge the very stressful planning she was supposed to be doing.

Wedding planning.

The past several months had been strange and chaotic enough, turning all their lives upside down with preternatural chaos. Vampire attacks, Werewolf pack takeover attempts, and people being taken away to a Fae realm were just a few. Now Shane, her fiancé and the leader of their pack, was determined to marry her as soon as possible.

The sentiment was sweet, not wanting to spend any more time not being joined in all ways, but the timing was terrible. Their house was still not completely unpacked. They had the remnants of a vampire nest killing humans in the city left and right since their master's disappearance and subsequent death. The St. Louis pack members were still in the process of being sentenced and banished by the Sha, meaning Shane and several other pack members were regularly traveling between Kansas City and St. Louis. But Vee was expected to not focus on any of those pressing matters or be given time to simply catch up on her own work and locksmith shop. No, Vee was instead told to look at venues, choose flowers, and go…

Vee gulped just thinking about it.

Dress shopping.

Her phone started ringing again, but this time it was coupled with a gentle nudge from the bond between her and Shane. With a sigh, she turned the blow torch off, slipped her gloves off, and reached behind her to the phone. Shane's name illuminated the screen.

"Yes, Shane?" she answered, turning back to the piece she had been working on. The ornate and delicate floral pattern on the key she was replicating was nearly there; she'd just need to use some hand tools to do the finer lines and details. No big deal ... except that she had to do it three times over. The order for her customer was for three more keys to match as closely as possible to the original.

"Cora called," Shane said, his voice laced with his own weariness. Getting a call from Cora on a rampage was not something even the bravest and strongest Werewolves could walk away from unscathed. And a rampage she had been on. When Cora Byers started planning something, she was a machine. The timetable Shane gave probably didn't help matters. Mid- October was merely weeks away, and the pressure was mounting.

"Did she?" Vee murmured, flipping the unfinished key in her fingers. She wasn't surprised Cora had reached out to Shane. If anyone could break Vee out of her hiding, it was him, but it was a bit harder, even for him since he had been gone so much lately. Especially after having been stolen away into a Fae realm, Vee had a hard time with his absences. If she wasn't determined to keep her shop open, she would just close it and go with him, but she had built this by herself, made it what it was, even if it was small, and she would be damned if she would give it up now just because she missed him.

"You were supposed to meet at her house for dinner fifteen minutes ago." Vee glanced at the clock over the door.

"Shit!" she hissed, pulling the rest of her gear off. Yes, she had been ignoring the calls, but she hadn't thought it was for this long. She just needed a few minutes—apparently that turned into hours—to get lost in her work. "I was trying to get a little more work done on those keys."

"And maybe trying to avoid additional conversation about the wedding?" Shane asked, though the amusement that filtered through their bond betrayed the hard tone in his voice. She knew he found some enjoyment in her discomfort. They would never be able to get away with eloping. Being part of a werewolf pack meant you essentially had an immediate family of thirty and an extended family that pushed you to nearly a hundred. Anyone not invited would be offended. And Cora...

"If you were here, you'd want a break from it too," she snarled, pressing her phone between her shoulder and her ear so she could pull her boots back on.

"How bad could it be?"

"Do I like daisies or tulips? What about orange? It would bring out the gold and amber in our eyes, Shane! Do we think duck for the reception of two hundred?" Vee asked, rattling off actual questions Cora had posed over the last week. Vee didn't even like duck, but somehow by the time Cora was done, Vee had agreed to whatever Cora suggested just to finish the conversation.

"Two hundred?" Shane asked, sounding as if she had said the sky was falling. Vee laughed darkly. He had been busy, but he had no idea what Vee had been dealing with, not really.

"Yes, Shane! She's imagining some huge monstrosity! Do I come off as an *orange* girl to you?"

There was a moment of silence while Vee regained her breath, moving through their basement and up the stairs to the kitchen, where Patrick sat with his homework strewn about the kitchen island. Even the bond was still, as if Shane was too shocked to even feel anything before he burst out in laughter. Patrick's head whipped up from whatever he had been studying at the sound of his father's laugh.

"Are you going over there?" he asked through chuckles.

"Of course, I am. I love her despite the fact she's going to give me an aneurysm," Vee said sharply, not particularly loving that Shane had the advantage of being across the state, dealing with the remnants of the St. Louis pack, to get himself out of Cora's planning clutches.

"You're coming too, Patrick," Vee said, placing a hand on her hip and gesturing for him to get up.

His grin faltered, eyes going wide. There were several reasons Patrick may not have wanted to go to Cora's house. The increasingly obvious relationship with Lori, Cora and Thomas's daughter, perhaps was one, as well as the fact that Patrick had thus far only had to be on the sidelines of Cora's planning. If he was there for dinner, he was certain he would be roped in somehow.

"I have to study," he said, his voice slightly panicked as he gestured to his scattered schoolwork.

"Perfect. It will give us an excuse to leave before I'm up until midnight looking at fabric swatches for linens I don't plan on using," Vee said, grabbing him roughly by the arm and pulling his massive frame off the stool he was sitting on. Vee was surprisingly strong when she wanted to be, and right now, there was no way she was going to that house without an exit strategy.

"I'll have Thomas talk to her," Shane said, as they stopped in the entry for Patrick to put his shoes on.

"I'd rather you just come home," she said, her voice quiet, having not really meant the words to slip out.

A desperate need overwhelmed her from him, along with frustration. They both hated this, that he had been going back and forth for the last few weeks, giving those wavering St. Louis pack members their final opportunities to join with them instead of being forced into a life as a lone wolf. Since being bonded, they had never spent this much time apart, other than the stretch a few weeks prior when he was trapped in a Fae realm. They had said when he returned, "never again," but that turned out to be impossible. At least they knew the other was alive and safe, but the distance was nearly unbearable.

"I'll be home tomorrow," he said back, as Patrick took her hand comfortingly. But the little vibration of a new text message going off pulled them from their sad bubble a moment later.

[Cora: If I don't see you here in two minutes...]

"We have to go," Vee grumbled, frowning down at the text message.

"Don't let it go on too long, Patrick," Shane said, knowing his son could hear.

"I'll try my best," Patrick said, pulling open the door for him and Vee to cross through their yard into Thomas and Cora's.

The food was delicious, as always. Cora seemed to always make the most delightful meals, and when she and Marcus were in the kitchen cooking for the pack, no one was left unsatisfied. Thomas and Tommy weren't at dinner, both having been tracking down the last vestiges of the Vampire nest that needed to be taken out. The last few weeks they had been tracking down every last Vampire and systematically ridding Kansas City of their population.

Ethan, Shane's oldest son, had also stayed in town to help with that effort. Shane hadn't yet forgiven Ethan for his part in the Witch Gwen Tallon's plot to kill Vee six months prior, but he allowed the additional help on the condition that Ethan was to stay away from Vee, especially when Shane was gone to St. Louis. Vee had only seen him a few times in the past few weeks because of that, and for that, she was thankful. It was a difficult position for her to be in; a wedge between father and son, made even more complicated because Patrick, too, was at odds with his older brother for it.

"I was thinking next week," Cora said, as she and Vee gathered the remaining dishes from the table to bring them to the newly finished kitchen for Patrick and Lori to clean with the rest.

There were still parts of the house in mid-construction with all the renovations Cora had in the works, but everything had slowed down with the current state of the pack, and the fact that Toby, the head of the renovation company they used, had his entire crew killed in the St. Louis pack's plot and subsequently turned into a Werewolf himself. One man, even with super strength, wasn't enough to get everything finished in the timely fashion Cora had envisioned.

"Next week?" Vee asked, pausing to try and think if she missed any parts of the conversation.

"For dress shopping. Margaret and Frida should be back by then, and the kids have a three-day weekend, so they should be able to help at the shop," Cora said, as she continued into the white kitchen without a falter in her stride.

Vee, however, was gripping the plates in her hands so hard she was afraid she might break them, stiffly walking to the nearest counter and setting them a little extra carefully down before she took in a breath. For some reason, the idea of going dress shopping was the worst part of the whole wedding planning. Excruciating was what it sounded like. She would not only be the center of attention all day, but she'd have to try on dress after uncomfortable dress. White dresses, at that, with nothing to hide behind or beneath. She'd be like a beacon, a great neon sign, saying, "Look at me."

"I am not missing the dress shopping to work. Patrick can handle the shop on his own," Lori shot back, sending a glare toward her mother.

"I was just trying to make Vee feel better about not being in the shop for a day," Cora snipped right back, narrowing her eyes at her daughter's tone before turning back to Vee, having handed Patrick her stack.

"I don't think—" but it didn't matter what Vee thought, as the phone in Vee's pocket began ringing. She pulled it out, looking at the number and realizing it was Anton. Not exactly the name Vee was expecting to see, but a little happy for the distraction.

"Vee," she answered, her gaze locking onto Patrick's at the sink.

"There's something you need to see," Anton said, her voice low and quiet.

"I'm in the middle of something," Vee said, watching as Lori also paused, turning from the sink to watch Vee.

"Ethan is with me. He didn't think you or Patrick would answer if he called."

"That does nothing to entice me to stop what I'm doing," Vee said, trying to keep her voice even, despite the desire to snap at her.

Anton had become a distant ally. She had given them information, though not very detailed information, and warned them of the Vampire Lazare Duflanc, but only when Ethan came back to town did Anton join the efforts to unburden the city of the increasingly monstrous remnants of Duflanc's nest, who had been murdering humans at an alarmingly increasing amount. It was causing the humans to start wondering. And humans questioning odd deaths could start them on a path to finding out about the preternaturals, something that needed to be avoided at all costs.

"This is important," Anton insisted.

"I promise no harm will come to you, Vee," came Ethan's voice from the background. Patrick let a low growl rumble in his chest, stepping toward Vee.

"I make no promises. Where?" Vee asked, holding up a hand to keep Patrick from tearing the phone from her grasp.

"Gregory and Wyandotte," Anton said quickly before hanging up.

Vee sighed, looking down at her phone. She wasn't sure what this was, or why Anton couldn't have just told her a little more over the phone, but she assumed it had to do with the Vampire hunt.

"This is ridiculous! How are we going to plan your wedding when there's always interruptions?" Cora said, breaking the silence that had stretched between them all for a few moments.

"Cora—" Vee started, but Patrick was already storming toward the door, his phone already in his hand as he violently called his dad. The glass on the phone shattered under his fingers, but he didn't flinch as he pressed it to his ear, opening the front door and walking back toward their house.

"You've got this, Cora. I trust you and Lori. But I need to go," Vee said, giving them both an apologetic look.

"I'll come," Lori said, drying her hands hastily and moving to leave the kitchen.

"Stay with your mom," Vee said, glancing at Cora who looked like she was furious, but only Vee could feel the churning of deep-seeded anxiety within her.

Cora had not taken almost losing Thomas and Tommy well, and they immediately began hunting Vampires, giving her no relief other than when they came home at night. Part of the reason Vee didn't push back on all of Cora's many, many outlandish ideas was because planning this wedding was a good distraction for her.

Lori's eyebrows drew in, her heart-shaped face a little scrunched, and the seriousness of her expression seemed so opposing to the bright pink hair she was sporting this week. Finally, after a moment where Cora began pulling all the dishes Lori and Patrick put in the dishwasher to load them again, Lori seemed to understand.

"Thank you, Cora," Vee murmured, gaining a nod from Cora's turned back before she raced out the front door, seeing Patrick climbing the steps to the apartment above the garage that Durran stayed in.

"Of course they didn't say why they needed us to meet them. Why would they, Dad?" Patrick said, his voice oozing with sarcastic hostility.

"You're taking Durran?" Shane asked over the phone.

"Taking me where?" Durran asked, just as Patrick was about to knock.

Durran was perched on the roof, their wings out instead of their customary black duster to disguise them, looking down at Vee and Patrick, who stood on the little landing before the door to the apartment.

"Anton called me. She says she and Ethan need to show me something," Vee said, being far more used to Durran showing up in strange places at odd times than Patrick.

"And you said you would meet them?" Shane asked over the phone.

"She said, 'I make no promises'; it was actually kind of badass," Patrick said, having calmed a bit from his temper, giving Vee a wry smile. She rolled her eyes.

"Thomas and Tommy are out right now taking out the last Vampire from Duflanc's nest. What could those two possibly need with you that can't wait until I'm back?" Shane growled. Vee could feel his urge to come home becoming stronger.

"We might as well go see. They should know better than to think Vee would go anywhere alone," Durran said before standing to their full height, rolling their shoulders and wings for a moment before letting the glamor fall back over them, masking the beautiful, glistening black feathers from view.

"Shouldn't Min be in the city?" Shane said, his voice still rough with frustration.

"He took Toby and Jack to meet with George. Toby is still worried about his wolf around him," Durran said, as they lithely jumped down in front of Vee.

Toby had only been a Werewolf a few weeks and seemed to be a rather dominant one at that. George was quite the opposite unless it came to real estate. It wasn't unheard of for dominant Weres to mistreat submissives, but usually their human counterpart was equally as terrible. Vee had no qualms about trusting

Toby, but she couldn't change his own mind; he'd just have to get comfortable at his own pace.

Jack, on the other hand, was still recovering from being abused and tortured by his former pack. The Jack Vee had known as a teenager had been a dominant wolf, but the one she saw in the basement shortly after the battle between the packs had been a completely different person. The two of them had been staying between her house and the Byers home, but both were eager to get back to their own space. It was Cora that suggested they get something together. The two of them, new to the pack and feeling a little on the outside still, could stick together.

"I'll text him," Vee said, turning and heading down the stairs and rounding on the garage.

"Call me when you're done. I'm coming home. There's no need for me to stay another night. The Sha can handle this without me," Shane said, before hanging up the phone.

"Your car or mine?" Patrick asked, looking at Durran as he tucked his phone back in his pocket.

"Mine," Durran said, not even pausing their stride as they went to where the black Buick sat on the round of the cul-de-sac.

BOOK CLUB QUESTIONS:

1. It's clear Vee's magic is changing the pack in this book, and the impact of that is still revealing itself. What are some things you noticed that have already changed?

2. Why do you think Shane is regularly so shocked/pleased that Vee is invested in their relationship?

3. Durran seems to be much more at peace about Vee's relationship with Shane. Why do you think that is?

4. How well do you think Midi the cat will fold into their lives?

5. How do you think the Sha gate being in their back yard might impact events in the future?

6. Vee seems to have more control over her abilities in each book. What do you think is causing her to gain that control?

7. What problems, if any, do you think Toby being in the pack will cause?

8. Min went from being somewhat hostile and unsure of Vee to calling her his sister. How do you think their relationship might change as time goes on? What do you think changed his opinions of her through this book?

More books from 4 Horsemen Publications

Paranormal & Urban Fantasy

Amanda Fasciano
Waking Up Dead
Dead Vessel
Dead Show
Dead Revelations
Dead Carnage

Beau Lake
The Beast Beside Me
The Beast Within Me
Taming the Beast: Novella
The Beast After Me
Charming the Beast: Novella
The Beast Like Me

Chelsea Burton Dunn
By Moonlight
Moon Bound
White Moon
New Moon Rising

J.M. Paquette
Call Me Forth
Invite Me In
Keep Me Close

Kait Disney-Leugers
Antique Magic
Blood Magic
Heart Magic

Lyra R. Saenz
Prelude
Sonata
Scherzo
Ragtime Swing
Midnight Cumbia
Sea Song de la Corsaire
Falsetto in the Woods: Novella
The Devil's Trill

Megan Mackie
The Finder of the Lucky Devil
The Saint Liars
The Devil's Day
The Digital Mage

Paige Lavoie
I'm in Love with Mothman
I'm Engaged with Mothman

ROBERT J. LEWIS
Shadow Guardian and the
Three Bears
Shadow Guardian and the
Big Bad Wolf
Shadow Guardian Boys
That Went Woof

VALERIE WILLIS
Cedric: The Demonic Knight
Romasanta: Father of
Werewolves
The Oracle: Keeper of the
Gaea's Gate
Artemis: Eye of Gaea
King Incubus: A New Reign
Rebirth
Judgment
Death

DISCOVER MORE AT
4HORSEMENPUBLICATIONS.COM